Carmichaels' Diamonds

Frances Parker-Smith

First published 2020
by Rowanvale Books Ltd
The Gate
Keppoch Street
Roath
Cardiff
CF24 3JW
www.rowanvalebooks.com

A CIP catalogue record for this book is available from the British Library.
ISBN: 978-1-912655-52-6

To my best friend,
Sue

Prologue

"I'm not like him," cried the boy. Tears ran down his face.

"Look in the bloody mirror, lad," the skinny policeman barked, gripping the boy's thick, dark hair and pushing his face into a mirror. "Admit it. You did it."

"No, I di… didn't!"

"Where were you? Last evening?"

"He was wiv me," cried his mother, Mary, a tall, good-looking woman with high cheekbones, sparkling blue eyes and dyed black hair. She dressed eye-catchingly, showing off her attributes to best effect. Tears ran down her cheeks.

"You're a lying cow!" yelled the skinny policeman, eyes bulging, trying not to lust after her body.

"How do you know?" a gruff voice bellowed from the open doorway. "Let the boy and mother go."

"But sir…?" The skinny policeman turned towards the inspector.

"Apparently there's a disagreement between the Michaels and Carmichael." The inspector's firm voice took a low tone. "Trying to frame the lad."

"Who's fucking told you that?" The skinny policeman glared at the inspector. "It's him. I know it's him." He grabbed the boy's collar. "Daddy's come to help you." He twisted the boy's head so their eyes met. "Clever Daddy's pulling strings from the inside." Sarcasm dripped from his voice.

"Let the boy go," demanded the inspector.

"It's him. I fucking know it."

"Take your son home, Mrs Carmichael," the inspector told Mary in a low, sympathetic tone, his eyes roaming up and down her body.

She grabbed her son's arm and dragged him out of the room. The boy turned and eyeballed the skinny policeman. A slow smirk spread across his youthful features.

"This isn't over, you fucking whore!" yelled the skinny policeman.

"It *is* over, Lawson. Now fucking listen. You'll leave them alone. Got it?" The inspector's voice was suddenly threating.

"You fuckin' 'er now?" Lawson growled, eyes bulging with defiance.

A large hand gripped him by the throat and pinned him against the wall, lifting him off the floor. He gasped for air, his hands trying desperately to free his neck.

"Now listen to me, you piece of shit. If you so much as look at her and the boy, I'll fucking see to you. Got it?"

Lawson was shaking his head.

The large hand released his throat. Lawson fell to the floor, gripping his neck and gasping for air, his face glowing red.

"That newsagent wouldn't pay," he gasped. "He fucking owed—"

A large boot thudded into his gut. He howled, rolling into a ball, writhing with pain. Another kick to the kidneys.

Lawson saw stars, and then blackness.

He struggled to open his eyes. His head hurt and his body ached. He was cold and wet, and he suddenly realised he was lying in his own urine.

He had no idea how long he had lain there.

He slowly eased himself to his feet. His head swirled and his legs buckled. The cold floor greeted him like an old friend.

Chapter One

The large open-plan office was dark. A figure lurked in the shadows, watching.

Jasper Carmichael stood gazing through the rain-drenched windows at the town he called home. Ordinary people had long gone home, most tucked up in bed asleep.

His phone buzzed.

"We 'ave to leave, sir."

"Cancel!"

"Problems?"

"Yes."

Don, his driver, had been with him since the early days. Jasper had bought him a house that needed refurbishment. Years of renovation had turned it into a luxurious house that he now shared with Milly, his wife. Don was old-school, loyal; he was one of the few people Jasper trusted.

Jasper had moved from London with his best friend and business partner, Jack Swain, before the death of his father, Colin. Colin Carmichael had been the top man of the Families Gang—a gang of different families trying to make a living in post-war London.

Colin had been the mastermind behind many successful diamond heists. However, he made a big mistake when he double-crossed his partner. Colin had fallen into the greed trap, keeping the diamonds and giving his partner glass. His enraged partner wanted revenge and, with the help of a policeman, Colin Carmichael was put inside.

Jasper had been the world to Colin Carmichael. Jasper was a true Carmichael, and now he was out of London, he had every chance of being the best Carmichael ever. Just before Colin died, he'd had one last talk with Jasper. He'd suggested Jasper should move away from the gang life and set up a new business in Wellsbury. He entrusted him with a wooden box; inside were velvet pouches of diamonds and Colin's black book.

So Jasper and Jack moved their fledgling wheeler-dealer business to Wellsbury. Jack had a natural eye for making money. His antiques business had done well, but he saw a golden opportunity in investing in rundown property, refurbishing and selling at a profit. He had been right. Jasper's property business had made them millions.

However, when Max Wilson, a forceful member of the Families, had sweet-talked Jack into thinking that he would be a useful contributor to Carmichael and Swain, Jasper and Jack's relationship had deteriorated. The bond between Jasper and Jack had been under pressure since Jasper became head of the business. The antiques side of the business was in decline and Jack did nothing, so Jasper had appointed himself head of Carmichael and Swain. The company had made a lot of money; the property side had gone from strength to strength since Jasper had developed an overseas network of business associates. Jasper was well aware that Max Wilson wanted to oust Jasper and take over his company and advance the Wilson business.

The shadow moved deeper into the dark office. His eyes fixed on Jasper, who was deep in thought. He silently cursed when he heard the word *cancel*.

Jasper moved towards his wall safe, hidden behind a panel in his drinks cabinet. He hesitated; the labels on the drink bottles were not facing forward as he had left them. When he opened the panel, a small length of cotton fell from the keypad. The pad had been wiped clean; someone had tried to break in.

It was time to empty the safe. Jasper had removed his not-so-legal transactions—the offshore bank and shell companies—some time ago, and now it was time to remove the last remaining item.

A wave of satisfaction passed through the shadow when Jasper lifted the box from his safe. The wax seal Colin had melted over the lock was still intact.

Jasper's fingers lightly circled the lid of the box that held the secrets of Colin Carmichael's success—his black book and the coveted diamonds.

He fingered the wax seal.

Excited, the shadow moved closer, intending to take the box.

The stillness of the office was shattered when the door swung open and Don's heavy footsteps echoed.

"I'll drive you home. Milly's not expecting me," he declared.

His eyes widened and settled on the box. Many long-serving Carmichael and Swain employees, as well as the London gangs, had speculated of the box's existence. Old Man Carmichael's box, where he'd hidden his black book and diamonds.

Trying not to stare at the box, he strolled over to Jasper's overnight leather holdall. He was surprised to see his boss's worried expression and sore eyes. What was going on?

The shadow carefully moved back into the dark shadows. He hadn't expected Don's arrival.

"What do you know about Kate Reynolds?" Jasper unexpectedly asked.

"Kate?" Don's surprised tone was louder than he'd anticipated. "Had it rough. Highflyer at school and uni, so I'm told. Gave up a well-paid job to look after Old Man Reynolds. The old bastard hasn't got a good word for her, but she saved that flower business."

"That all?"

Don's eyes fixed on his boss's fingers, which were slowly moving around the wax seal. "Nah! Married that slob Eric. Pregnant. Gossip 'as it that she fell down the stairs. More like pushed. She lost the baby, and not long after, they divorced."

Jasper placed the box into his holdall along with his laptop and a wad of papers and cash that lay on his desk.

"That Nigel James fancies his chances," Don continued, his eyes on the small holdall.

"Sleeping with her?"

Don was surprised by Jasper's concerned tone. "Nah. She's eager to leave though. Make her a good offer and that whole block will be yours."

Jasper closed the safe.

"Now you're not going to Miami, go to the mayor's do. Jack's going. I'm sure she'll be there."

The shadow disappeared into the office as Jasper switched off his desk light. He watched Don and Jasper silently walk towards the emergency exit sign before standing.

***

Later that night, Don sat in his office, sipping a malt.

"He 'as the box," he said to the blank laptop screen.

"Are you sure?" asked the thick South American voice.

"Wax seal over the lock."

"Colin." The voice was suddenly angry. "Where's the box now?"

"In his holdall."

"Increase surveillance."

The call ended.

Chapter Two

Jasper Carmichael sat on a wooden bench, alone outside the George, sipping warm lager and trying to eat a stale sandwich that lodged in his throat. His eyes were fixed on the flower shop opposite and the woman smiling and chatting as she helped unload a delivery of flowers. Her long blonde hair was tied back. Her over-washed jeans and worn fleece didn't do her justice.

He had been watching Kate Reynolds for some time. He liked her confident manner and the friendly, helpful way she treated people. Kate Reynolds was liked and highly thought of. He wished he was. Even his dad had been, by the community he lived in. But the good people of Wellsbury were wary of him. Rumours and gossip surrounded Jasper Carmichael, some true, others not. He had tried to put his past behind him, start a new business, but old acquaintances had a habit of resurfacing. The Carmichael reputation hung over him like the sword of Damocles.

The young, inexperienced Jasper flashed into his mind. In those days, he'd been nothing like his dad.

Colin Carmichael had apparently died in prison, but Jasper hadn't been allowed to see his body. His mother had identified Colin's body. But she'd never cared; her tears weren't for Colin, just his money. Her meal ticket was dead.

A lump formed in Jasper's throat as he recalled

his father's last advice to him, the advice that had started him on the path to Carmichael and Swain's international success. And with that success came power, money, confidence and self-assurance. Jasper Carmichael got whatever he wanted. And he wanted Kate Reynolds.

He pulled at the cuffs of his grey Armani suit. He owned several of these suits, handmade white shirts and Italian leather loafers. He lived well, only eating in the best restaurants; he owned many of them in Wellsbury.

Loud banter from the bar drew his attention. He heard Kate's name followed by raucous laughter.

"What's this about my ex?" shouted the overweight barman, wiping his hands on a dirty cloth.

Jasper knew immediately who he was—Eric.

"That solicitor fancies his chances with your ex."

"Wasting his time. Frigid as a nun—and that's insulting the nun!"

Loud laughter again filtered from the bar.

The hairs on the back of Jasper's neck stood as eyes suddenly settled on him. He was a little overdressed compared to the George's normal clientele, but that didn't bother him; he had no intention of talking to them.

"They reckon that property company, Carmichael and Swain, is after the shop. Rumour has it that they already have the row." The customer paused, making sure Jasper had heard. "You should have stayed with her. She'd be worth a bob or two." He grinned.

"Hey, Eric! You think you could persuade her to give you some?" said another customer.

More laughter.

Not if I can help it, thought Jasper. Again, he pulled on his cuffs.

"Thought I'd find you here."

Jack, Jasper's so-called best friend and back-stabbing business partner, slipped onto the bench beside him.

Jasper purposely ignored him, and an awkward silence developed.

"We'd make a lot of money, Jas," Jack said hopefully, following the direction of Jasper's gaze.

He hated being called Jas.

"The council's desperate to develop the whole area. We're the only company interested."

Silence.

"It's a done deal, Jas. All you've got to do is buy her out." Jack nodded towards Kate.

Silence.

"I dropped our application off. My contact's impressed and expects the council to agree."

"Money's tight. The bottom dropped out of the property market."

Jack didn't like Jasper's comment. It wasn't what he wanted to hear.

"Sell some," he retorted. "Go to the bank. Get a loan."

Jasper cringed. He no intention to let a bank own part of Carmichael and Swain.

Just at that moment, Nigel James pulled up outside the flower shop. He purposefully strode over to Kate and kissed her.

"Did she cringe just then?" Jack's words mirrored Jasper's thoughts. Kate didn't appreciate Nigel's affections.

"Get me everything on her solicitor, Nigel James," Jasper uttered so only Jack could hear.

Jack smiled. *At last, he's interested*, he thought.

Chapter Three

At the mayor's reception, Jasper stood with Jack, sipping cheap, warm wine and watching the great and good of Wellsbury mingle.

Jasper and Jack were as different as chalk and cheese. Jasper's tall form stood head and shoulders above Jack. Even when they were at school, Jack had never cared about how he looked. Uncombed hair, ill-fitting uniform, dirty shoes. Whereas appearance had been everything to Jasper: neatly cut hair, fitted uniform and polished shoes. Even then, Jasper knew he was a cut above the rest.

"Here she is," Jack said so only Jasper could hear. Their heads turned.

Nigel James had his hand resting on the small of Kate's back. Declaring ownership, Jasper thought. But not for much longer.

Jasper and Jack watched Kate skilfully leave Nigel and work the room. Heads were turning, and Nigel glared at each and every one. Kate looked stunning in her cerise, knee-length, V-neck dress. When she laughed, she flicked her long blond hair, exposing her neck. A young waiter offered her a glass of white wine, and she briefly smiled at him before greeting more guests with an air-kiss and a smile. *She's good*, thought Jasper as his trousers tightened.

"What do we know about the solicitor?" he asked Jack, deliberately looking away from Kate.

"Friend of the family."

"Fucking her?"

"As far as I can find out, no. But he wants to. Some say he wants a ring on her finger." Jack paused and looked up at Jasper questioningly.

"So who is?" Jasper asked.

Jack hesitated. "Why the interest?"

"Just answer the fucking question."

"I've been digging. Found no skeletons, except Eric. She had the usual boyfriends at Oxford Uni. They ended with uni. Celibate since Eric. He says she's frigid… That's her ex." Jack nodded towards the overweight bald man. "Weren't married long. Gossip 'as it that he got her pregnant. She fell down the stairs. Lost the baby. Some reckon she was pushed—they were heard arguing—but he denies it. They divorced. He moved in with that buxom piece; they run the George." Jack turned and briefly studied Jasper. "She was destined for a city job, then Old Man Reynolds took bad."

"She looked after him?"

"Yeah, and saved the business. I was talking to an old biddy that knew Old Man Reynolds. Bastard by all accounts. Treated Kate like shit. After she lost the baby, she was ill for some time, physically and mentally. Can't have children. Lost a lot of weight, I'm told. That's when Nigel stepped in."

At every opportunity, Jack had nagged Jasper to buy Kate Reynolds out so they could get on with the shopping centre. Jack had made it his business to find out everything about Kate— her weaknesses, the skeletons in her closet— so with subtle persuasion they could negotiate a less than market price for the property. Kate Reynolds was well liked, and her life story was well known, particularly if you frequented the

George, where her ex was only too willing to talk about her. Jasper thought the George was the source of Jack's local knowledge, but he never mentioned Kate's loyalty and trustworthiness. It was these qualities that attracted Jasper to Kate. *But could she fuck?*

Since Beth, he had relied on Joanne's escort business to relieve his sexual tension, but he needed a woman in his apartment, waiting to satisfy his sexual appetite.

He didn't like going to Joanne's and making appointments. Joanne's girls, as she referred to them, met their clients either at their homes or hotel rooms. But Jasper was sick of fucking strangers. He needed a woman waiting, one he could trust—and fuck all night if he wanted. No questions asked.

He continued watching Kate mingling while sipping her wine. She had moved closer to him. He admired her form and her smile, which spread to her sparkling green eyes. Her dress was simple but very effective, with its long V-neck dipping to show off her cleavage. Her heels enhanced her shapely legs. Kate had good taste. Jasper had only seen her in well-worn jeans and fleeces before.

Her head turned slightly so their eyes momentarily met. Still smiling, she flicked her hair, exposing her neck and high cheekbones. He imagined his head tucked into her smooth long neck, trailing kisses. Kate Reynolds was teasing him. A half smile played on his lips.

"Council 'ave been trying to buy her out." Jack followed Jasper's gaze. "But she runs rings round them."

"Everyone has their price," commented Jasper, still fantasising about kissing Kate's neck.

Kate's eyes finally locked onto Jasper's.

"You bastard, you've been waiting to eye-fuck her," Jack exclaimed.

Jasper grinned.

His thoughts were interrupted by Jack's contact from the council, Rupert. Another bald, overweight man.

"We liked your plans, Mr Carmichael." His low, silky voice made Jasper cringe.

"Good," Jasper politely managed, his eyes still focused on Kate.

"There's just one problem," Rupert said, rubbing his hands together.

"Kate Reynolds," Jasper guessed.

"She won't budge."

"I'll sort it, Rupert. Leave it with me."

Rupert half smiled and slinked away towards the loud tones of a woman calling his name.

"Thought you were due in Miami," Jack commented, a little surprised.

"I might have to cancel."

"But Miami's a big deal, right?" Jack impatiently added.

"The Miami office can handle the immediate issue."

"We need money, Jasper." Jack's voice was slightly raised.

Jasper turned to his business partner, irritated. "With the Miami operation closing, I need another project."

"We need the fucking money."

"Let me worry about money," Jasper said dismissively.

Angry, Jack walked away in a huff before an argument ensued.

Even watching Jack, with his long strides and stiff posture, irritated Jasper; he was tired of Jack interfering with the company finances. Jasper watched as Jack pulled his phone from his jacket pocket and started talking, confirming what he already suspected: Max was pulling Jack's strings.

Jasper was becoming impatient. He'd had enough of this polite mingling; he needed a lay. He looked for Joanne, but she was too busy networking. Drumming up trade.

His mind briefly lingered on Beth. They had been good together. He paid for all her designer clothes, salon treatments and anything else she wanted. They ate at the best restaurants, drank the best wine. He had a cellar full of the stuff, after all.

Their relationship had begun when he was still at school. Jasper had a fiery temper. He was always getting in scraps—fighting was his release. Then he discovered sex and Beth. She was sex on tap; he had never wanted another. He didn't love her. Emotional love wasn't something he needed. But he wouldn't have minded a child with her. As far as he knew, he was Colin's only child—it was his duty to continue Colin's line. But his relationship with Beth ended badly when he caught her in bed with Jack and Richard, his half-brother.

Jasper emptied his glass; these maudlin thoughts were depressing him. He went in search of another drink, not this warm wine but a malt. There was only one person at the bar, Kate, chatting and laughing with the barman as if she knew him. Jasper scanned the room, looking for her keeper. Nigel was walking towards a passage with the banker's wife, Michelle. *Well, well. There's more to Kate's solicitor than meets the eye*, he thought.

Jasper slipped onto the bar stool next to Kate,

carefully edging closer to her. Her green eyes were on fire as laughter filled her face. She glanced at him as if expecting him to join her.

"Another, Kate?" asked the barman, still laughing. He met Jasper's gaze. "You'll 'ave to excuse us—Kate and I go back."

She turned towards Jasper and held out her hand. "Kate Reynolds, Mr Carmichael."

"At school together," the barman continued, pouring a generous malt for Jasper and a white wine for Kate. "Top of the class. Highflyer."

"Mr Carmichael doesn't want to hear about our school days," Kate said as Jasper shook her hand.

"On the contrary—I'd love to," he replied, sipping his malt.

She was still smiling when their eyes locked. Green on blue. The chemistry was immediate and mutual.

"Your shadow's returning," she said in a low voice.

From the corner of his eye, Jasper glimpsed Jack and Max.

"Dinner?" he tentatively asked.

Her eyes widened. "Let me cook." Her words escaped through a smile.

Her cheeks flushed as he returned her smile. "Mine or yours?"

Her stomach flipped as he leaned close, his lips grazing her ear.

"Mine. Six thirty," she stuttered as a nervous flutter descended to the top of her thighs.

She turned back to the barman and continued talking, but her mind was elsewhere.

Chapter Four

The next day, Kate was unusually busy. Although some customers bought flowers, the majority wanted to gossip about Jasper.

"'As he made you an offer?" one asked.

"He's quite taken with you," another commented. "His eyes followed you everywhere."

That was the trouble with Wellsbury—everyone knew your business.

Kate was running late. The morning's delivery had been delayed, but Kate hadn't the heart to complain to the flower delivery man. He had apologised, explaining that he'd taken on extra deliveries due to illness.

Kate's head whipped round when the shop door abruptly rang.

"Is it true?" Nigel angrily asked, eyes bulging.

"Is what true?"

"You're meeting Carmichael."

"Well... yes. Why so angry?"

"The town's full of you and Carmichael eye-fucking at the bar."

"I haven't got time for this," she said impatiently, returning her attention to the flowers.

"I felt a right idiot in the George."

"If you hadn't been too busy fucking Michelle, I'd have told you."

Nigel stormed across the shop, and she flinched away from the anger in his eyes. He raised his hand, and her breath caught. He was going to hit her—*Nigel* was going to hit her. Her tears stung.

"I wouldn't do that, old boy."

Nigel froze as Jasper Carmichael's calm, menacing voice drifted into the shop. He stood in the doorway, tightly gripping a bottle and a large brown envelope.

"Nothing to do with you."

"Wrong. It's everything to do with me." Jasper's voice became more threatening.

"You think you own the bloody place."

Jasper walked to the counter, placing the wine and envelope on top. "I don't like to see women slapped about."

"You mean like this?" Nigel's hand hit Kate's face with such force she stumbled back against the shop window.

Jasper pounced on Nigel before his hand left Kate's cheek. As Jasper's hand tightened around his neck, Nigel's face reddened, gasping for air.

Kate screamed, "Stop!"

Nigel fell to the floor. He crawled to the open shop door and onto the pavement. He curled into a ball, coughing and spluttering. Jasper stood over him, casually pulling his Armani jacket sleeves back over his shirt cuffs. He slowly lifted his gaze to the loud gasps from the crowd that had gathered outside the George. Eric's shocked expression caught Jasper's eye. Eric's chest was heaving, gaping mouth gasping for breath, as he rubbed his hands on a dirty cloth. Their eyes briefly met. Eric took a step back; there was no mistaking Jasper's hateful expression.

Jasper left Nigel lying on the pavement and casually walked into the shop. The silence was overbearing; Kate had disappeared. He locked the door and listened. Sobs drifted from a dark corridor.

Jasper walked along the corridor to a small

living room at the back of the shop. Kate was sitting on a well-worn sofa, head in hands. Jasper slid beside her, gently pulling her into his shoulder.

"He's never done that," she said between sobs.

"He's losing you."

She turned to face him. "He's never had me."

"He thinks differently."

She pulled away. "I've got food to prepare."

Jasper's fingers lightly touched Kate's reddened cheek. "Go and shower. I'll order in." His voice was slow and uncharacteristically caring.

***

Dressed in clean jeans and a fitted white blouse, Kate watched Jasper pour white wine into two crystal glasses.

Jasper looked up, smiling. "That's better." *She's definitely fuckable, even dressed in jeans,* he thought.

Kate looked at the dressed dinner table. "What's this?"

"I thought you needed…" He hesitated; he hadn't the words. Jasper had never done anything romantic. "Marco's suggestion." He gestured at the set table. Two lit candles stood in the centre.

Kate's eyes looked over her living room and kitchen. Marco turned from the hob, smiling.

"This is an absolute pleasure, Miss Kate," he said in his thick Italian accent.

Jasper pulled a seat away from the table. As Kate sat, he leaned into her, his lips caressing her ear. "I didn't know you had a fan club. I'm not used to competition."

Kate flushed while her stomach flipped.

"*Bon appetit,*" Marco cheerfully said, winking at Jasper.

Kate gazed at her full plate of well-done steak, green vegetables and carrots with boiled baby potatoes and English mustard—not horseradish—lightly covered with onion gravy.

"How did you know?"

"Marco. I rang for a takeaway, but Marco wouldn't hear of it. 'Miss Kate deserves better'." Jasper mimicked Marco's Italian accent. "'She likes steak and lots of vegetables.'"

Kate's eyes sparkled as she smiled, her mouth full of tender steak. Jasper felt a nervous quiver in his stomach. Women never made his stomach flutter.

"Shall we talk about the offer?" Kate said between mouthfuls.

"Not at the moment." He flashed his Carmichael smile. "I prefer to watch you eat."

His trousers unexpectedly tightened, reminding him that he was in desperate need of a woman.

Their eyes met, green on blue. A warm glow settled at the top of her thighs.

"When I was growing up," she said, changing the subject, "we lived in the house that Don lives in—Dad moved into the flat above."

"And you live here! Why?"

She nodded. "Can't be bothered with moving up there. As soon as this is sold, I'll be moving on."

"And Nigel?" Jasper couldn't help himself. He wanted to hear about their relationship from her. Nigel obviously thought Kate was his.

Kate smiled, looking down at her empty plate. "That was delicious. Thank you."

Jasper cursed. Nigel was off limits.

***

Jasper impatiently paced while Kate read the sales document.

"This looks okay. But Nigel will have to read it."

Fucking Nigel again, Jasper thought.

"It's not all in there," he said, somewhat hesitantly.

Kate's green eyes flashed in surprise.

"I, er… need a very special personal assistant. An assistant that's loyal to me. Check files, organise the archives."

She looked expectantly. "And?"

"A housekeeper."

"You offering me a job?"

Jasper looked away. This might be a deal-breaker.

"I have one very important particular requirement."

Their eyes met. Jasper tried to read Kate's eyes.

"Sex."

"Oh! No."

"Let me finish. Since I finished with Beth—"

"You visit Joanne's establishment," Kate interrupted. "Gossip."

"Don't judge me." Jasper's blue eyes watched every flicker of emotion on Kate's face. "I get stressed. My temper flares. Easily. I need release. I used to get into fights; Colin suggested sex, and Jack found Beth."

An uncomfortable silence hung between them.

"I work hard. Long hours. I travel. I don't want to mess around booking fucking appointments at Joanne's. I want a woman waiting for me."

"I'm not that woman."

"How do you know? Eric fucked you against a wall and got you pregnant."

Kate reddened. How did he know?

It was as if he could read her mind. "He brags about it. The whole fucking town knows." Jasper was becoming agitated.

Upset, Kate raced to the door. Her hand rested on the door handle. "I think you should go."

In one swift, unexpected move, he pinned her against the door and crashed their lips together, long and hard. She broke away, but before she could speak, he kissed her again. This time, she didn't fight him. She opened her mouth, allowing their exploring tongues to touch. Her hands feverishly ran through his salt and pepper hair. She moaned when his hand slipped beneath her top.

Any doubts about Kate Reynolds being frigid were quickly dashed from Jasper's mind. She wanted him.

"This is not a good idea," she stuttered.

But Jasper's mind was elsewhere. His fingers deftly flicked open her jeans and expertly trailed inside her panties.

She gasped. Her hand hastily grabbed his. Thoughts of Eric and the torment of the miscarriage flashed through her mind.

"No!" she snapped.

"No?" he repeated in a sharp tone. "*No* isn't in my vocabulary."

She placed both hands on his chest and pushed. "Housekeeping. That's not me."

But he wasn't listening; he was busy enjoying the delights of her neck.

What's he doing? she thought. *I've got to stop this.* But her body betrayed her. Sexual desire that had lain dormant deep inside stirred. Her best efforts at relieving pent-up sexual tension had failed. Her body craved a man.

"I need someone to watch my back for three

months," he said as his fingers eagerly searched her folds. "I know how to treat people, and I certainly know how to satisfy a woman. You won't be disappointed on either account."

But she wasn't listening. Her body had taken control.

Her fingers fumbled for his zipper. She gently stroked his hardness, and he moaned. He lifted her into his arms.

"Bedroom."

He lay on top of her, his arms supporting his weight, gazing into her shining green eyes. His erection twitched at her folds.

She rested her hands on his firm chest. He looked a little surprised.

"It's been a while," she mumbled.

"I know."

She raised her eyebrows.

"I know all about you and that slob Eric. You haven't had a man since." His words were soft and caring as his fingers gently pushed wisps of hair from her forehead. "I have no intention of hurting you."

He had no idea where the words came from. But he needed this woman's loyalty, and a rough fuck wouldn't get him that.

"In that case, don't make me wait," she murmured.

She wrapped her legs around his waist. A satisfied grin spread across his face as he slowly entered her.

She gasped at his fullness. Her fingers dug into his broad shoulders. He withdrew, his eyes trying to gauge her discomfort. After a long moment, he leaned into her, planting soft kisses on her cheeks.

"Relax."

Her mind flicked back to the last time she had felt such fullness. Her uni days. His fingers caressed her forehead.

"Oh, babe. You're so tight and wet."

He claimed her soft mouth, drinking in her gentle moans as he began to move.

With every movement, he hit her most sensitive spot, awaking the embers that simmered deep inside. Warm comforting sensations pulsed as her mind drifted.

"I'm so close," she moaned.

Her mind and body finally surrendering to pleasure, she screamed his name.

"Babe," he yelled as he filled her.

They lay still. Hearts racing, lungs gulping for air.

"What have we done?" she uttered.

"I don't know. But I've had the best fuck of my life." He grinned.

"Me too," she said, pulling him into a kiss.

***

Warm water cascaded over them as he slowly and gently soaped her body.

"This is a first." His soft words drifted into the warm water. "I've never washed a woman."

She smiled. "Also for me. Never shared a shower. Never been washed."

Swift and sudden, he pinned her against the tiles, hooked her legs around his waist and plunged inside her. Their mouths crashed together, swallowing cries of delight.

Jasper thought of the many delights he would share with Kate Reynolds.

***

"Sleep with me." His words had been hesitant. He had no idea where they had sprung from. He'd never shared a bed. Not even with Beth.

"Jasper, I don't think…"

"Don't think."

Another first, he thought.

Their naked bodies nestled together, as if this was how it should be.

***

He left early the next morning. He had a presentation to prepare for, but Kate Reynolds filled his thoughts.

They had talked and laughed. She'd teased him. Jasper couldn't remember the last time he had laughed so much. When she continued teasing, he'd pulled her onto the carpet and rough fucked her until she screamed his name.

This is how it's going to be, Kate, he thought. *I'll fuck you till you can't walk.*

Chapter Five

Kate leaned over the kitchen worksurface, chin resting on her hands, with a cup of piping hot tea next to her, her hair still wet from showering.

She couldn't remember the last time she'd felt this good. Lack of sleep, tiredness and an aching body were pushed out of her mind. Jasper Carmichael had given her so much pleasure.

Is this how it should be? she wondered. *What have I been missing?*

Her eyes momentarily closed as she reached for her tea. Maybe she wouldn't open the shop, and just go back to bed. If only the bloody phone would stop ringing.

The phone rang again. With eyes firmly closed, she hit the answer button. "Kate Reynolds."

"I thought I had the wrong number," an unfamiliar female voice snapped. "Mr Carmichael wants you to attend the new shopping centre presentation."

Kate's eyes sprang open and she stared at the phone.

"I'm sorry." The voice took on an apologetic tone. "It's mayhem here. Mr Carmichael was due to be in Miami, but he's cancelled and we're in chaos. He's reorganised everything." She paused for breath. "But that's no excuse. I'm sorry. I'm Amanda, Mr Carmichael's PA. He's asked me to invite you to the lunchtime presentation."

Kate was more than a little surprised. She wasn't really interested in a stuffy presentation, preferring the idea of sleep. "Me?"

"Yes. He's very insistent."

Kate said nothing, mulling over the offer.

"Are you alright? Only, Nigel said you hadn't opened the shop."

At the mention of interfering Nigel, Kate's hackles rose. "What the fuck is it to do with him?" she snapped.

"I'm sorry," said a surprised Amanda. "I didn't mean to upset you."

"No, I should apologise! My outburst was uncalled for. What time is this presentation?"

"It's starting soon, and people are starting to gather."

"I'll be late."

"I'm sure that won't matter. Will you please just show your face?"

Kate was beginning to feel a little sorry for Amanda—she was obviously at the rough end of Jasper's tongue—but a boring presentation still wasn't appealing. Sleep was more important than smiling at a group of boring businessmen.

She quickly refreshed her mind; what was at stake? If this could get her closer to a new life away from Wellsbury, she would go. She scanned the room for the sales contract she'd signed. Jasper had been more than generous, but he'd added the proviso that the sale depended on her accepting the housekeeping job. Crafty bugger.

The job came with other duties, mainly admin, and a non-disclosure agreement. That was of no consequence; Kate didn't do gossip. But she was a little curious as to why Jasper was being so cautious. She pushed that to the back of her mind, and a wicked grin spread across her face as she thought of a weekend or two with sex on legs.

"Please." Amanda's pleading voice echoed

into her ear. "He's in such a mood, and it's taken ages to contact you."

"Okay. Give me half hour. On second thought—forty-five minutes."

***

Kate had just finished drying her hair when the shop door shuddered with a heavy knock.

"Kate Reynolds, open up!" a loud voice boomed.

"What the fuck do you think you're doing?"

Kate cringed; that was the second time she had used that word today. She was so annoyed.

"Ms Reynolds?"

Her mouth opened but no words escaped. She opened the door and Don walked in. Her eyes settled on the black Range Rover parked on the pavement.

"This isn't necessary. I can drive myself."

"Mr Carmichael. He's the boss. I just follow instructions."

"Just give me ten minutes."

Don smiled as he watched Kate disappear towards the rear of the shop. So, this was the woman who had made his boss smile. He'd looked well-fucked this morning, and so did she.

***

Jasper twisted his wrist and stared at his Omega watch. *Where the hell is she?*

The presentation about the shopping and leisure centre had gone badly. The businessmen liked the idea but were reluctant to confirm if they would be willing to open retail outlets. Jasper needed one of them to convince the others of the benefits of his project. That was when Kate came into his mind. She was one of them. They would listen to her.

A feeling of relief welled in him when he caught a glimpse of blonde hair being flicked back and Amanda rushing towards the door. Don stood guard-like while Amanda shook Kate's hand and smiled.

A young waiter hurried towards her, offering finger food and wine. Amanda was talking as she guided Kate towards the shopping centre model.

Only the top button of Kate's shirt was open. Jasper inwardly smiled; he had marked the top of her breast when she cried his name for the third time. Memories of sex with Kate Reynolds came flooding back. She was tight and wet. His cock had strained to be inside her. Her full breasts were just the right size; he wouldn't have to pay for enlargements. He grinned, beginning to lust for her, but he would have to wait. He had more pressing matters to deal with.

***

Don, who knew Jasper's every mood, watched with interest as Jasper's glowing blue eyes followed Kate. After sex, Jasper was always settled. But something was different this time.

He had heard panic in Jasper's voice when he phoned to ask him to pick up Kate. Don's wife had cursed—he had promised to take her shopping.

Amanda came over to stand beside him.

"Thought you were babysitting," he said, looking down at her.

"She'll be fine... He was pretty insistent that she was here."

"He was panicking when he phoned me," Don added.

They both watched Kate, who sipped white wine while studying the model.

"Big bust up this morning," Amanda whispered.

Don looked down at her with surprise. Could this be the reason for the change in Jasper?

"We all heard it. They didn't like Jasper being here—he's taken over the project."

Don raised his eyebrows. *That's unusual.*

"Jack and Max demanded him to release funds. The antiques side is struggling." She paused. "Everything's changed since Max bungled his way into the company. He's too thick with Jack... They're trying push Jasper out."

"And you know because...?" Don asked.

"Jasper's cancelled Miami," Amanda confided. "He's needed there. But this project is make or break."

"He must know Jack's been fiddling," commented Don.

"Someone's been going through Jasper's office."

Don's mind flicked to the box Jasper had removed from his safe.

"Richard said Jasper couldn't cope with more work. Got to agree. If he doesn't slow down, he'll crack."

Don changed the topic. "Do you know if he's bought the shop?"

"That's another thing. Jack's been pushing for the development. Jasper's resisted until now."

Don and Amanda's eyes rested on Kate as she walked through the crowd.

"I wonder if it's her?" Amanda said.

"He was with her all night," Don commented.

"He told me that he was employing someone

to oversee the project while he's away."

"What?"

Amanda nodded. "When I went in the conference room, he was sat with his head in his hands. Asked me to phone Kate."

***

Jasper was tiring of being polite to the business leaders and the good people of Wellsbury. They were obviously not in favour of his planned shopping centre, most being content to live in the past and be left behind by other towns that were only too willing to modernise using outside investment. They needed persuading.

The room suddenly hushed, and all eyes turned to Nigel, pushing through the crowd so he could greet Kate. He smiled and planted soft kisses on her cheeks. Her surprised look didn't stop him from slipping his arm around her. Jasper cringed.

Jasper watched with some interest as two businessmen he considered old-school skilfully manoeuvred Nigel to one side and guided Kate to the food table. It was obvious they had no intention of Nigel having Kate all to himself. When two more businessmen joined in the discussion, Jasper inwardly smiled. He couldn't hear their conversation, but when Kate deftly moved the group back to the model of the proposed centre, he knew his plan to use Kate to influence them was working.

Jasper uneasily watched as fingers were pointed and voices raised, but Kate seemed undeterred. He instructed a waiter to refill Kate's glass in the hope that this would encourage the flow of discussion.

"What the fuck's going on?" Jack said into Jasper's ear.

"You better hope she's persuading them to agree to the centre," Jasper whispered. "And for fuck's sake, keep Max away from her."

Jasper caught the waiter's arm. "What's she saying?" he asked.

"Didn't hear."

"Don't lie to me, son," Jasper said impatiently.

"She asked them what they want, derelict buildings or a new development."

"She wants the fuckin' money," commented Jack.

"Of course she wants the money. Wouldn't you?" snapped Jasper.

From out of nowhere Max sidled up to Kate. His thick index finger pointed at the model. Jasper could just hear what he was saying.

"Your shop's here."

Max's gravelly voice made Kate visually shudder as she looked where he was pointing. She moved slightly. He was too close for her liking. He took a step closer. She could now feel his breath on her neck.

Jasper and Jack hurried towards Kate and Max.

"I'm Max. A partner in Carmichael and Swain."

I know who you are, thought Kate. *Everyone in Wellsbury knows who you are.*

She kept her gaze steady on the model, pretending to listen to the discussion surrounding her.

"Have you signed?" His voice was low but unmistakably aggressive.

She said nothing.

"Ah, that's why you're here! Nigel was surprised to see you," Max added.

Kate's stomach churned. Max frightened her. Where the hell was Jasper?

During her time running the flower shop, Kate had experienced all types of people, but she had never experienced the likes of Max. He instilled fear—another reason to take the money and leave.

"Kate! Good of you to come." Jasper's friendly voice went a long way to settling her churning stomach.

Their eyes briefly met.

"Impressive, isn't it?" Jasper continued, nodding towards the model. But Kate wasn't listening, Max still had her full attention. "I see Max has pointed out your shop. It's key to our development."

Jasper slipped his arm around her waist and gently squeezed, claiming her for all to see. From the corner of her eye, she saw Max's body stiffen. Jasper pretended not to notice and continued to point out various features of the proposed development.

"This is not only a shopping centre but a place for people to relax and enjoy. There are places to eat and drink, areas for entertainment, cinemas, a luxury hotel and apartments."

People listened and watched as Jasper reiterated his rehearsed speech on his proposed shopping centre.

His hand settled on the small of Kate's back as he guided her around the model, pointing out the hotel, cinema, shops, restaurants and apartments. He occasionally leaned into her, his warm breath grazing her neck.

The young waiter appeared and offered them more wine. Jasper handed Kate a glass, giving her his best smile.

"What do you think, Kate?" shouted one of the old-school businessmen.

"I think it's better in Wellsbury than another town. It's got to be better than what we've got." There was a slight quiver in her voice, but no one appeared to notice. Jasper did. She glanced towards the doubters. "I see jobs, new businesses, shoppers, an influx of people eager to experience urban living."

"You would say that—you're selling the shop," commented another voice. "You'll be leaving with money in your pocket."

"Yes, I'll have money, but it doesn't mean I'm leaving," she lied.

***

Several glasses of wine later, a tipsy Kate stood in Jasper's office. It was a corner office with large windows on two sides, giving him uninterrupted views of Wellsbury.

She couldn't resist admiring the view, and Jasper couldn't resist wrapping his arms around her waist.

"You had them eating out of your hand." His soft words caressed her ear.

She turned, giving him an approving smile. Their lips met.

He took her hand and eased open an adjoining door.

"I would like this to be your office."

"Mine?"

"My very private and personal assistant needs an office."

It was very small compared to his. Doors to three sides and a window to one. In the far corner, a kettle and microwave sat on a newish work surface.

"That leads to the side car park," he said, pointing to the door opposite the one to his office. "That goes into the main office."

"But it's only for a few months," she commented, staring at the computer on the desk.

"That's yours. You'll have access to company finances. I'll need you to check some accounts." He hesitated. "I want the old company archives sorted."

She turned and their eyes met.

"The pay will be considerable. Also..." He hesitated, as if carefully choosing his words. "My apartment needs a sitter while I'm away. And I need sex. And after last night, I've no worries about that."

She blushed a deep red.

"It's only for a few months." Jasper's voice took a nervous tone. He pulled her close to his body, their lips grazing. His fingers stroked her hairline. "I need someone I can trust to watch my back while I'm away. The vultures are gathering."

The door bounced open.

"What the fuck's going on?" Beth snarled, looking daggers at Kate and Jasper. Jasper had never been so tender with her.

"'As she fucking signed?" said an unpleasantly familiar voice—Max.

As Max, Jack, Richard and Beth pushed into the room, a hostile tension followed them.

Why is Beth here? Kate thought.

"We need money, Jasper." Even Jack's voice had an aggressive edge.

Jasper ignored him. "I have something to say." He moved to stand behind his desk. "While I'm away, Kate will oversee all money issues." His tone was firm.

"What the fuck?" exclaimed Richard.

"I want fresh eyes on our business." Jasper's eyes briefly rested on Jack, his business partner. Once upon a time they had worked together as a team, but now Jack worked against Jasper thanks to the influence of Richard, Jasper's half-brother, and Beth, his discarded lover. Richard wanted money to feed his drug habit and Beth wanted revenge for being kicked out of Jasper's bed.

Jasper's eyes settled on Beth. "Why are you here?"

Beth reddened. "I have every right. You fucking dumped me."

"You have no right." Jasper's tone was abrupt. "Now get the fuck out."

"You don't know this girl," growled Max.

"I want fresh eyes on our business."

Kate reddened. Jasper had put her on the spot. A hateful undercurrent swished between the partners. Were these the vultures Jasper had referred to?

"Money is going to be tight until Miami is closed," Jasper continued.

"What about my antiques?" Jack's voice hadn't lost its aggressive tone.

"Make do until Miami is sorted."

"You're hanging it out to dry. Just like you've always wanted," Jack snapped, thumping Jasper's desk.

"That's not true, Jack, and you know it." Their eyes met like two men about to fight. "The property market's slowed. Many are losing money. I prefer to wait until it picks up."

"What were you doing in the Caymans?" Max growled.

Jasper was taken aback. His mind immediately flashed to the supposed secret Cayman Islands meeting. Faces appeared before him as he tried to guess the whistleblower.

"We know all about your secret dealing with the Cayman crew," continued Max.

"Were you going to tell us?" asked Richard.

"No need. You appear to already know."

"My contacts tell me you've bought property." Max's snide tone put Jasper on the spot again.

"Yes. People that I've known for years have serious financial problems."

Jack's temper flared. "You fucking bought more property. When you knew the antiques are running at a loss."

"In a few months, the market will pick up and I will sell. And make a bigger profit."

"Profit for Jasper Carmichael or Carmichael and Swain?" Max sneered.

How much does Max know? thought Jasper.

"My contacts tell me your friends aren't happy with you," Max confidently added.

"They had a choice. Just like you lot have a choice." Jasper's impatience showed in his voice. "They decided to sell to me and cut their losses. I had to make instant decisions: wait until the property market rises and make a big profit, or sell and maybe lose money."

"Where does she come in?" asked Beth, clearly not interested about the ins and outs of the property market.

"Kate will be my personal assistant and apartment sitter."

A tense, hostile silence surfaced.

"Your personal assistant and apartment sitter," Max scoffed. His cruel eyes made Kate shudder. "Well, I need some help, and she'll be underused while you're away." He laughed. "Particularly in the pussy department."

"Shut the fuck up." Max had stirred Jasper's

temper. "For your information, I'm paying Kate's wages, not C and S."

Kate was the colour of beetroot. She didn't want to be in the same building as these people, but she felt sorry for Jasper. He was in a desperate situation. He couldn't trust these people; they wanted control of his company.

He was offering her stupid money for three months to babysit his apartment and do admin work. The icing on the cake was mind-blowing sex. She could cope with that. But Max was another question. He frightened her.

Richard's loud voice brought her out of her thoughts. "When?"

"I'm flying out tonight. Kate will move in. The shop will close. When I get back, I expect detailed quotes from contractors."

"No way!" shouted Jack.

"Make it happen. The council won't be a problem. I've met a number of contractors that are very eager for the work."

"You're fucking gambling with the fucking company," exclaimed Jack.

"I always have."

Chapter Six

A booming knock made the apartment door shudder. A peeved Kate pulled it open and glared at Don.

"The boss said earlier start," announced Don. He had been given specific instructions to babysit Kate until he was convinced she could cope.

He lingered awkwardly in the doorway. "Jasper doesn't like me inside."

"I'm not Jasper. And I haven't finished my tea," she said, swirling the teapot and wishing he would go away.

"We've got a busy day."

"I know," snapped Kate. "First stop: the shop."

"The team is already there."

"Team?!"

"Jasper wants you settled here by the end of the day."

Now he had her attention. She stared at him. She didn't like her day being organised by someone else. And she hadn't finished her morning tea.

Don watched her as she sipped her tea while fingering the credit and debit cards lined up on the granite worktop. She then picked up her iPhone.

"I'm a fish out of water, Don," she admitted.

"Aye."

His sympathetic tone did nothing to alleviate her nervously churning stomach. "I'm not welcome here."

Don didn't know how to answer. She *wasn't*

welcome. Jasper had given her business responsibilities that Jack, Richard and Max thought should be theirs. Beth hated her because she had taken her place in Jasper's bed. Nigel hated her because she had agreed to sell the shop without him being present and, more importantly for him, she was sleeping with Jasper when he thought it should have been him.

"How long have you known Jasper?" she asked.

"Me and the family came with him from London. He's been good to us."

She nodded, slowly arranged the cards in her purse and walked to the door.

***

Jasper had insisted she gave the shop keys to him. And now she knew why.

The shop was a hive of activity. Flowers were being loaded into a white Transit van. A Luton van was being loaded with her possessions.

"Kate Reynolds!" bellowed a rough-looking bear of a man.

"Yes?" she meekly replied.

"Bruce. I work for Jasper." He strode towards her and gripped her hand.

She looked round for Don. He was leaning against the Range Rover as if he hadn't a care in the world. He certainly didn't show any signs of wanting to help. She momently hesitated as a daunting realisation sank in. None of Jasper's employees would do more than the bare minimum to help her; they wanted her to fail. But they didn't know Kate Reynolds and her steely determination.

"There's just your personal stuff to pack," Bruce the bear-like man continued.

She glanced at the removal van. Neatly packed inside was the furniture of her small ground-floor flat. Her initial reaction was to shout at Bruce, but it would have been futile. The furniture would be of no use when she started her new life anyway. She wandered into the van.

"What you looking for?" shouted Bruce.

Then Kate saw what she was looking for. Her beach painting. She had worked on it through her uni art classes. Her group had made several trips to the beach, and each trip had inspired her more. It was the only survivor of her father's destructive rampage, the day he destroyed nearly everything she held dear. Her paintings, her uni work. *Bastard*.

She held the beach painting in both hands and gazed at it, her eyes filling with memories. She liked painting; her art teacher had told her she had potential.

"Where are you taking my furniture?" She tried to sound concerned, but she didn't care. The only thing she cared about, she held in her hands.

"Jasper owns a row of lock-ups. Your clothes and stuff will go in the apartment."

"I don't have a great deal."

"Just as well he's given us another job."

"Keeps you busy then."

"Good bloke is our Jasper."

I wouldn't know, she thought. The only thing she knew about Jasper was he gave her deep, satisfying orgasms. Her tender breasts and sore sex were testament to his skill.

***

"It's true then." An angry voice Kate knew well echoed through the empty shop. "His solicitor's been in touch. Sending a courier with documents for approval."

Kate paid Nigel no attention. As far as she was concerned, he was to approve the sale of the shop. He had no need to know about her agreement to be Jasper's personal assistant and housekeeper.

"It's more than I expected," she offered in way of response.

"You could 'ave screwed him for more," Nigel angrily retorted.

We've been screwing all night, she thought. After she'd signed the non-disclosure agreement, they'd had sex in bed, the shower and, just before he left, the kitchen.

"You're moving in then?"

"It's temporary, Nigel," Kate snapped.

"I don't understand why you're getting involved with the likes of Jasper Carmichael."

To be honest, neither do I, she thought. But Jasper did intrigue her. Living in his apartment was like living in a luxury hotel. Had she given in to the temptation of money and sex? For some reason, she didn't care. She didn't want to reach ninety and regret not experiencing the likes of Jasper Carmichael.

"The police are showing more than an interest in him."

She hadn't known that. But it wouldn't have affected her decision. She'd neither known nor cared.

Bruce stood by the open door, patiently waiting for the keys. Kate took one last look around the place she had called home for more years than she cared to remember. Her sanctuary after her marriage had ended. The work that healed the emotional wounds from losing her baby. The work that had hidden the abuse from her demanding, unloving father. She had never been good enough for him. He'd never appreciated her saving the business and the care she had given him. He died a bitter old man, and she hadn't shed a tear.

She turned to meet Bruce's stare and dropped the keys into his open palm.

"Do you know what you're doing? This is not like you, Kate." Nigel's angry voice followed her as she walked to the Range Rover. "Is he fucking you? He has a reputation. Eric—"

At the mention of Eric, anger flashed across her face.

"Fuck Eric. What's it to do with him? For that matter, what's it to do with you? Just make the sale legal."

"But fucking him after all the women he's had…"

"Pot calling the kettle, Nigel. You and I go way back, remember? I know you've been fucking Michelle for years." Kate slammed the passenger door.

A shocked Nigel stood and stared at the Range Rover as it disappeared into the distance.

***

Kate shook out her favourite V-neck cerise dress before slipping it onto a hanger. Her only other dress, the same design but lilac, was already hanging in the wall-to-wall wardrobe of Jasper's guest bedroom.

She had stood her ground today, making it perfectly clear to Don and Joanne she wasn't going to be pushed around.

After they left the flower shop, Don had driven her to Joanne's Boutique. Joanne's expensive designer clothes were well known in the town. It was important to Jasper for his staff to be smartly dressed—grey suits and white shirts. And Joanne was the sole supplier of those clothes. She also operated a very successful escort business. Again, Jasper was one of her best customers.

Kate had given in to Jasper and Joanne's demands and agreed to adhere to the company dress code while at the office. Grey skirt and jacket and white blouse, although Kate had insisted upon a round-neck shirt. When Joanne urged her to buy a black cocktail dress, the atmosphere went from tense to hostile. Kate didn't like black. It didn't suit her. When Joanne and Don put pressure on Kate, she refused.

"You can't wear fucking jeans to the Carmichael office," Joanne had admonished.

Her choice of words only added to Kate's lack of co-operation.

Kate carefully slid the new matching bra and panties to the back of her underwear drawer. They were all her size and more revealing than she would have liked.

"Jasper's very particular about lingerie," Joanne had commented, grinning. "He'll expect them to be matching."

There was nothing wrong with her everyday M&S underwear. White lace half-cup bra with lace-trimmed knickers. Jasper hadn't grumbled when he removed them. But he'd had other things on his mind. She grinned.

How many times Jasper had fucked not only Joanne but her escorts? Kate put the thought out of her mind. It didn't matter. In a few months, Jasper Carmichael would be a pleasurable memory.

Kate settled into the overstuffed couch, glass of red wine in hand, and thought about Don. She had an uneasy feeling about him, even though he was one of Jasper's trusted friends.

He had waited till they were alone in the car before advising her to accept Joanne's clothes and not to argue. He added that since Jasper and Beth had broken up, he and Joanne had become close. He was a regular user of her escort business, and when all her girls were busy, Joanne took their place. But Kate had already known.

From Joanne's, Don drove to Kenny's Garage, where a brand new Evoque was waiting for her.

By the time Don left, they were barely speaking.

If Don or Joanne thought they were going to boss her around, they had another think coming. The only person she took orders from was Jasper, and that was only for three months.

Her musing was abruptly interrupted by a high-pitched sound indicative of an old-fashioned phone.

"Joanne tells me you were difficult."

She recognised Jasper's voice but was taken aback by his impatient tone.

"I wasn't difficult."

"You didn't like the clothes."

"I don't like black. I agreed to the uniform," she corrected.

Silence.

"Tomorrow, Amanda will give you keys and stationary supplies. It may be a good idea to buy your own tea." He paused. "She was adamant that you're working for me and not Carmichael and Swain and as such, not eligible for free drinks."

"That's petty."

"I agree."

"Thank you for the Evoque. Bruce and his

team emptied the shop. Flowers sold."

Silence.

"When will you be back?" she asked.

"Jack, Richard, Max and Beth will try to interfere. Don't let them." He sighed.

"You're tired."

"A little. Keep the doors locked. I've changed the code to the apartment, so you should be safe."

"Any idea when you're back?" she asked again.

"No."

"Take care," she said, her voice full of concern.

She didn't quite catch what he said, but it sounded like *miss you*.

Chapter Seven

The rain was pouring down when the flight left Miami. The pilot informed the passengers to be prepared for a bumpy ride and to keep seatbelts on.

There would be no desperately needed sleep for Jasper.

He cast his mind back to those early days, when over drinks in a George Town bar, a group of disillusioned property dealers had formed a property consortium. Buying and selling with this group of entrepreneurs had made him and Carmichael and Swain a lot of money. Money that Jack and Richard had squandered on drugs and alcohol. And now, to get Carmichael and Swain financially sound, he had gone against the spirit of the consortium.

He had watched and waited until the hotel came on the market. The owner of the ocean-front hotel had had his line of credit stopped by the bank. Jasper had tried to give the impression of sympathy for the owner's plight, but he had his own business to save. So, to save his company, he bought the hotel with money he didn't have. He anticipated the profit from a quick re-sale of the hotel would solve all immediate financial problems.

If only the consortium members had waited for him to arrive in Miami. If only they had been patient, as he had advised, and waited for the right moment. But he was losing influence within the group. It was common knowledge that his Miami operation was in trouble.

Jasper's arrangement with like-minded property dealers had made him rich. However, since his Miami operation was in trouble, he had lost favour with his business associates. Consequently, he anticipated that they wouldn't be interested in the hotel. His gut told him to tread carefully. The behaviour of his group of dealers was out of character. In the past, when one of the group was in trouble, they rallied to help. But no one offered to help Jasper over this rough patch he was experiencing. It was as if they had an ulterior motive: the demise of Jasper Carmichael.

Jasper could have approached the consortium's sole South American associate, Anton. But Anton was dangerous; his business reached every corner of the world. Anton's empire reminded Jasper of a spider's web—once caught, you never got out. Anton had strict rules that must be obeyed. Jasper was well aware of the consequences if you crossed Anton, but this didn't deter him from seeking another group of South American investors.

He felt confident that his dealing with these new South American investors wouldn't be traced.

***

Kate cheerfully gazed around her new surroundings.

I could get used to this, she thought as she sat sipping her second cup of morning tea. *Even if it is only for three months.*

Granite tops, fitted cupboards that opened with a slight touch, a six-burner hob that looked as if it had never been used, stainless steel utensils that hung from a beam.

My new home will probably have something similar. Not as expensive though.

A loud ping from her new iPhone jolted her out of her musings. She sighed. No peace for the wicked.

A message from Jasper: *Appointment. Dr Lomax. Eight. Before surgery.*

Second message: *Ask no questions. Remember the non-disclosure agreement.*

Kate thought about telling him to get lost, but on second thought, she could put up with his bossiness for a few months.

***

Dr Lomax's practice was in the expensive part of town, a converted Victorian villa.

"Go straight through," the glamorous receptionist instructed, more interested in the colour of her fingernails than Kate. "He's expecting you."

Dr Lomax sat behind an expensive antique oak desk, his head down, reading a file.

"Kate Reynolds," he said into the file, and pointed to the seat in front of his large oak desk. "You must be important." His eyes were still focused on the file. "Jasper's called in one of his favours." He finally lifted his head, and their eyes met. "Jasper and I go back. He set me up here."

He's miffed, thought Kate, *that Jasper's called in a favour.*

"Your GP was annoyed about me having your records. Healthy, except for a miscarriage."

"Yes. I fell down some stairs. Lost my baby."

"How did you feel about that?"

"How do you think I felt?" Kate snapped. "I'd just lost my baby. I was devastated."

Kate's impatient tone made Lomax stop and stare at her.

"No hysterectomy." He raised his eyebrows. "How do you feel about that?"

"At the time, the doctor advised against it. They considered the operation life threatening. I was weak. I'd lost a lot of blood. My mind was messed up."

"It clearly states that the uterus should be removed."

"I know what the file recommends. It took me a while to regain my health; I couldn't face the operation. It was doing no harm."

She had no intention of recalling the pain and anguish she had suffered after losing her baby, the mental torment that followed, how she had shunned men until Jasper Carmichael. She wasn't going to share her inner self with a soul, least of all Dr Lomax.

"Right, let's have a quick look."

"What?"

"Jasper's requested a full exam. Go through the door. The nurse will help you."

Twenty minutes later, the nurse helped an angry Kate get dressed.

"He's not normally like that," the nurse had whispered. "He's a caring, thoughtful man."

But the nurse's comments did nothing to ease the humiliation that Lomax had inflicted on Kate. She'd been naked, legs apart, while Lomax made comments about Jasper fucking her. He described Jasper as an animal with no regard for the delicate female form.

"He fucks like an animal," he had admonished as he inserted a cold instrument inside her. "I can see he hasn't changed."

Kate refused to react to Lomax. He was wrong. Jasper was gentle, considerate—not an animal. He had waited while she adjusted to his size. His slow movements sent warm, comforting, sensations through her body. Jasper had healed her.

"I've sent Jasper a message confirming you're fit and healthy," Lomax said after the examination. "No problems down below." He smirked.

"What?" Her loud exclamation made Dr Lomax stop and stare.

"You must be special. He's never done this before. Not even with Beth."

"I don't understand."

"He's just bought your flower shop?" Lomax continued.

"What's that to do with this?"

"You're now working for him. A very important role, I'm told. All a bit odd to say the least."

"I don't know about that. It's just temporary." Her tone was matter of fact.

"Do you know where he is? I'd like to post a report."

Alarm bells rang in Kate's head. It seemed suspicious—why did he really want to know?

"Dr Lomax, Jasper operates on a need to know basis. And I don't need to know where he is. As for the report, send it to his home address."

She stood, turned and left.

Lomax walked to his office window, watching Don walk towards Kate.

"She's going to be difficult," he said into his phone. "Mind of her own."

"Will he get her pregnant?" said the voice, trying to hide his South American accent.

"I agree with her GP—it's unlikely she can have children."

"I detect a but."

"Doctors can be wrong. Particularly where fertility is concerned. There's no guarantee. She still has all her parts."

"I don't want a fucking description," the voice cursed. "Did you ask about Jasper? He's not where he's supposed to be."

"She didn't know."

"Is Don there?"

"Yes. He was waiting," Lomax said, his eyes still on Kate.

The line went dead.

Lomax switched to his mobile banking app. He was five thousand pounds richer.

***

"Everything alright?" Don asked. "You look angry."

They stood by Kate's Evoque.

"I'm fine," she said. "Just too much prodding and probing."

Don reddened and nodded. He felt awkward discussing women's private parts. "You need me at the office?" he enquired.

"I'm not going to the office."

"Do you think that's a good idea?"

"The apartment is still upside down. There's no food. Amanda can wait."

"Have you heard from Jasper?" Don asked.

Kate gave him a curious look. Why did they all think she knew where Jasper was?

"No!" Her loud, impatient tone took Don by surprise. "I'm sorry. Lomax asked the same question. Jasper operates on a need to know basis. And I don't need to know." *And even if I did know, I wouldn't tell you*.

"Only, he's given me time off, and Milly wants

to go away," Don continued.

Kate stared into his confused eyes. "Is that unusual?"

"Yes! He's acting out of character."

She hesitated. She hadn't expected Don to be so frank.

"I'm sure everything will be alright," she said. "Take a break. Spend quality time with Milly."

"You should know Joanne's emailed him. Complaining."

"About?"

"Your lack of co-operation." He turned and began to walk back towards the car. "Watch your back," he said over his shoulder.

Chapter Eight

"I'm glad you have time to go shopping, but I have an office to run," Amanda's angry voice bellowed into Kate's earpiece. "Jasper may be paying you, but that doesn't mean you shouldn't be here."

Kate ended the call. She had neither the time nor inclination to listen to Amanda. Jasper was her boss—and that was only for a few months—not the staff at Carmichael and Swain.

She pondered on how Amanda had found out she'd been shopping. *Don,* she thought.

"Well, fuck Don and Amanda," she cursed.

Her phone rang again.

"What now?" she yelled.

"Stop annoying my staff." Jasper's stern voice caressed her ears. "When you finally go to the office, you'll find a table full of dirty, dusty files. The IT technician should have installed a scanner, printer and copier. Scan the files onto a USB stick. Apologise to Amanda."

The line went dead, but not before she heard a flight called.

***

Kate stared at the chaos of her office. The dirty files weren't on a table, they were on her desk. *Amanda,* she thought.

An hour later, the files were on the table and Kate sat eating a biscuit and drinking tea. The door to the main office burst open.

"Where the fuck is he?" Jack yelled. "He's not in fucking Miami." His eyes moved to the dirty files on the table, widening with recognition. "What the fuck?"

"What are you doing with these?" snapped Max, who had followed Jack.

Kate watched him run his fat fingers through the dust. "Sorting," she remarked in a matter-of-fact manner, eager not to provoke either of them.

"So, you've got control over Carmichael and Swain's finances," Max said.

Kate didn't answer.

"We need an injection of cash," Jack sheepishly commented.

"Just transfer this amount into the antiques account," Max said, dropping a folded piece of paper onto Kate's desk. "There's a good girl." His patronising tone riled her.

She ripped the paper into several pieces and dropped it into the waste bin without reading it.

"I work for Jasper. Not you."

Max went bright red and clenched his fists. "You'll regret that, bitch!" he yelled as he stormed back into the main office.

***

Jasper was relaxing in his Mitchem safe house, sipping a very large brandy. He was very pleased with himself.

He couldn't believe how smoothly the sale had gone with the South Americans. The consortium members had more or less told him to fuck off, so all the profit from the Miami hotel was his.

At that very moment, his laptop pinged. An email from Kate.

How long would it take her to discover his

double dealings, now she had access to the C&S archives and company files?

I have a new table, she wrote. *A large, new table covered in old dusty, dirty files. My new sparkling clean uniform is now dirty. I'm dirty. I can't stop sneezing. I'm leaving :)*

He grinned.

I should leave. Lomax humiliated me. Probing and prodding. Comments about our sex. I'm not going to him again. Find another doctor.

Max tried his luck getting me to transfer money. And why have you sent Don away?

He stopped grinning. He hadn't sent Don anywhere. And what had Lomax been up to? Max trying to get money was not a surprise though.

Jasper felt his temper trying to surface.

His thoughts turned to Kate. Her medical file had pricked his conscience. When the ambulance crew arrived on the night of her miscarriage, she'd been lying unconscious at the bottom of the stairs. She had lost a lot of blood. Reading between the lines, her hospital treatment had bordered on neglect. It was obvious that the doctor who initially examined her didn't expect her to live. Her baby was dead. It wasn't until the duty consultant read her notes that Kate's chances of survival increased.

What made his temper boil was that no one had visited her until Nigel James appeared days later while she was recovering. Nigel fucking James, who no doubt realised that Kate would need a shoulder to cry on. Kate was Old Man Reynolds' only child and would inherit.

His mind turned to Eric. Jasper was convinced he'd pushed her. He'd caused her suffering.

Jasper vowed to make Eric grovel.

He strolled into his wet room and folded his

clothes into a neat pile before standing under the fast-flowing water. His outstretched arms supported his aching body while the warm water worked its magic on his back.

His brandy-induced thoughts returned to those that had betrayed him.

Beth, Jack and Richard. He had trusted them. He had never looked at another woman, and God knows he had turned many away. The image of Beth lying in the king-size bed he had fucked her in, screaming her head off with Jack plunging between her legs, Richard's head buried between her large, full breasts, which Jasper had paid to be enlarged. Richard's full condom discarded on the floor.

Richard looked up. "You should have phoned, old boy."

He then returned to sucking her breasts.

Jasper had snapped. He tore Jack off her and pushed Richard away. Jack went to punch him, but he should have known better. His fist met Jack's cheek with such power that Jack was out cold. Richard scurried away, his tail between his legs. He had never seen his brother like this, but Jack had.

The next day, the mansion was divided. Jasper had his own apartment modelled to his high standards. He hadn't touched Beth since and only just managed to be civil to Jack and Richard.

But what was Don up to? Jasper hadn't sent him away. His gut churned as Colin's advice came into his mind: *Listen to your gut.* And his gut told him to be careful. Don was his most trusted employee. He'd known Colin, he'd moved with Jasper to Wellsbury. Jasper had bought him a house and refurbished it. He'd been more than a little surprised when Kate had told him it had been her family house. *Small world.*

Was Don in cahoots with Max Wilson? Jasper disliked the man, but Jack and Richard had made it perfectly clear that Max's inclusion on the Carmichael and Swain board was not up for negotiation.

The Wilsons and Colin Carmichael were gangland rivals, back in the day. Since Jasper had moved, he'd only had minimal dealing with the Wilson brothers, Charlie, Max and Matt. As far he was concerned, they were scum. They had made their money in drugs and the sex trade. That was probably how Richard and Max had become friends.

Jasper had resisted Jack and Richard's requests for Max to have access to the company finances. They had argued that when Jasper was away, the company had cashflow problems. Jasper had solved that by giving Kate access to the finances. He hoped he hadn't made the wrong choice.

Unconsciously, he thumped the wet-room's tiled wall. Blood trickled from his knuckles. Betrayal had this effect on him.

He needed sex. A lot of it. *Kate.* He needed to pin her against the shower wall and fuck her, hard. He needed to hear her scream. She was tight and wet. Her soft, curvaceous body and large breasts were natural and inviting, and she didn't fake orgasms.

He wrapped himself in two bath sheets and collapsed onto the bed.

Chapter Nine

Kate was looking forward to the weekend. While Jasper was away, she'd have plenty of me time. A lie-in. Clothes shopping, maybe—her well-washed jeans were past their best. A bottle of wine and an evening watching a film on Netflix. Jasper had subscribed to so many channels, she was spoilt for choice.

Shopping didn't take long; she wasn't one who enjoyed walking in and out of shops. But she did enjoy wandering around the Saturday open-air market. It was a colourful, vibrant place to be. Kate knew most of the stall holders and enjoyed the friendly banter she shared with them. Their fruit and veg was fresh, their meat and eggs locally sourced.

A tinge of sadness filled her. She would miss this when she left Wellsbury.

She pulled into the George car park and wandered over to the demolition site where the shopping centre would stand. She couldn't believe her eyes; the flower shop was a pile of bricks. She couldn't help feeling a little sad. Her gaze wandered over the site, taking in the rubble that had once been buildings. *That was quick,* she thought, as her eyes settled on a crane and wrecking ball. A group of men were guiding it onto a trailer. She stood for a while, realising the destructive power of the machine. She pulled her new iPhone from her pocket and took photos, making a mental note to find out who had authorised this demolition work.

"Are you Kate Reynolds?" boomed a rough Irish voice.

She turned and was face to face with a very large man. His big, weather-beaten face hadn't seen a razor for days. His small black eyes wandered up and down her body.

"Eric said you're the one to see."

"About?"

"We've been here a week. And no bugger from Carmichael's been."

"It's Jack you want."

"You in charge of paying?"

He pushed sheets of dirty, crunched-up paper into her hand. A quick glance at the figures, and she saw they weren't right.

"Jack never checks my figures. He pays what's owed. Eric said you're a tight one." He sniggered, eyes moving up and down her body. "In more ways than one." He grinned.

He was provoking Kate, and it worked. She pushed the dirty papers into his overhanging stomach.

"You can take these and your snide comments back where they came from." She nodded at the pub. "If you want payment, you need proper clean paperwork, presented to the office."

"Jack never fucking bothers."

"I'm not Jack," she snapped.

She turned away, but another deep voice shouted to her. "Are you Carmichael and Swain?"

Not again, thought Kate, more than a little irritated.

She turned to be confronted by a tall, clean-shaven man with shining brown eyes.

"Luke Jones. I own a salvaging company." He gripped her hand. "These bricks, wood—what you doing with them?"

"Got a contract with the council," interrupted the Irish man. "They take it away."

That sounds a bit off, thought Kate. No one had mentioned the council being involved with demolition.

Luke Jones was very persuasive. So much so that Kate spent the rest of Saturday with him, wandering around his extensive plant, awestruck by the sheer size of the operation and his knowledge of demolition and salvage.

"We operate a shift system, twenty-four hours, seven days a week."

Kate nodded as if she understood the need for a twenty-four-seven shift system.

"We only shut down over Christmas." He grinned. "I'd be in the divorce court if we didn't."

They were watching a skip driver expertly reversing into a recycling bay.

"I'm hoping to go into plastic recycling. I've submitted plans to the council, but I need a backer or another big contract. That's where Carmichael and Swain comes in."

She turned to give him her full attention.

"There's a big road-building programme in the pipeline. The bricks from your demolition site are of poor quality, but they can be crushed and used for road-building." Luke pointed to a conveyor belt at the far end of the plant, delivering bricks to the crusher.

Kate was pleased when he suggested coffee in his office, where she could examine all the approved paperwork for his business operation, including health and safety.

"We work to the book here," he said.

Kate lifted her eyes from the paperwork.

"Before any demolition, the site has to be

surveyed, types of construction material used have to be identified. Use of the empty building…" He paused. Kate had gone still, her grip on the paper tightening. "The presence of wastewater, hazardous material, drainage, flooding. We have to consider people. Noise, dust, impact of traffic… You get my drift, Kate.

"From your expression, I take it that you were unaware of the demolition. I'm afraid that doesn't alter the fact that Carmichael and Swain have broken the law. It's a council decision how best to proceed."

***

Kate drove straight back to Carmichael and Swain's offices, intending to find out how they had acted on previous building projects. But as she drove past Joanne's, she nearly crashed her car. There, parked outside the building, was Jasper's Range Rover. There was no mistaking that it was his.

Kate's mind went into overdrive; Jasper never parked his car where it could be seen, and she didn't know that he was back in town.

Putting the thought to the back of her mind for now, Kate continued on to the office. She surprised the security guard when she drove up to the main gate.

"No one's here," he shouted.

Kate shook her head, and he raised the barrier to let her pass.

It was obvious that Carmichael and Swain would be getting a visit from the council. How on earth Jasper was going to talk his way out of this was beyond her; the best the company could hope for was a fine.

Somehow, Carmichael and Swain's cowboy reputation had to be buried. Once inside her office, Kate turned to the mass of files. Somewhere amongst them must be records of how Carmichael and Swain had conducted itself on other building projects.

She opened a bottle of red wine and began the monotonous task of organising the files.

Chapter Ten

Monday started badly for Kate; she had tossed and turned all night. Jasper hadn't returned to the apartment. Her concern had gone into overdrive when she saw his Range Rover parked outside Joanne's. Jasper never parked his car where it could be seen.

Her stomach hadn't stopped churning. Jasper had admitted he needed a lot of sex, particularly when he was stressed. She obviously wasn't enough for him. She tried to convince herself that she had no claim over Jasper just because they'd had sex. She would just have to accept that she didn't meet his exact sexual requirements.

She took her time dressing for the office. A satisfied smile filled her face as she gazed at her reflection. Her intention was to catch Jasper's eye, and she knew she looked good in Carmichael grey. The grey skirt fell over her hips, resting just above her knee. Her white lace bra was visible under her fitted white blouse, open to her cleavage, and the grey heels showed off her shapely legs.

There was no sign of Jasper's Range Rover when she arrived at the office. She was thankful she was alone so no one could see her disappointment.

Kate had just finished writing a report on the implications of Carmichael and Swain not complying with demolition and health and safety protocol when she heard Jasper barking out instructions to whoever had the bad luck to cross his path.

"Conference room. Now," snapped Amanda from the connecting door.

Kate stomach churned. She looked a little dazed.

Amanda mistakenly thought she was going to defy her. "Now!" she commanded. "And bring that." She nodded at the laptop. "And that file you've had your head over."

Kate jumped up and turned to grab her jacket, which hung over the chair back.

"You've no time to mess with that or your shoes. He's in a black mood."

The conference room was a large oblong room with a long mahogany table in the centre. Jasper sat at the middle of the table with his laptop open and a pile of files next to it. Jack, Richard, Max and Beth were opposite. And to Kate's amazement, Joanne sat by the door.

Amanda scurried to a small table in one corner, leaving Kate hesitantly searching for a chair.

"Here!" Jasper impatiently snapped, pointing to a chair next to him.

She reddened, momentarily hesitating before confidently flicking her long blonde hair back and slowly walking to her seat.

Jasper glared at her feet. "Shoes!" he barked.

"I left in a hurry."

Jasper raised his eyebrows in surprise.

"Oh! They're under my desk," she sheepishly answered as Jasper pulled her chair closer to him so that their thighs rubbed. If she wasn't mistaken, his tense expression relaxed. She blushed slightly as his hand rested upon her knee.

He turned his laptop so she could see her

report on Luke Jones displayed on his screen.

"I've only just finished it," she said. "Are there mistakes?"

Before Jasper could speak, Jack blurted, "We didn't expect you."

Jasper didn't answer. His mind was on Kate and the Luke Jones report. He didn't like reading about Carmichael and Swain's cavalier attitude towards the authorities. This was Jack's doing. But ultimately Jasper was responsible—he should have kept an eye on Jack.

If he had been with Kate last night, he wouldn't be on the backfoot now. And he could have fucked her. He had promised himself that, after Beth, he would never tie himself to one woman, but as tempting as Joanne's escorts had been, he had preferred a bottle of Scotch and sleep.

"We need funds." Richard's harsh tone brought Jasper out of his musing.

"Kate, tell me about the shopping centre," Jasper continued, ignoring Richard.

"Um... Been confusion over demolition," she nervously answered.

"What do you mean?" Jack snapped. "The demolition is finished?"

"It was done without paperwork."

"Fuck paperwork," snarled Jack.

Jasper glared at him. "I'm expecting a visit from the council."

"Considering the confusion..." Kate said hesitantly. "Jones Waste will survey the site and submit the correct paperwork to the council—"

Jack was on his feet, bellowing. "You 'ave no fucking right interfering! You just sign the bloody cheques."

"Explain." Jasper raised his voice, keeping his eyes on Kate. Jack sat.

The tense atmosphere went from bad to worse as she explained how the Irish contractor had confronted her demanding payment. He had shoved dirty papers into her hand with scribbles on. When she mentioned Jones Waste and health and safety, Jack exploded again.

However, Jasper's reaction was more measured. He was also concerned that the council hadn't received the correct paperwork. This project needed the cooperation of the council.

"Were these contractors on site?" questioned Jasper.

"Luke Jones was wandering around the site, but the Irishman had come out of the George."

"Have we used either of them before?"

"There's no paperwork showing that we've used either of them before," Kate replied in a self-assured manner. "I wasn't going to pay for any work that hadn't been sanctioned."

"Luke Jones is too expensive," barked Jack.

"So, who's the Irishman?" retorted Kate.

"Patrick's a reliable sub."

"And how am I to know that when there's no paperwork?"

"There's fucking paperwork." Jack was becoming irate. He didn't like being questioned by Kate.

"I've been through all the archives and there's no mention of Patrick. If that's his name."

"And when did Supergirl do that?" snapped Max.

"This weekend."

Silence.

"Your private assistant has overstepped her paygrade," growled Jack. "Max can take over."

"All shopping centre funds will go through Kate," Jasper repeated, his patience wearing thin. "Have we got value for money, Kate?" he asked.

"I don't know. But I didn't doubt Jones when he told me that C and S have treated waste disposal in a cavalier manner."

"That's a fucking lie!" shouted Jack.

"Jones has all the correct up-to-date certificates. Has Patrick?" Kate wasn't going to let Jack get one over her.

"And when did you see them?" Sarcasm spilled from Jack's voice.

"Yesterday."

Jasper froze. If Kate had driven to the office yesterday, she'd have passed Joanne's. And his car had been right outside.

"Have you agreed anything with him?" asked a distracted Jasper, not daring to look at Kate.

"Not yet. I told him to see you."

"Why did you go to the site?" he asked, perplexed.

"I just…" Kate hesitated. "Wanted a last look. But it was a pile of bricks." That was all that remained of her unhappy past.

"Is that all you're going to fucking say?" shouted Jack. "Letting pussy override me!"

Kate began to stand, but Jasper put his hand on her leg.

"I thought the shopping centre is a make or break project?" Jack stood, his hands leaning on the table, glaring at Jasper. "Every penny counts. And she takes it upon herself to employ Jones. More cost!"

Max stood, following Jack's lead. "I thought she was temporary!" he bellowed at Jasper.

Then all hell broke loose. Richard's voice joined Max and Jack's accusing shouts. Beth, who'd been glaring daggers at Jasper, stood abruptly, spitting venom. Joanne was shouting something—Kate couldn't hear what, didn't want to know what. When Amanda chimed in shouting something about stationery, it all became too much. Kate felt the room start to vibrate. She thought no one noticed her slip out of the room, but Jasper did, his eyes piercing her back.

She hurried towards her office and slammed the door. Her heart was racing. She felt hot and sticky.

This wasn't her. A voice at the back of her mind told her to leave. The money from the shop would give her a comfortable new start. She was only being greedy, wanting more money and sex.

She walked into the small bathroom and splashed cold water over her face.

Kate knew where the argument was going. A temp doesn't override the founder of the company without consequences. And she was sure that Beth and Joanne would remind Jasper that she was frigid.

She hung her head, tears and cold water dipping into the sink.

She didn't hear him enter the small bathroom, but she felt his presence. She spun around to face him.

His temper was raging; he needed release. He needed to fuck. He suddenly took a step back. The sight of Kate sobbing floored him. Her red wet cheeks, her puffy eyes. His right index finger affectionately traced her hair line and her head moved into his hand.

"You know what I want," he whispered.

She nodded, words failed her, she was too scared to admit that she wanted it too.

When it was done, they stood forehead to forehead, calming.

"You are a bastard," she finally uttered, pushing against his chest.

She gasped when he pulled out of her.

"You have no idea," he retorted, throwing her a towel.

Chapter Eleven

Jasper skidded to a halt in front of his apartment. Loud music was booming from the main house, accompanied by the customary screams and laughter. A Richard orgy.

His younger stepbrother's craving for sex had put him in prison on a rape charge. After a few months he'd been released for good behaviour, but the damage was done. He had been introduced to drugs and to Max Wilson.

Jasper stepped out of his Range Rover and was a little surprised that Kate's Evoque was missing. The apartment was in darkness. He raced inside. Kate's work clothes were strewn over the bedroom floor. He picked up her ripped panties. Blood. He stood and stared. Fucking blood. He'd made her bleed.

He was responsible for this. A conscience Jasper had never known he had surfaced. Guilt spread through him.

He searched his mind for excuses. He blamed that meeting. He was losing control over the business; he should have been at the office during the weekend instead of Kate. Max knew too much about his private dealings. Joanne and Beth's perpetual interference in his life had tipped him over the edge.

He threw Kate's wardrobe door open. Empty.

"Fuck! Fuck!" he shouted, thumping the wardrobe door.

His inside pocket vibrated.

"What?" he snapped.

"She's by the river," said a thick voice.

"Don!"

"Hurry. One of Max's cronies has also found her."

"Don!" Jasper yelled into the mouthpiece.

The line was dead.

***

Don had obeyed his master and followed Kate. She had parked at the confluence of the Well and Bury. She sat in the car, staring into space. Something had upset her.

A quick call to Amanda told him all he needed to know: the hostile meeting, Kate's interference with the shopping centre demolition. Amanda went into detail about Jasper fucking Kate in the bathroom. It was the talk of the office: Kate had left Jasper.

***

Beth stood at the mansion landing window, talking to Amanda. There was no sign of Kate, either at the office or the mansion. She felt a satisfactory glow spread through her: Kate had left. She couldn't handle Jasper's need for rough sex. Beth was the only one who could quell Jasper's sea of anger; she gave him what he wanted. It was just a matter of time before he returned to her.

***

But Don knew Kate hadn't left Jasper. Yet.

Don was leaning against a tree, mulling over

the situation. He liked Kate; she would be good for Jasper, but by all accounts, he had shown her what a bastard he was.

Max had approached Don when it became clear that Jasper trusted Kate with the details of his business. Don would be handsomely paid when he gave Max the information he wanted: what Jasper was up to and why he had entrusted the company finances to Kate. Don suspected that Jasper was preparing to leave Wellsbury and wind down the company, but he had no proof—just a gut feeling based on Jasper's out-of-character behaviour.

Don wasn't stupid. The Wilsons' drug business was going nowhere without expansion. They needed Jasper's extensive network to survive.

But Max had suggested that Don would receive a considerable bonus if Kate had an accident and Jasper got the blame—which he would, considering his fiery temper and reputation. The police would relish the opportunity to put him inside, just like his old man.

Don was greedy, he had shaken hands with Max. He would have to careful; if his South American boss got an inkling of his deal with Max, he would be toast.

Don had known Jasper's parents. His dad, Colin, used to just turn up and use his considerable charisma to win over the Families. Whenever they had a job planned, it was always changed to Colin's plan.

Colin had a particular knack for sussing out lucrative diamond heists. He would spend time with young Jasper and his pseudo-wife until the diamond haul was divided up, then he would disappear. One of the Wilson family had tried to follow him once, but Colin was too good. In the end, the Families lost interest in Colin. As long as they had money to splash around, that was all that mattered.

Everyone was happy until the last diamond heist, when Colin crossed the Families. They sought revenge, and Colin was put inside for a murder he hadn't committed.

Initially, Jasper and his mother survived on money from Colin's empire. However, when Colin died, the money ran out and his mother made money the only way she knew—entertaining men. The last one she entertained was that skinny copper, Inspector fucking Lawson. He was obsessed with Jasper, blaming him for the murder of the newsagent who'd been swindling Jasper and Jack. Nothing could be proved, and the skinny copper was taken off the case. But he wouldn't let go. He slowly became Mrs Carmichael's main client and ultimately fathered Richard.

Don's musing abruptly ended when Jasper's Range Rover skidded to a halt nearby. Jasper leapt out, opened the driver's door of Kate's Evoque and pulled her into his arms.

Don's mouth opened wide as he watched Jasper cup Kate's face, taking his time kissing her eyes, cheeks and lips before claiming her mouth. This wasn't the behaviour of the Jasper that Don was familiar with. This was a lover apologising. Jasper had hurt Beth many times, and he'd never been sorry.

Don watched them stroll to the riverside bench. Jasper never let go of her. He kissed her hair and whispered in her ear. And when she kissed him back, he pulled her onto his lap and their kiss deepened.

Don had seen enough. Kate was more than pussy for Jasper; they were lovers.

He made a phone call.

"I told you never to ring this number," barked the voice in Don's earpiece.

"There's more to this Kate relationship. He's like a man in love."

"Jasper?!" the voice shouted in disbelief.

"They're sitting on the riverside bench. Kissing and whispering."

"This changes everything."

Don's phone went dead.

Don then dialled Max. "They're by the river. Should be home soon."

***

Don walked into his darkened house and checked his wife was fast asleep before tiptoeing to his office. He poured a very large malt and settled into his high-backed desk chair, preparing himself for the wrath of his South American boss as he switched on his laptop. Money ruled Don, and this guy paid more than Jasper.

"You've taken your bloody time," barked the deep, South American voice. Don's boss was an impatient man. "I want to talk about Colin."

"Colin? What the fuck!"

His boss took no notice of Don's comments or raised voice. "You knew Colin."

"I was a kid."

"When did Carmichael appear in your little community?"

"You should talk to Cohen."

"Tell me."

"It was just after the war that the Cohens noticed him."

"Where did he come from?"

"No one knew. He just appeared."

"Diamonds were his business?"

"He knew about diamonds. There was a rumour that he was involved with getting the diamonds out of Holland before Hitler got his hands on them."

His boss considered this. "Go on."

"Colin never mentioned it. But if that's true, he must have been a teenager."

"Where did he meet his whore?"

"She wandered into the local, looking for a meal ticket. Love at first sight, some said. But no one looked at her while she was Colin's."

"And Jasper?"

"He's a Carmichael. He gets more like Colin every day."

"He's in love with this Kate?"

"Jasper needs someone to fuck. The property side is stagnant. Jack, Richard and Max Wilson want him out. I would say that Jasper wants out. Kate is watching his back. Keeping an eye on the finances and sorting the archives."

"Archives?"

"Mainly Colin's old records. My contact tells me she's putting them in date order." Don paused for a long moment. "I suspect they will be put on a computer and the paper records destroyed."

"Jasper's preparing to leave."

"That's my guess," confirmed Don.

"Colin's intel was always spot on. He knew the exact time diamonds were arriving in Hatton Gardens. Did he have a silent insider?"

Don was becoming impatient. "I don't know."

"The Cohens always fenced his diamonds." The South American paused. "Except the last job."

"No one knows where those diamonds are."

"Jasper does." The angry voice echoed.

"They were uncut." Don raised his voice. "They haven't turned up. We've 'ad feelers out for years." Don's impatience was increasing. "Colin pulled a fast one. Get over it. You 'ad the last laugh. You and Lawson got 'im inside. He died inside. End of it."

"Jasper visited him. Where?"

"He was a kid, for Christ's sake." Don raised his voice.

Silence stretched, long and uncomfortable, before it was shattered by the South American. "Colin got him off the newsagent murder. Lawson's convinced he did it." His loud, angry voice made Don move away from the screen. "Where did he get the money from to move and start a business?"

"Look, I moved here with 'im and Jack. They were broke."

"But Jasper always comes through. Just like he has a guardian fucking angel. If he fell in a barrel of muck, he'd come out smelling of roses. I want him watched. Get more men."

The screen went blank.

Don poured another generous malt. He stared at the black laptop screen, slowly sipping. His thoughts fixed on his South American boss's obsession with Jasper and Colin's diamonds. Colin had double-crossed his boss—Don knew that. He'd palmed him off with paste and kept the real ones for himself. The police and insurance company searched in vain, but they made sure the diamonds were too hot to handle. No fence would touch them. The diamonds were still at the top of their wanted list.

Colin had never taken anyone into his confidence. But had he taken Jasper?

Don emptied his glass, still pondering on the likelihood that Jasper knew where the diamonds were and was just waiting for the right time to fence them. He'd watched Jasper take the box from his safe. The safe that Max had failed to open. Did that box contain the diamonds?

He switched off the lights and tiptoed towards the bedroom; he didn't want to wake Milly. He quietly removed his clothes, his mind still replaying the South American's last comment. If Jasper fell in a barrel of muck, he'd come out smelling of roses.

"Jasper's been good to us," Milly murmured as Don snuggled up to her. She'd been eavesdropping again.

"I know." His fingers pulled her hair away from her neck. His lips found her soft skin. "Go to sleep and stop worrying."

Chapter Twelve

They lay in the bath, her back to his front. His hand drifted towards her sex.

"Does it hurt?" Jasper murmured into her ear.

"Not really."

"Forgive me."

"I do."

"No. Don't just say it."

She turned over. Water splashed over the side. Her heavy breasts pressed into his chest. He sighed.

"I forgive you." Her words were soft and sincere.

She pressed their lips together. Their mouths opened, and their tongues danced.

***

Jasper left Kate sleeping. He was ashamed of rough-fucking her. She was hurting, but he still had an overwhelming desire to be buried deep inside her.

Work was the antidote for Kate Reynolds. Bare-chested, he sat at the kitchen work surface, hunched over his laptop. His fingers flew over the keys.

He stopped when he heard her light footsteps. He watched her refection in the oven's glass doors. Her robe was open, revealing her soft, curvaceous body. She was smiling. He sighed when she slipped her arms around him, pressing their skin together. Her warm breath caressed his neck.

"Breathe," she murmured while her hands trailed around his chest.

He leaned back into her as she planted soft kisses on his neck.

"I want you," she whispered. "I've never felt like this."

Kate's emotions were laid bare. She needed comfort, love. She needed Jasper Carmichael.

He quickly shut his laptop, swirled round and pulled her onto his lap. Their mouths fused as his fingers glided up and down her spine. Delightful moans escaped from her mouth, making Jasper's heart skip a beat.

He carried her to the bedroom, their mouths still joined. He gently laid her on the bed, gazing admiringly at her form. She stretched her arms towards him. His eyes uncharacteristically filled. The old Jasper would have already been fucking her, but not this time. He wanted to convince her he was sorry. She was more than a quick fuck.

He carefully lay atop her, leaning on his elbows, gazing into her loving green eyes. Her hands rested on his broad shoulders. His desire twitched against her sex, eager to taste her delights.

"Jasper, please." Her hands entwined in his hair.

"I'm not sure about this," he said softly.

A look of surprise flashed across her face. "I need this. I need you," she murmured.

Her soft, loving voice and sparkling green eyes melted his concern.

His fingertips glided over her warm skin. His mouth worshipped each breast in turn. A loud gasp escaped her mouth when his fingers entered her folds.

"My love, you're too tender. I'll hurt you."

"No! I need this." Her voice was almost pleading.

Kate relaxed and delightful cries filled the room as he carefully caressed her most sensitive spot. He slipped inside her and gently moved. His passionate kiss swallowed her cries as his hardness filled her.

"Jasper."

They moved together, her hands gripping his shoulders. Waves of uncontrollable pleasure spread through them.

She fell asleep in his arms. He kissed her forehead. He had never felt such contentment and happiness.

***

The drive to the office seemed to take forever. Kate gazed over to a scowling Jasper.

"Let's play hooky," he unexpectedly blurted.

The Range Rover continued past the office, heading out of town.

"I was a mess after I found Beth in bed with Jack and Richard," Jasper began, taking Kate by surprise. "I had to get away. I needed to be alone. Think. My thoughts were filled with Jack and Richard. I was losing my grip over the company. They had become confident, going against orders, making friends with people I despised— the Wilsons.

"I deceived them. They thought I was in Bristol viewing prospective properties, but I was looking for an isolated bolt hole. I stopped for a pint of real ale and sandwich at a roadside pub. The place was deserted, except for a couple of locals that were leaning on the bar, gossiping about Alwyn's boatyard that was about to close. Apparently, Alwyn owed the bank.

"'He's never been any good since Mary died,' commented one.

"'Those kids are no good. Drained him dry,' said another.

"'He's let things go,' added the landlord. 'The place is falling down. Those city types that come in here flashing their wallets won't give it a second glance. If only he had the money to turn it around.'

"And for some reason, I went in search of it. I was about to give up when I noticed a weed-strewn track. The Range Rover bounced from one rut to another. Any hard core had long since disappeared.

"The track opened into a yard with large buildings either side. Pushed to one side of the yard were large rusty chunks of metal that were losing the battle against encroaching weeds.

"I poked my head into the large building. They were obviously workshops, for refitting boats.

"A neglected yacht was leaning towards the shoreline. It was in need of some TLC. It looked as if it had been there some time. The chain that secured it to the concrete jetty had rusted through in several places.

"It was low tide and the yacht was surrounded by mud. And the channel leading to the sea was a small stream.

"'What the fuck do you want?' yelled a rough voice.

"A small, stocky, scruffy man was aggressively walking towards me. I gave him my best smile and enquired about the yacht.

"Over cups of sweet tea that made my stomach heave, I listened to Alwyn's sob story.

His business had declined after his wife died of cancer. She was ill for a long time, he explained, and his children, a boy and girl, had just left him to cope. He couldn't work the yard and nurse his wife. I felt awkward; I didn't know what to say.

"But he offered me the whole lot. The yard, the boat, and a cottage I hadn't seen. It used to be a holiday cottage but had fallen into disrepair.

"'It's low tide. The water comes right up to here,' he mumbled, pointing to the concrete jetty.

"We followed the shoreline track until a single-storey cottage appeared. I stopped and stared. It was my isolated bolt hole.

"'You can get to it from over there.' Alwyn pointed to the field behind the cottage and the row of cottages. 'Not used much. You just bounce over the field. Best if you have a Land Rover, mind.'

"There wasn't much to the cottage. One bedroom, bathroom, kitchen-diner. But remarkably, it had mains water and electricity.

"'Needs gutting and bringing into the twenty-first century,' Alwyn had commented.

"I pretended to mull over Alwyn's proposition.

"'Pay the bank,' he said. 'Pay for the yacht refit. I'll be happy. I'm getting on. Retire to my small cottage.'

"It wasn't all plain sailing though," continued Jasper as they stopped in front of the cottage he'd been describing. "The bank put me through the mill, so to speak. They took their time investigating Miles Phillips of nineteen Glen Way, Waltham."

He opened the passenger door. His smile stretched across his face.

"Welcome to my bolt hole."

He planted a soft kiss onto Kate's welcoming lips.

Chapter Thirteen

A week later, Jasper was lounging in his luxurious leather armchair, feeling very pleased with himself. His European business had been very successful. He no longer had any commitments in Europe, and the profits had been transferred into his personal Cayman account.

His mind drifted to Kate. She had proved to be everything he'd expected and more. She had organised the shopping centre like a pro, but unfortunately, she had upset Jack, his shady contractors and Max. A satisfied smile filled his face; she was even better between the sheets.

His private phone rang. It was Don.

"Jasper." His voice was hard and cold.

"What's up?"

"Those bastards have roughed Kate up."

Jasper sat bolt upright.

"When?"

"Just now. She was unloading groceries when he grabbed her. Wanted the combination to the office safe."

"Who?"

"Max. But they all watched. Ripped her clothes off. Generally abused her."

"Did he...?"

"No. She passed out and they just left her."

"Where is she?"

"Hospital. Richard phoned. He was waiting." *Only half a lie,* thought Don. "He's shit-scared what you'll do. He was a mess. In need of a fix."

Silence.
"They'll be waiting," Don added.
But Jasper didn't answer.

***

"What now?" barked the voice of Don's South American boss.
"Max has roughed Kate up. It's a hospital job."
"What the fuck? Where's Jasper?"
"The last I heard he was stuck in Europe. There's no flights. The French are on strike—two-hour wait for Eurostar."
"Find him," barked the voice.

***

Jasper's temper boiled to the surface. Kate was his. They had no right touching her; they should have left her alone. Richard was right to be shit scared; they'd all regret messing with Kate. Max couldn't wait to get his hands on Carmichael and Swain, but he had just made a big mistake.

Jasper calmly walked into his bedroom and changed into black, casual clothes. He opened his bedroom safe and slipped five hundred pounds into the inside pocket of his hoody. He switched off his phones and removed the batteries and SIM cards. He methodically placed his phones, gloves, cap and change of clothes into his satchel, locked his Mitchem safe house and started the black Ford Focus that was hidden in an enclosed carport. With any luck it would be still dark when he arrived in Wellsbury.

He drove through the early hours, hands clutching the wheel tight, until the Carmichael Mansion came into sight. He followed the wall that surrounded the mansion until a little-used gate appeared. The gate was well disguised; Jasper was one of only a handful of people who knew of its existence. He put his shoulder to the gate, forcing it open. He gazed upon the garden, deciding on the best route to his apartment.

He sprinted around the garden, trying to avoid the security lights, to his apartment. He stood silently, listening and looking. The security lights hadn't come on. *Trap* flashed into his mind.

Putting aside his concerns, he slowly entered his apartment. By torchlight, he opened the alarm control-box, carefully switching off the alarm and cameras and resetting the code.

He took a moment to regulate his breathing and cover his shoes.

He walked, catlike, to the dividing wall between the apartment and main house. His books were neatly arranged along this wall. He pressed one heavy volume and the shelf moved outwards. He slipped through the gap and stood, listening for any movement. Only when he was satisfied did he step out of the disused fireplace and into the hall of the house.

There were no lights on, except one shining through the living room door. He stepped inside. Jack, Richard and Beth were asleep, naked in front of the dying embers of the fire. There was no sign of Max. His senses jumped to full alert, then the faint splashing of water caught his attention. Max was at the pool.

Jasper stood in the shadows and watched Max swim the length of the pool. He tied a towel around the tip of the pool pole. He switched off the lights and waited. Max didn't seem to notice.

A nervous quiver rose into Jasper's mouth as he bided his time. He would only have one chance. Max was a big, strong man and could easily overpower Jasper. Surprise was his greatest weapon.

Max slowly lifted himself out of the pool, water dripping off his muscular frame as he balanced on the slippery tiled surface.

Jasper charged towards Max, holding the pole lance-like. Max's eyes widened in surprise. He staggered on the slick floor.

The pole hit him in the stomach, knocking him off balance. His arms flailed as he tried to catch hold of the pole. He fell backwards into the pool.

"What the—" escaped his mouth before he crashed into the water.

He surfaced, shaking his head, glaring at the hooded figure who was coming at him again.

"Carmichael!" he gasped as Jasper pushed him back underwater.

Max groped for the pole, but Jasper had the upper hand as he pushed Max to the bottom of the pool. Unexpectedly, Max pushed the pole away and resurfaced. He was disorientated, too close to the edge. Violently shaking his head, he caught the hard surface of the pool side.

Before Max could recover, Jasper forced him back underwater. Max was still shaking his head, gasping for air. His evil eyes opened wide as he desperately tried to grab the pole while moving back to the safety of the pool's edge. Dazed, his grip loosened on the pole. His head hit the pool side with such force that blood trickled from a large cut. Jasper pushed him away from the safety of the edge and watched him slowly slip under the water.

Jasper dropped the towel into the water and calmly clipped the pole into the wall bracket. He didn't give Max a second look as he walked back into the house.

On his way to Jack's office, he peeped into the living room. Jack, Richard and Beth were still sleeping.

The untidy state of Jack's office hadn't changed. He smirked as he punched a code into the wall safe; Jack hadn't bothered to update the code. His smirk morphed as he stared at the neatly stacked documents and bundles of sterling within. It took a moment to register the depth of Jack's deceit. He hadn't expected this, but he couldn't dwell. This had taken longer than he had anticipated; he was running late.

He quickly scooped the contents of the safe into a cheap plastic holdall that was discarded by the side of the desk. His eyes scanned the documents on the desk. *Shit*. They were draft legal papers for the demise of Carmichael and Swain.

With the bulging plastic holdall, he hurried to the front door. To his amazement, it was ajar and the alarm off. *Careless, careless,* he thought as he raced back to the Ford.

He joined the flow of early-morning commuters. He stopped, bought the customary coffee and filled up with petrol. He paid cash. He took his time using the toilet facilities, wrapping his black clothes in a bin liner and throwing them into an industrial waste bin.

He was feeling tired when he parked the Ford in the enclosed carport at the Mitchem semi. He placed the satchel and holdall on the kitchen table and collapsed on the bed.

Chapter Fourteen

Jasper couldn't settle. Sleep evaded him. Kate stood before him, smiling; he could taste her lips, hear her cries as she lost control. When he opened his eyes, she stood at the bottom of the bed. He wanted to see her, he wanted to hold her.

Jasper had never felt a pain like the one that lingered deep inside; the concept of emotions was anathema to him. When he wanted something, he just took it. When he craved sex, he fucked until he was exhausted. But he'd never had a lingering pain. He convinced himself that, when he fucked Kate, the pain would disappear. But for now, he comforted himself with the knowledge that Max wouldn't harm her again.

***

The police were all over the mansion. Jack, Richard and Beth had been questioned along with June and April, the cleaners. It was June who had found Max.

"Where's Jasper?" bellowed a voice from the past.

Jack whipped round. He was no longer skinny—he had filled out with age—but the hateful features of the skinny policeman were still recognisable.

"Not here," Jack stuttered, not believing his eyes.

"Hello, Jack. Long time no see." Inspector Lawson smirked.

He strode over to Richard. He hadn't seen his son for twenty years. The resemblance was uncanny.

Richard cowered.

Lawson couldn't believe this weak specimen was his flesh and blood. He was shaking, eyes bloodshot—as much of an addict as his mother. He sniggered, but she'd been a good fuck.

"Sir." His musing was broken by Lockwood. "There was an incident here. Yesterday. A woman was assaulted."

"Where's Don?" asked Lawson, his eyes never leaving his son.

"Not here."

"Who's the woman?"

"Kate Reynolds. She works for Jasper."

"Who did the assaulting? Jack?"

"I called the ambulance." Richard's voice quivered. He didn't recognise his dad. He couldn't remember him; he had just started school when his dad mysteriously disappeared.

"Max." Jack's word seemed to fill every room.

So, Jasper's woman had been assaulted by the dead Max? Lawson's mind raced to the consequences. The Wilsons wouldn't rest until they had revenge. Jasper was already in the frame.

"I've sent an officer to the hospital," Lockwood continued, but his words were lost on a preoccupied Lawson.

***

Kate was sat on the hospital bed, waiting to be discharged, when the message came through.

Memorise these numbers and delete.

She was deleting the message when Don arrived with an M&S carrier. She raised her eyebrows and quickly looked inside: matching bra and panties, jumper and jeans.

"You can't go back to the apartment in a hospital gown," he said sympathetically.

She looked at him, smiled and mouthed 'thank you', but Don's eyes were more interested in her phone.

"The police are outside," he said.

"Hello, Don," said a familiar voice.

Don whipped round, coming face to face with the policeman who had tried to put Jasper away all those years ago.

"Still doing his dirty work, I see," mocked Lawson, his eyes firmly fixed on Kate and her new clothes.

Don clenched his fists, stifling a desire to thump Lawson. *He hasn't changed,* he thought. *He's still a jumped-up prick.*

"Where's Jasper?" Lawson barked, his words directed at Kate.

"She's knows nothing," interrupted Don, taking on a protective role.

Kate's cheeks reddened.

"Max was found in the mansion's pool," the inspector continued, his eyes still on Kate.

She flinched, her hospital breakfast rising. She didn't know if it was the shock of Max's death, after he'd attacked her, or the accusing tone in the inspector's voice. Did he think Jasper killed Max? But Jasper was away?

"You can't cover for him this time." The inspector moved towards Don, pointing his index finger.

Kate was bewildered. What the hell was going on?

"I don't have to cover. He's not here," Don retorted.

"Who roughed you up, Ms Reynolds?" The inspector swirled around to face Kate, trying to catch her off guard. His snarling tone emphasised *Ms Reynolds*.

"She knows nothing." Don's impatient tone did nothing to stop Lawson glaring at Kate.

"Shut the fuck up."

"It was dark. I didn't see them. I woke up here," she choked. Her tearful look at Don said it all. *What's going on?*

"This is Inspector Lawson, Kate," Don said. "We all go back a long way."

An uncomfortable silence descended.

"Max was found in the pool. Your lover did it." The inspector's harsh, venomous words were all that was needed for a tear to trickle down Kate's cheek.

But a tear didn't deter Lawson. "Now! Where the fuck is he?"

"Sir!"

The inspector glared at Lockwood.

"He's just arrived at his London apartment. The local police said he arrived in a taxi."

The inspector angrily turned to Lockwood. "His Range Rover?"

"Still there."

"I don't suppose one of those plods felt if it was warm?"

"Cold as ice. He wouldn't let the officer in—said they would have to get a warrant," Lockwood blurted. "Apparently, he looked very tired. Dishevelled. The taxi picked him up at St Pancras."

"Dover! Jasper never slums it on a ferry."

"The French are still on strike. Eurostar was overbooked. No flights."

"I want to know his movements in Europe.

Who he visited, had dinner with, slept with. Check the CCTV. That bastard's up to something."

"The CCTV was down at Dover. We picked him up at St. Pancras."

"Fuck!" shouted the inspector.

Chapter Fifteen

A nervous Kate sat in the passenger seat of Don's Audi, watching the sights of Wellsbury flash by. Don didn't seem to care that he was breaking the speed limit.

"What's going on?" she tentatively asked.

Silence.

"Don! Tell me." Her voice rose with anger.

"In a nutshell, Inspector Lawson blamed Jasper for the murder of a newsagent. He was a teenager. Him and Jack were wheeler-dealing; the newsagent owed 'em money. At the time, Jasper and his mother were desperate for money."

"Did he do it?"

"No one knows."

For a moment, Don was silent. There was clearly more to the story, and Kate waited for it.

"Lawson was mysteriously taken off the case. He blamed his boss, who he claimed was fucking Jasper's mother."

Kate gulped in surprise. "Where was his dad?"

"Inside. It was more likely his old man. He was a…" Don hesitated. "He was a powerful figure, in the criminal world. He ran things from inside."

Kate's eyes widened in disbelief.

"The thing is, while his dad was inside, Lawson started to fuck Mrs Carmichael. He's obsessed with Jasper. Richard's his son."

Another gulp from Kate.

"Jasper and Jack moved. Lawson stopped fucking Mrs Carmichael. Richard knows nothing."

They had stopped outside Jasper's apartment.

"That's some story."

"That's not all of it."

"There's more?!" Kate raised her voice in disbelief.

"The rest's Jasper's to tell." He took her hand. "You should know this: I've worked for Jasper for years—he's a good, fair boss—but he changed after Beth. But with you he's different. He appears to care."

She opened the car door, walked towards the apartment and slowly punched the new code into the panel. Her eyes filled and a single tear trickled down her cheek.

Once she was safely inside, she slumped on the couch and sobbed. Had she fallen in love with a possible murderer?

She'd tasted Jasper's temper. But he was sorry and pleaded with her to forgive him.

He had loved her in a most tender manner— she had never experienced the like of it. Her whole body ignited to his gentle touch. When she closed her eyes, she could still feel his fingers meandering, their tongues dancing with expectation, the sensations from his fullness that travelled to her inner core.

Jasper wasn't acting. He was loving her, giving himself to her.

Her thoughts lay heavy in her mind as she curled up on the couch and slept.

***

The contents of the plastic holdall lay on the dining table in Jasper's apartment. He fingered the money. Max's money. The Wilsons would be after him.

There were too many documents for him to read fully. But from what he had read, Jack and Max were preparing to oust him and take over C&S. But for some reason, the property in Miami held them back.

He glanced over to a sleeping Kate. She cringed whenever she moved. *That bastard won't hurt her again*, he thought.

He stuffed the money into his over-full safe. A trip to the bank was needed, he thought, returning the documents to his leather satchel.

Kate had suddenly become restless. He gently caressed her forehead. Her eyes slowly opened, and she smiled.

His strong arms carried her to his bedroom. He carefully laid her on his king-size bed.

She pulled his sleeve. "Don't go. Hold me."

He kicked off his shoes and nestled her into the crux of his body. His lips found her neck, and his hands cupped her breasts. Her eyes closed as she relaxed into the safety and warmth of Jasper Carmichael.

***

The aromatic smell of freshly brewed coffee filled the bedroom. Kate slowly opened her eyes. Jasper took her hands and brought them to his lips. His eyes brimmed with concern—or was it love?

"Jasper," she murmured.

Their lips hesitantly met. His arms stretched to her shoulders, lifting her to him. The kiss deepened, her fingers threading through his soft hair.

He broke away.

"I'll make it all up to you. I promise."

"I need a shower," she said absentmindedly. "I smell of hospital."

Chapter Sixteen

Loud angry voices greeted Kate as she walked towards the kitchen. Her hair was wet from her long, hot shower. She didn't pay the voices any attention, automatically lifting the teapot from the shelf and dropping in two bags of Morning Breakfast. The kettle was already hot, and a flick of the switch soon brought it to the boil.

With her hands wrapped around a cup of hot tea, she reluctantly looked at the two men eyeing each other as if they were about to go three rounds.

"Warrant." Jasper's voice was curt and loud.

Lawson didn't answer, just waved a piece of paper in front of Jasper.

"This is for the fucking office. Get out."

The inspector brushed him aside. "Richard's a mess."

"What do you care?"

Lawson turned to look at Kate. "How's this one match up to the others?" he snarled, determined to rile Jasper. When he got no response, his lip curled. "Your fucking dad was no good. But we put 'im away. And that's where you're going."

Tension thickened as both men glared at each other.

"I know he got you off. He had something on the governor, and it was more than fucking your whore of a mother."

Jasper fists were tightly clenched.

"You went to visit him. Crying on Daddy's

shoulder." Sarcasm dripped out of the inspector's voice.

Jasper still didn't answer, his knuckles turning white.

"I hear you're still friendly with his old cronies. There's rumours that they're active." He took a step towards Kate, and Jasper took a step towards him. "They need a leader. Carmichael blood. Someone who knows a thing or two." The inspector paused, his eyes moving to Kate then Jasper. "Richard, my son." Disgust oozed from his voice. "Fucking useless. Drugged up most of the time—that's when he's not fucking. That's his mother in 'im." He paused again, fixing Jasper with a penetrating stare. "That leaves you."

He moved his gaze to Kate. "His old man's gang were notorious for murder, burglary. But we got him and most of his gang."

Lawson turned towards the door and paused.

"Don was part of it. But Don always works for the biggest penny."

He opened the door.

"When the Carmichael temper gets the better of you, that's when you strike. First was the newsagent and now Max. Of course, there may be others that we don't know about. The newsagent was fiddling you and Jack. Max was into drugs—not your scene.

"You've been handling Max. Not sure you'll manage the Wilson brothers. So, what did Max do? That's puzzled me. But now I've seen you together, I know. He roughed up her." He pointed at Kate. "Is she your Achilles heel, Carmichael?"

He slammed the door.

Jasper unclenched his fists and kicked over a small glass coffee table.

Kate poured another cup of tea and dropped

two slices of bread into the toaster.

"Fuck's sake! Say something," he yelled.

"What do you want me to say?"

A heavy silence descended between them.

"Let's walk," he said, throwing her a jacket.

Their steps crunched on the gravel drive. His head was bowed, eyes focused on the gravel.

"I've never trusted anyone like I trust you."

Her stomach gave a nervous flip.

"It was going to be Beth, but somehow the time never seemed right... And then she didn't feel right."

"And I do?" Kate interjected, unable to hold back her surprise.

"Beth was pussy. Good pussy, mind, but still pussy. I never trusted Jack, even as teenagers. Jack was always in it for Jack. And still is. Came close to trusting my old man."

He stopped and gripped her arm. "I watched you for months."

She gasped. His strong arm suddenly pulled her into his shoulder.

"My old man wanted me to take over. I'm a natural." He nervously laughed. "I'm a Carmichael. They're all watching and waiting for the Carmichael evil to surface."

He sat on a stone seat facing the mansion, and she willingly nuzzled into him, resting her head on his shoulder. He smiled and kissed her hair. She felt good.

"I've wanted out for a long time. These businessmen Jack and Richard keep trying to introduce into the business are trouble with a capital T. Jack and I started the business; best mates at school. We were teenage wheeler-dealers, specialising in antiques. Jack's good at spotting business opportunities, and he suggested with my ability with money, we should try buying and selling property. At first, we concentrated on properties that needed renovation. Over the years that's changed. I now own property all over the world: new developments, bankrupt office blocks, houses. I'm good. I make a lot of money. As a result, I control the business. Jack and Richard hate it. It's their own fault the antiques side is starting to lose money."

He paused as he gathered his thoughts.

"I began to lie. I told Jack I was going to Miami, but I was in the Caymans, Virgins or Nauru. I found an agent; the agent found a bank and supplied encryption software, PIN numbers and account numbers. No questions, he said. The bank is NRJ. It's offshore, strictly no questions. Mr Smith, if that's his name, is my contact. I must deposit ten thousand pounds a month. That hasn't been a problem until now. I can't leave the office again. Jack's already having me watched."

"Is this legal?"

"No questions, remember? I'm on the fence, so to speak."

"Jasper!"

"The authorities have me on their radar but have left me alone, until now."

"Where does your money come from?"

"No questions, Kate... Let's say it's money I have salted away from the business. Deals that went through my personal books and not the business's. The business has made a profit and so have I."

"And now you have enough. You're going to disappear," she mumbled.

"Lawson's after me."

Silence.

"I still own property in London, the Shires,

Florida, New York. I'm selling some as we speak."

"So, you're running two businesses."

"You know?" He was surprised she had already worked it out.

"I suspected. Where do I fit in?"

"You've already highlighted hidden discrepancies in the company accounts that I suspect Jack and Richard had buried. They counted on me not having the time to be so thorough. The accounts weren't adding up. Hence, I employed you.

"Jack was in charge of all our building projects: materials, contractors and such like. I suspected he had a deal with some contractors. Charge more hours or more materials, and the company paid. Jack took a cut and so did the contractor. He gave himself away when he was so angry that I had taken over the shopping centre project."

Kate's stomach nervously churned. Would she be expected to falsify invoices? She had never done anything unlawful, not even a speeding ticket.

"We're going to disappear, my love. A new life. Either together or alone."

Where did that come from? he thought. *Would life be so bad with Kate?*

"You have no family. I have no family. No one would miss us."

Silence.

"I have no idea why I trust you." His mouth pressed to her ear. "So far, my judgement hasn't been wrong. But I have to earn your trust."

"I trust you, Jasper. I don't know why. I don't care about the newsagent or Max."

"They were both evil. And Max hurt what's mine."

His kiss was long and hard. Her hand cupped

his head, holding their mouths together. A tinge of conscience settled in the back of Jasper's mind. He hadn't lied to Kate, but what he'd failed to tell her about his activities could put him inside for a long time.

Chapter Seventeen

Routine had settled into Kate's life. She liked living in Jasper's luxury apartment; she had it to herself most of the time. Jasper was often away, doing whatever. He would return at any hour and require sex. A lot of it. The thought of sex with Jasper always brought a smile to her face and a nervous quiver to the top of her thighs. If she was tired the next day, she wouldn't bother with work. No one missed her, and if they did, no one dared mention it.

After the last chaotic meeting, Jasper decided on private meetings about the shopping centre, sometimes in his office but mostly in the apartment. She didn't have to prepare for the meeting; she knew exactly what contractors were responsible for what, and all the costs involved.

However, Jasper took her by surprise when he asked for a detailed report on the archives, so she started the time-consuming and tedious task of scanning the archives onto her laptop. Saturday afternoon or Sunday morning was the best time for that, when she wouldn't be disturbed.

Jasper surprised her when he spent a weekend burning the old paper records dating back to Colin Carmichael's time, sparked by Kate mentioning that she hadn't found Colin's so-called black book that recorded all his criminal activities. Jasper already knew she wouldn't find the black book—he had it—but he didn't want any papers referring to Colin falling into the wrong hands.

But this particular weekend, she wouldn't be going into the office.

Soft kisses trailing along her neck awakened her. She was still half asleep when he entered her for the first time. Her breasts ached, and she was sore, very sore.

He now stood above her holding a breakfast tray.

"I thought you need a bit of pampering after last night." An evil grin spread over his face.

He carefully handed her a cup of tea.

"You've changed," he said in a matter of fact way.

Changed, she thought. *That's an understatement.*

"How?"

"You're comfortable sitting in front of me naked. When we first met, you covered yourself."

"It's pointless now. You know my body better than me."

They were both smiling.

Kate was surprised when Jasper said, "How do you fancy a trip to London next week?"

***

She had never travelled first class before. Room to stretch, a table to work on, Wi-Fi, empty seating. *No overcrowding here,* she thought. But she wasn't really interested. Her aches and pains from Max's beating had been replaced by Jasper's mind-blowing sex that left her sore and even more tired. Muscles she'd never known she had were aching. Sex with Jasper was worth the aches and pain, but she did need a long nap.

But how could she nap when adrenaline was surging? Lying in the bottom of her designer satchel was £10,000 that she was going to deposit in NRJ Bank.

Nigel's angry voice sprang into her mind. He had warned her about Jasper's seedy life, as he put it. And now she was becoming part of it. What would Nigel do if he knew how deep she had become in Jasper Carmichael's business activities?

She was posing as Helen James of Kingsworth. Jasper had already deposited money as Gary James. Her passport and driving licence were both in Helen's name. All she had to do was to hand over her ID and deposit the money.

A taxi would be waiting at Euston to take her to the bank. It would wait while she paid in the money to Mr Smith.

"Is this legal?" she had asked.

"No questions, remember."

He had then returned her laptop, which he had updated with information relating to his business and private accounts.

"Everything is encrypted. You must memorise the passwords."

The contents of Kate's stomach had risen into her mouth as reality sank in. Jasper was trusting her not to be a grass either to the police or other interested parties. The Wilson brothers had come to mind.

"Hey!" he had said, putting a comforting arm around her. "Everything will be fine. In a few months this will be over. I've had to bring it all forward because of the police interest. We carry on as normal: meetings on the shopping centre, you checking files and archives, me going abroad."

A lone tear had meandered down her cheek. He had gently wiped it away with his thumb and planted a soft kiss on her lips.

The taxi driver met her on the platform.

"Jasper said look out for the best-looking woman in first class," he said, smiling, trying to put her at ease. "Call me Tom. Me and Jasper go way back."

A Carmichael gang member, she thought.

The bank didn't look like a normal bank, Kate thought. It could easily be mistaken for a large Georgian house. However, the brass plaque did help: NRJ Bank, London.

The doors were locked so she rang the bell. An attractive woman greeted her. Kate followed the stiletto heels that clicked along a wooden floor to an office.

"Mrs James for you."

A small round man stood from his desk. "Mrs James. We meet at last."

His small, fat, sweaty hand gripped hers. He smiled but his smile didn't reach his eyes. They were lusting after her cleavage. Jasper had insisted she wore a white, figure-hugging dress with a deep V.

"Smith likes tits," he had laughed.

Jasper wasn't lying; Smith's eyes were firmly fixed on her cleavage. His face had become hot and reddened. If she wasn't mistaken, he was fidgeting. She dared not glance at his crotch.

She lowered herself onto a chair, lifted her designer satchel onto her lap and unlocked it. Mr Smith scurried back to his desk and grinned.

"Didn't think Gary would make it this month. There've been rumours," he commented as Kate leaned forward, placing the money on his desk.

"You must wear a lace half-cup bra so, when you lean forward, he can get a good tit eyeful," Jasper had instructed. *"I want him distracted. He*

mustn't pay too much attention to the cash."

Jasper knew Smith well; he was lusting at her half-cup lace bra.

"Lunch?" Smith asked as he buzzed for his glamorous assistant. She didn't look at Kate or Smith. Kate watched as she collected the money, turned and left the office. Smith hadn't paid any attention to the fifty-pound notes, just as Jasper had predicted.

His lustful eyes met Kate's when he handed her a receipt.

"Lunch?"

"I'm married."

"It's just lunch. Gary won't mind."

Kate looked at her Cartier watch.

"A bit early for lunch."

"I have a table and room. The hotel is very discreet."

Kate stood, rearranging her dress, which had ridden to her hips. She blushed.

Smith caught a glimpse of her stocking tops and readjusted his trousers. He was very skilled in the art of seduction. She would need a lot of coaxing. He would slowly remove her jacket, taking his time planting soft kisses on her neck and shoulder. He would continue kissing her neck while inching her dress zip down. Her dress would drop to the floor and she would be his. He imagined that she would protest when his hand slipped inside her panties, but he was well-versed in the female erogenous zones.

"Maybe next time."

Her curt reply brought him back from his sexual musing.

He reluctantly moved around the desk and opened the door, his bulging crotch on display.

"Pity," he said, smiling, taking a last glimpse

of her ample breasts, imagining his head buried in them.

***

"She's been a long time." Jasper's concerned voice echoed into Tom's earpiece. "Smith's already confirmed."

"She's here. A bit flustered." He placed his phone in the cradle but left the call open. Kate settled into the back seat. "Getting worried—been a long time," he said.

"Bathroom," Kate gasped, thankful she was back in the taxi.

"Everything okay?"

"Yes!" She was visibly shaking, and her stomach's contents were continually rising into her throat.

Tom watched her through the rear-view mirror.

"He's a lecherous bugger." Tom smiled.

"You can say that again."

"Tried it on, did he?" Tom said, grinning. He could hear Jasper cursing.

Chapter Eighteen

It was Sunday. Archive day.

Without thinking, Kate picked up the office phone as it rang. "Kate Reynolds."

"Thought you'd be there."

She immediately recognised the voice. And stopped. "What do you want, Nigel?"

"No need for that tone."

She didn't dignify that with a response.

"How are you? Recovered from your beating?" His snarky tone didn't go unnoticed. "You've papers to sign."

"What papers?"

"You're angry."

Silence.

"Your picky boyfriend insisted that I amended the sale documents."

"I'm busy."

"I'm in the office all day. Call in when you've finished. Your hotshot's out of town."

She slammed the phone down.

She cast her mind back to the sale documents. She thought she'd signed the papers, but she did remember that Jasper hadn't been happy.

He was away so she sent a text, but he didn't reply.

It was late afternoon when she parked outside Nigel's building. She looked up towards his front office. The window was open, so she knew he was still there.

She sat in the car for a long moment, trying

to recall the sale documents. Jasper had already deposited the money in her account. The more she thought about it, the more convinced she was that she had signed.

Kate was too lost in her thoughts to notice the black BMW parked opposite.

***

"She's where?" Jasper's surprised voice was on speakerphone.

"Outside Nigel's office. She's been at the office all day."

Jasper searched his messages. And there was Kate's; he hadn't bothered to read it.

"Here she goes."

"What's she wearing?" Jasper imagined her in a tight white blouse and fitted grey skirt that hugged her hips.

"Jeans and a very nice fitted white blouse."

White suits Kate, Jasper thought. But what the hell was she doing wearing jeans to the office?

"Is the listening device set up?" said Jasper, recalling that Nigel's office should have been bugged since the flower shop sale.

"Yes."

***

Kate politely knocked on Nigel's door before walking in. He sat at his desk. His eyes wandered up and down her body. They stared at one another, and an awkward silence developed.

Nigel made the first move. He pushed papers towards her. "Picky bastard, your lover."

Kate didn't react to his comment. Without giving the papers a second glance, she folded them and slipped them into her pocket.

"I'll go through them and get back to you."

"So it's true then? The two of you are fucking like rabbits." She didn't rise to the bait. "I deserve an explanation."

"You deserve nothing. I sold the shop and you didn't want me to."

"I'd 'ave got more out of him."

"Time was running out. How was I supposed to live? Trade was dropping. I wasn't breaking even."

"I'd have looked after you. You could've moved in with me. If you wanted a housekeeping job, you could've kept house for me."

"What?!"

"He's going to prison, you do know that? You'll go with him. One slip and the police will 'ave him."

The door unexpectedly opened and in walked two men. Kate immediately recognised Lawson.

"We meet again, Ms Reynolds," said Lawson, holding his ID so Kate could see it. "Take a seat while I talk to you about Jasper Carmichael and his two friends."

Kate preferred to stand as a heavy silence descended in Nigel's office.

***

Jasper's phone vibrated in his pocket. A nervous quiver passed through him.

A message: *Lawson's got her.*

He inwardly cursed.

***

"Do you know who you're involved with? Do you know the type of business he's involved in?"

Lawson's stern tone made her nervous, but

her stoic expression didn't slip.

"Carmichael, Jack and Richard are fences."

Silence.

"Jewellery, painting, antiques, but mainly money laundering. Jasper's the brain. The other two haven't got it."

Silence.

"Do you know where he is?"

Silence.

"They'll all be in the Caymans. Jasper's working, Jack and Richard are supposed to be negotiating deals with new clients. When Richard's not fucking and snorting," Lawson continued.

Silence.

"Why so quiet?"

Silence.

"I'm prepared to offer you a deal. Be our mole. Help us put them behind bars, and you'll go scot free."

Silence.

"Jasper's good. Covers his tracks. Books on a plane then, at the last minute, switches."

Silence.

"Drives to London, leaves his Range Rover in the underground car park, switches cars then disappears. Never uses the same car twice. Devious bastard, is our Jasper."

Silence.

"Think about it." Lawson paused and took a moment to study Kate. "You can contact us through Nigel."

Kate pushed past the two policemen and left.

"We're too late," Lawson said. "He's got to her."

"Leave Kate to me," Nigel said confidently. "I know how to handle her."

***

Jasper's phone vibrated again.

She's back in her car. Looks a bit hot and flustered. Head in hands. There's three of them looking down at her.

Jasper cursed; they weren't going to leave Kate alone. As Lawson had skilfully noticed, she was his Achilles heel.

His phone buzzed again.

"What now?" he snapped, not bothering to look at the number.

"That's no way to greet an old friend."

Jasper immediately recognised the gravelly voice. Zak Cohen, a diamond expert, just like Colin and now him. He wouldn't use the term old friend, more like a passing dealer.

"This is a surprise. It's been a while."

"Didn't know your latest pussy was Kate Reynolds... Nice."

"What do you want, Zak?"

"Off limits, is she? I heard Lawson was poking around after Max—"

"Zak!"

"'ave something that you'll be interested in."

"I don't think so."

"Don't turn your fucking nose up. Your old man would never do that."

For a moment, Jasper was thrown.

"I'm not in the market."

"Never look a gift horse, Jasper. Usual place. Old times' sake."

The phone went dead.

Chapter Nineteen

Kate had lost count how many cups of tea she had drunk. She spent all night tossing and turning.

This business with Nigel had unsettled her. They had known each other for many years; he had been a friend in her darkest hours. He had never been aggressive towards her until she'd got involved with Jasper Carmichael.

What else had he hidden from her? It couldn't be anything about his long-standing affair with Michelle. She had been best friends with Michelle and knew that Nigel had taken her virginity and Michelle's eldest was his. Michelle had hoodwinked poor Dan into believing he was the father. Dan's family was old-money and rich.

Nigel must have been peeved about Kate's relationship with Jasper. Maybe his attitude would have been different if she'd told him that the job was temporary.

In a few months, she would have enough money to do as she pleased. She slowly convinced herself she could handle Nigel.

However, she wasn't so confident about Inspector Lawson. His threats had unnerved her. She had never been a grass, and she didn't have any intention of being one now. Her loyalty was with Jasper, whatever he was guilty of.

Her laptop pinged. A new email from Jasper. Her stomach flipped. He wanted her to deliver another payment to Smith. He didn't say why. She didn't need to know. Tom wasn't picking her up, and she would have to collect the money from a storage locker.

Instead of a quiet day at the office, she would be visiting the lecherous Smith. She cursed.

There wasn't a chance that he would have another eyeful of her breasts. Instead of a dress, she wore her grey trouser-suit and flats. The white blouse would only have the top button open.

The walk to the station calmed her. Walking always had that effect on her. She found solace in the thoughts of her new life away from Wellsbury and Jasper Carmichael. A cloud hung over her thoughts at the prospect of leaving Jasper. She had feelings for Jasper Carmichael—deep feelings, dangerous feelings—and this frightened her.

The saying *'You never know what you've got until you don't have it'* flashed into her mind. She could never have foreseen how much the flower shop had meant to her. It had been her safe place. She felt anchorless now she no longer owned it, and this added to her unease.

She settled into her first-class seat, shut her eyes and tried to recall Jasper's directions to the storage locker. She had no sense of direction, and Google wasn't any help.

Kate joined the taxi queue at Euston. She handed the driver a slip of paper with the address of Jasper's storage locker.

"Sure you want to go 'ere, love?" asked the taxi driver. "Noth' 'ere but derelict factories."

She nodded and slumped into the back seat.

Half an hour later, she was dropped off at the end of an alleyway. On impulse she asked the driver to wait, explaining she wouldn't be long. In fact, a feeling of fear had welled inside her. She could make out the metal door at the end of the dark and seedy narrow alley. The high brick walls reminded her of Charles Dickens novels. Her grey flat shoes slipped on the uneven cobbled surface. Kate began to shiver.

She stood, staring at the metal door with a picture of a large finger pointing to the doorbell. It was a long moment before she pressed the doorbell. She didn't notice the two cameras above her head.

A tall, scruffy, bearded man grunted as he opened the door. She took a step back. His dirty, hairy hand snatched the slip of paper from her. He stared at the numbers she had copied from Jasper's email.

He grunted, and she followed him along a dimly lit warehouse with rows of lockers that were not dissimilar to old left-luggage lockers. Her stomach somersaulted when she glanced at the back of his jeans; a gun was sticking out from the waistband.

She jumped when he suddenly stopped and pointed.

She opened the torch application on her iPhone and gingerly walked along a very narrow passage to the end locker. She tentatively punched the code into the keypad. In the middle of the locker sat twenty folded envelopes. For a brief moment, she hesitated, considering what Jasper had instructed her to do and the danger he had put her in. She glanced behind her; the grunting man's intense stare sent a cold shiver trickling down her spine.

Kate's heart raced as she walked towards him. He could attack, even kill her, and no one would know.

"Everyfink alright?" he growled, his black eyes resting on her red complexion and the beads of sweat on her forehead.

She nodded, too frightened to speak.

***

"Yo pussy's bin," the grunting man said into his phone.

"Problems?" Jasper impatiently answered.

"She's shit-scared."

He now had Jasper's complete attention.

"What did you do?"

"Nothin'."

"We're done," Jasper said angrily.

His phone skidded across the carpet.

Jasper's black mood had just got blacker. For some reason, he felt guilty for sending Kate on a job that he should have done. He had put Zak before her.

Against his better judgement, he'd accepted Zak's proposition. He convinced himself he'd done it for the money, but deep down, he knew that he'd need Zak's diamond-cutting skill sooner or later.

It was a simple enough job. The next time he was in the Caymans, he would open Zak's safety deposit box and collect twenty envelopes.

He didn't know Zak had been to the Caymans, but they'd never confided in one another and had not been in touch for some time.

***

"Where to now, love?" asked the taxi driver, watching a dishevelled Kate slump into the rear seat.

"NRJ Bank," she uttered.

"That's the other side of the city."

"I'll take your word for it."

The taxi stopped around the corner from the bank's main entrance. The driver mumbled something about the traffic. Kate wasn't surprised there was another entrance to the bank.

She pressed the bell below the brass nameplate and a smiling, stiletto-heeled woman promptly answered. She explained that Mr Smith was still with a client and directed her to a very plush waiting area. Kate returned her smile and hurried to the bathroom.

She closed the cubicle door and sat with her head in her shaking hands. She only had a few minutes to calm before meeting Smith and put all thoughts of the gun-toting grunting man out of her mind.

The mirror reflected what Kate had already suspected: she was a mess. Cold water calmed her red sweaty face and a hairbrush controlled her hair. After reapplying her makeup and straightening her clothes, she looked almost respectable.

She returned to the waiting area and sank into an overstuffed chair. The glamorous woman miraculous reappeared, apologising profusely. This was apparently very unusual: Mr Smith rarely ran late.

Her words went over Kate's head. She wasn't interested.

Ten minutes later, Kate's churning stomach began to settle; she wasn't sure if that was thanks to the overstuffed chair or the cappuccino with an extra shot.

A loud voice caught Kate's attention. A voice she was all too familiar with. Jack was strolling towards the main entrance, shaking Smith's hand. The coffee cup chinked in Kate's trembling hand. But neither of them noticed; they were too engrossed in congratulating each other. The doors opened, and Richard and Beth were standing on the steps leading to the bank. Jack nodded and patted the satchel hanging from his shoulder.

"We'll finish it next week," said a smiling Smith in a loud, confident voice.

What the fuck? thought Kate. They'd been double-crossed.

Without thinking, she slipped out the side door and began to follow Jack, Richard and Beth. The streets were becoming crowded, and she had to walk quickly to keep Jack in sight. They stopped outside an overcrowded coffee shop. After a brief discussion, they went inside.

Kate slinked inside and leaned against the wall so she could keep an eye on them. She clicked onto the NRJ Bank app. Jasper's words flashed into her mind:

"Whatever you do at the bank. Check," he'd said, waving the phone in front of her.

She choked when the red withdrawal number came up. The coffee she'd drunk in the bank welled up into her mouth. Her eyes turned to Jack, who was patting his satchel.

That bastard Smith had double-crossed Jasper. He had some deal going with Jack and had emptied Jasper's account. How much of Jasper's £500,000 did Jack have? She had no idea what £500,000 looked like, but she suspected Jack's satchel wouldn't hold that much.

Her mind was whirling. How did Jack know about Jasper's account? For a brief moment, she studied Beth. That devious bitch who'd fucked Jasper had betrayed him.

Kate was incensed. They had not only stood

by and watched Max punch and kick her, tearing her clothes, exposing her breasts, but they were also betraying Jasper.

She mingled with the crowd, her eyes fixed on the overconfident traitors standing around a table waiting for their coffee, laughing and joking.

Jack handed Richard the satchel. Richard's face lit up. Beth leaned over and stared inside. Their eyes met and they couldn't contain their delight.

Jack let his guard drop as he pulled on the open satchel and smiled. At that moment, a young waiter was struggling through the crowd with their coffee. Richard moved the satchel to his lap.

"Celebrate!" Richard shouted over the crowd.

Their coffee glasses touching, all three said cheers together.

Kate watched as the satchel slowly slipped off Richard's lap and onto the floor. He didn't seem to notice. At that moment, a young man carrying coffee bumped into Jack, spilling coffee over his shirt and trousers.

"What the fuck!" Jack angrily cursed, aggressively turning to the apologetic young man.

Customers turned and stared at Beth dabbing Jack's clothes and Richard tugging the apologising young man away.

The satchel was unattended.

Without a second thought, Kate quickly walked towards it. Not looking at Jack, Richard or Beth, she lifted the satchel and walked into the crowd while they were too distracted to notice.

Her heart was thumping as she slowly manoeuvred her way out of the shop.

With her adrenaline surging, she slipped into the convoy of shoppers, fighting the urge to run. She was about to stop and regain her ragged breath when a taxi crawled by. It was still moving when she opened the door and jumped in.

"Eus...ton." The word came out in a series of gulps.

She sank into the rear seat and tried to calm and recover her breath. She didn't recognise Tom with his several days of stubble and a cloth cap. But Tom recognised her, even though she looked nothing like the glamorous Kate he had driven to the bank.

Tom stopped on double yellow lines outside the station and Kate handed him cash. On her way to the ladies, a store selling luggage caught her eye. A sale sign drew her. A brown leather holdall suited her needs. Once inside a ladies' cubicle, she began to calm.

While she was transferring the money into the holdall, a scream echoed.

"Get out!" shouted a female voice. "You pervert."

Kate waited until she was satisfied that the toilets were empty. She splashed water on her face, ran her fingers through her hair and straightened her clothes.

Tom had left the taxi and raced after her. He gambled on her going into the ladies. He waited and waited but Kate didn't appear. In the end he went into the ladies, only to be set upon by an irate woman.

As he was frantically searching platforms, shops and coffee outlets, Kate left the toilets behind a group of chattering women, binning Jack's satchel as she walked. She stopped in her tracks as she recognised a cap-less Tom milling around as if he was looking for someone.

She quickly joined a party of people walking towards the platforms as Tom brazenly walked into the ladies.

The comfort of first class went some way to relaxing her. She nursed the holdall as the enormity of what she had just done slowly sank in. And the reality that when Jasper checked his bank account, he would think she had betrayed him.

***

While Kate stood outside the apartment paying the taxi, Jasper was speeding along the M40 on his way to Wellsbury. With each mile, his temper was rising.

When he'd checked the bank balance, he'd exploded. His thoughts settled on Kate. She had betrayed him. Kate Reynolds had peeled away his layers, exposing his emotions. She had a lot of explaining to do.

Chapter Twenty

Jasper's Range Rover skidded to a halt outside the apartment. His temper was boiling. He took a moment to observe his surroundings. Kate's car wasn't there, and the apartment and mansion were in darkness.

In his mind, he rehearsed again what he was going to do. No nice fuck for her. He would plunge inside her, hitting her cervix while squeezing those full tits. He wouldn't come. He wouldn't care if there was blood. He'd wait till he fucked her from behind or, better still, fucked her tight arse. She wouldn't like that. He could hear her screams and tears begging him to stop. But she deserved more. A shower fuck. He'd pin her to the tile wall and ram into her. Betray Jasper Carmichael and you pay the price.

He tore into the apartment, revenge raging, when he came to an abrupt halt.

On the dining table sat a holdall he didn't recognise. Jasper snatched it open. He ran his hand through his hair. He couldn't believe his eyes. *What the fuck?*

He slowly paced the apartment, trying to put two and two together. But the only person who could do that was Kate. He stared at the carpet and followed the trail of discarded clothes. Her shoes lay by the door where she'd kicked them off; her jacket was discarded on the couch, trousers at the bedroom door, blouse on the bedroom carpet with bra and panties on top.

She lay on the bed with only a towel for cover.

**

Kate had been a nervous wreck when she'd opened the apartment door. She'd dumped the holdall on the dining table and torn off her clothes, not caring where they fell.

She slid to the tiled shower floor and cried. The warm water joined her tears as her body shook. Thoughts of Jasper filled her mind. What would he think of her? *Betrayal, betrayal,* repeated in her head.

She imagined two firm arms pinning her to the tiled wall and Jasper's soft lips kissing her, his hands lovingly caressing her body as he filled her. Time stood still as waves of uncontrollable bliss rolled through her, satisfying every fibre of body and soul.

"Jasper," she murmured between sobs.

**

He slowly removed his clothes, taking time to fold them and place them neatly on a chair. All the time, his eyes were fixed on the towel that covered a sleeping Kate.

He slowly and gently inched the towel away. He took a long moment to admire her naked form. Her high cheekbones, soft lips, full breasts, curvaceous hips. He prided himself that he knew every inch of her soft body. All thoughts of a revenge fuck melted. He covered her with a sheet and nestled beside her.

"Tell me," he whispered in her ear. He wrapped his arms around her and gazed at her erect nipples.

A murmuring of a sigh escaped her mouth.

"Tell me."

Her green eyes shot open. "Jasper?"

"Who else?"

A half smile struggled across her face.

"Tell me."

***

Jasper smiled at the unmistakeable ritualistic sound of Kate making her morning tea. He had noticed that if she didn't have two cups of Yorkshire first thing, she was exceptionally grumpy. He sat at his study's antique desk, reorganising his investments. The safe in his study was overflowing with cash, now that Kate had rescued some of the money from his NRJ account.

His temper rose at the thought of Smith and Jack dividing his cash fifty-fifty.

It had been approaching dawn when Kate had finally finished telling him everything. The grunting man, as she called him. The shock of seeing Jack, Richard and Beth at the bank. Following them and lifting the money satchel from the floor.

He wasn't surprised; they had a tendency to be overconfident and careless. However, he was surprised that Tom had been searching for her at Euston.

Jasper had thought he'd had Jack, Richard and Beth under control now that Max was dead, but he couldn't have been more mistaken. He'd had no idea that Smith had formed an alliance with them. Jack and Richard had suddenly become very confident. Sooner or later he would have to deal with them.

Jasper was surprised that he'd found himself comforting Kate upon his return home. He had never done that before, but she was traumatised. She needed him.

He didn't tell her about his temper. Or the punishment fuck he had planned.

He felt guilty; he was to blame for Kate's distress. He shouldn't have sent her into the jaws of the criminal world.

He had put Kate's life in danger. She had shown him deep loyalty that he hadn't known existed. The least he could do was find her a safe haven for when he disappeared, or she would be an easy target.

Kate was standing in the office doorway, looking over the steaming cup that she held in both hands. She had helped herself to one of his dress shirts. It was open and just covered her bottom. His gaze slowly meandered to the top of her thighs. The softness of her skin, full breasts, and warm, wet pussy. He would miss Kate when he disappeared. But most of all he would miss her breasts and pussy.

"You didn't say why you sent me to that god-awful place," she innocently said between sips of tea.

His erection strained for freedom. He mentally debated if he should have her on his desk, sore or not.

"Jasper!"

"You distract me."

She raised her eyebrows.

"Your hair's tousled, your nipples hard, and I bet you're wet." He pushed his high-backed leather chair away from his desk.

"We could make a deal." Her voice was mischievously playful.

"Go on." His eyes were on fire as he kicked his jeans, boxers and T-shirt to the floor.

"Tell me why you sent me to that prison, then we can christen your desk."

"It wasn't a prison."

He removed the empty cup from her hand and gazed helplessly at her breasts.

"I want you," he said in his husky voice.

Her hand reached for his erection. She smiled when he closed his eyes.

"Tell me."

He lifted her onto his desk and flicked the shirt off her shoulders.

"The prison, as you call it, is being demolished. Affordable housing." He was losing concentration. "I had to empty my locker. And you…" He didn't finish.

His mouth devoured first one breast then the other, his erection straining at her entrance, eager to taste her delights.

Chapter Twenty-One

The silver Rolls Royce Phantom was parked across the disabled parking bays at the Carmichael and Swain offices.

Memories flashed before Jasper's eyes. Memories he would sooner forget. The old Families always drove Phantoms, but Colin Carmichael never did. The old Families enjoyed showing off their wealth and power, whereas Colin had preferred not to announce his presence or his wealth.

Jasper took a long moment to consider the arrival of the Wilson brothers, Charlie and Matt. A display of power, he thought. He had expected them sooner; the Wilsons were big players in the Families.

Jasper had a fight on his hands. A fight for survival. The Families or the Wilsons or both were preparing to take over C&S.

He found Charlie and Matt in the conference room, sprawled in the comfy chairs, drinking his whisky and laughing with Jack, Richard and Beth.

"You're late, Carmichael," Charlie growled in a superior manner as his eyes settled on Jasper.

"What do you want?" Jasper lowered himself into a chair opposite the glaring Wilsons.

"We're taking Max's place," Charlie aggressively replied.

"Max didn't have a place," Jasper calmly said.

Charlie Wilson sat up and glared at Jasper. "Max had a place here."

"Max had no place here. He may have sat in on a meeting or two, but as for voting rights, he had none." Jasper's voice was firm and authoritative.

"My brother had a deal with Jack. And you're going to fucking recognise it."

"Your brother had no deal with Carmichael and Swain."

"Come on, Jasper," interjected Jack.

For a brief moment, Jasper's and Jack's eyes met.

Charlie stood menacingly over Jasper. His face flushed and his eyes bulged. "I represent the Families. Old Man Cohen's got family problems."

"The Families have no rights here. We're independent."

"Not anymore," Charlie growled. "Jack's already agreed."

Jasper slammed his chair back against the wall, just missing Charlie.

"Is that so?! Well, get this straight: if the fucking Families want to buy me out, dig deep."

Tension thickened as the two old Family rivals, Wilson and Carmichael, faced off with each other like two boxers.

A cough came from the open conference room door.

"Your pussy's 'ere," sniggered Matt.

Jasper's eyes briefly flicked to Kate; he ignored Matt.

"They tell me you're putty in 'er 'and." Matt grinned. "She must be some pussy."

Jasper clenched his fist, tight. Kate reddened.

Matt sniggered. "Max 'ad the hots for 'er. Nice tits, 'e told me." He cupped his crotch.

Jasper's knuckles started to turn white, and his eyes returned to Kate.

"Don't react," she mouthed.

A long, tense moment passed.

"We'll reschedule." Jasper's words were slow and controlled as he left the conference room.

"Matt, you fucking idiot!" yelled Charlie. "Stop taunting him."

Jasper just caught Charlie's words as he pushed past Kate and stormed towards his office, kicking over every waste bin he passed. He slammed his office door and then Kate's.

Jasper was seething. Matt Wilson was lucky to be standing after the comments he'd made about Kate.

He slumped into her high-backed desk chair. Two hands unexpectedly settled on his shoulders and slowly massaged. Round and round and up and down.

"I should fuck you." His words slurred slightly as he began to relax.

She leaned into his ear. "Later."

Jasper grinned and pulled her onto his lap.

"Fancy playing hooky?"

"Jasper Carmichael! How dare you suggest such a thing… again." Her voice was playful, eyes sparkling.

"Where are we going?" she tentatively asked.

"You'll see."

He hadn't told Kate many things. Sooner or later he would have to come clean.

Chapter Twenty-Two

Jasper took Kate's hand as they walked around the boatyard.

"We've been here before," Kate commented. "I can't believe you bought this." Her voice was louder than she would have liked.

She couldn't believe her eyes. The place still looked like a scrapyard to her. Chunks of metal were haphazardly strewn about, the weeds knee high.

"I thought that when I first saw it." Jasper smiled.

They stopped by the refitted yacht.

"Is this that...?"

"Yes." Jasper couldn't hide the pride in his voice.

"It looks finished," Kate commented.

Jasper put his arm around her shoulder. "Yes. Would you like to go sailing?"

"Do you know how?"

"I've joined a club. Lessons. I could take you up the coast."

"I don't know. I'm frightened of water. I... I can't swim," she stuttered.

Jasper pulled her round so she faced him. "You can't swim?! In that case, lessons." He planted a soft kiss on her lips. "Your lessons start now."

"Now?!"

He held her hand as he guided her along the plank to the boat. Jasper pulled the hatch door open.

"After you." He grinned with that glint in his eyes.

She stepped into the cabin. It looked like a living room and kitchen.

"Keep walking. The bedroom's in the stern."

As he closed the hatch, he caught a glimpse of Alwyn. It was the second time he had caught Alwyn watching him and Kate. His gut told him that he should pay Alwyn a visit. But that would have to wait; he had more important things on his mind.

***

Alwyn Jones slipped from his workshop and watched Jasper and that woman. Nice and cosy, he thought, as they strolled towards the yacht, arms wrapped around each other. His hand searched his pocket for the paper with a telephone number written on it.

He had met the man in the pub. He had bought a round of drinks and had been very keen to know if any strangers had been about.

Alwyn had run after him. The man had told him he would be handsomely paid if the right stranger appeared.

***

Matt Wilson was walking from the service station when he noticed Jasper filling his Range Rover with fuel. He stepped back into the drinks area and watched.

Jasper was talking on his phone as he slipped into the driver's seat. Kate looked surprised when he parked in front of the services' Travelodge.

"Jasper's at the services with 'is bitch," Matt said quietly into his phone.

"Don't do anything. Wait for us," his brother instructed.

Matt watched Jasper and Kate enter the last ground-floor room, next to the fire escape. With his ear pressed against the bedroom door, Matt listened.

When he heard the sound of running water, he kicked the door open.

Jasper sat on the bed, engrossed in his phone. He didn't have time to react before Matt punched his face.

Jasper slumped back onto the bed. Matt held him by his shirt collar and slapped him about the face. Jasper managed to push Matt off him, but Matt had the upper hand and pushed Jasper to the floor.

"Take that, you bastard." Matt's foot found Jasper's ribs.

Jasper's body lifted.

A loud cry came from the bathroom. Matt looked up. Kate was standing naked, eyes fixed on Jasper lying on the floor.

His big foot pushed Jasper to one side while he removed his belt. Matt had other things on his mind. His trousers and boxers fell onto the floor. He was determined to do what Max hadn't: fuck Jasper's woman.

She gasped in fright, stepping back into the bathroom.

Matt followed with a big grin across his face. He followed her, rubbing his hard erection.

"This is all for you," he gloated.

She began to cry, backing away from him. The tiled wall was cold against her back. Through tears, she looked past Matt to where Jasper lay, unconscious.

Matt grinned. "That bastard can't help." He grabbed her face, hard around her jaw, tilting her eyes to meet his. "But he'll watch as I fuck. Your cunt, mouth and arse."

Uncontrollable tears gushed down her face, and Matt slapped her. "Shut the fuck up. I'm going to fuck you until you can't fuckin' stand."

She closed her eyes, bracing herself for the assault.

But it never came. She screamed when Matt fell. She stood shaking as adrenaline soared.

Jasper pulled her into his arms. Blood dripped down his face.

"Shhhh," he whispered gently, stroking her hair.

After a long moment he tentatively asked. "Did he?"

"No."

"But he hit you." His thumb gently caressed her bruised face.

She nodded, gulping deep sobs.

"I'll kill that bastard."

"Jasper! No!"

She clung to him, her body shaking.

"He hurt what's mine." His words were barely audible.

Her stomach flipped as she sobbed into his shoulder.

"Get dressed." His tone was soft and caring. *I'll deal with Matt Wilson later,* he thought.

He retrieved Matt's belt from the floor and tied his arms to his ankles. When Kate's back was turned, he kicked him in the kidneys.

Chapter Twenty-Three

Matt sat on the bed, holding an ice pack to his head.

Charlie was pacing and cursing at his brother when Jack rushed in.

"CCTV tape gone. Registration book—pages missing. Paid cash."

"In a hurry," commented Charlie, shaking his head at his brother. "How the fuck did he manage all that?"

"I got lucky," murmured a despondent Matt, not listening to his brother.

"You should have waited, Matt," chided Jack.

"He's hurt. Bloody face," Matt mumbled. "I can't believe he's driving."

"She could be driving," Charlie added.

"He's dangerous. Can't believe you're alive," commented Jack.

"It was her. She was in the shower. He sat on the bed staring at his phone. He didn't hear me. I 'ad her pinned to the shower wall."

"You fucked her!" exclaimed Jack. *He's a dead man,* Jack thought.

"Nah. Nice tits. Was about to have her, then Jasper hit me."

Charlie was in another world, concentrating on how Jasper would react.

"You know he'll be after you," said Jack. "No one floors Jasper and gets away with it."

"Fuck Jasper. I can handle him."

"Max said the same."

"Best guess: where's he gone, Jack?" asked Charlie.

"London."

Charlie picked up his phone.

"London," he barked.

"He'll make a mistake," said a dejected Matt.

"You don't get it." Jack's exasperated words made both of them look up. "Jasper rarely makes mistakes. He thinks things through."

Charlie dropped his phone on the bed after reading the text message that flashed on it. "He's not at the London apartment."

"Let's go," said Matt.

"And do what? Fuck her and torture Jasper? I want his fucking network and his money. Not his fucking woman."

An uncomfortable silence hung in the room.

"We'll bide our time. We'll let Lawson harass him."

"You'll clean this mess up and go back to Wellsbury!" Don's angry voice bellowed. "You fucking idiot! It's cancelled, until Jasper makes a move."

Don had surprised them. They hadn't heard him move into the room. He stood just inside the door, hatefully staring at Matt.

Matt quivered.

"We don't know where he's gone," mumbled Jack.

"It doesn't matter. He'll 'ave to return to Wellsbury." Don turned and walked away.

***

"Where're we going?" asked a nervous Kate.

Jasper didn't answer. His head was thumping, ribs aching. He could barely give her directions.

Kate stopped the Range Rover on the drive of a 1930s semi. Jasper's minimal directions hadn't given her any idea of where they were, but she saw a shop sign with 'Mitchem' written on it.

"It's my safe house," he had reluctantly told her. And that was all she needed to know.

Jasper opened the passenger door and was sick. *This is not good,* Kate thought.

"Where's the nearest A and E?" she tentatively asked.

Jasper's look said all she needed to know. "Don't even think about it."

Jasper leaned against Kate as they slowly walked up the stairs to the bedroom. He gingerly lowered himself onto the bed. Kate flicked his shoes off, slackened his trousers and shirt. She sat on the edge of the bed, carefully wiping the cut on his forehead.

"It should be stitched," she said as she finally removed the last of the dried blood.

It had been her idea to stop and buy some groceries and medical supplies.

"This is going to hurt."

Their eyes met.

Jasper shut his eyes firmly as Kate gently fixed the closure strips and wound spray over his cut head. She cut off his shirt and gasped at the bruises already forming on his chest and stomach. With gentle, light circular motions, she slowly applied cream.

She left Jasper sleeping while she removed the groceries from the Range Rover.

The house was cold, and the central heating boiler didn't want to know. The fact that Jasper had insisted that the curtains remained closed and the lighting was very poor in the cubby hole that housed the boiler didn't help.

Kate sat for some time, staring into the dimly lit room, sipping a very welcome cup of tea. Her thoughts were confused. One minute they were on the yacht having mind-blowing sex, the next Matt Wilson broke into their room and attacked first Jasper and then her.

The Wilsons were bad news; they were preparing to take over Carmichael and Swain. And now their lives were in danger, Jasper was preparing to disappear and leave her, alone.

It was time for her to push her feelings for Jasper to the back of her mind and think of Kate.

Jasper was asleep, but there would be no sleep for her. She would have to keep an eye on him, just in case his head wound turned nasty and he began to vomit.

"Kate." His loud croaky voice startled her.

She must have dropped off. The blanket that covered her had fallen to the carpet.

"Do you feel sick?" Her words were soft and comforting. Her fingers stroked his forehead.

"Where were you?"

"In the chair."

"I need you by me."

"Jasper. That's not a good idea."

"Take your clothes off and snuggle beside me," he croaked.

She woke to the sound of cars and people. She had no idea how long they had slept; neither had stirred.

Her soft lips grazed his forehead.

"Breakfast?"

"Bathroom."

She helped him along the landing to the bathroom. He cringed at every step.

"I'll use the toilet, then shower me."

The warm water gave him some relief from

the pain, but he couldn't bear the flannel touching him.

He refused to go back to bed, insisting on lying on the large sofa in the sitting room. However, he managed a small bowl of porridge and coffee.

Jasper Carmichael was not a good patient. He reluctantly ate and drank. He insisted Kate slept naked by his side and showered him.

On the fourth day he insisted on a bath.

"Join me. Your front to my back."

On the fifth day Kate found him in the dining room hunched over his laptop, staring at the screen, running his hand through his salt-and-pepper hair. *More salt than pepper,* Kate thought.

"Coffee?"

He nodded.

"The house will need a thorough clean," he mumbled between bites of toast. "We leave for Wellsbury tomorrow."

"Is that a good idea?"

"I can't leave you alone. The Wilsons have shown their hand."

"You're leaving."

"Not yet. I have things to settle." He paused. "A trip to the Caymans. A holiday." His eyes left the laptop screen, and he smiled.

The next day they left the Mitchem safe house. Things had changed between them. There were long periods of silence. Jasper had a permanent scowl on his face, and he never looked at or touched her.

Kate was hurting deep inside.

Chapter Twenty-Four

"This isn't the way to the apartment," commented Kate.

Jasper had turned off the Wellsbury main road and into the old part of the town.

"Loft Lane! Look at it! No wonder it's up for demolition," Kate said.

He stopped by the old school, an architectural masterpiece of its time. It was built by one of the Victorian entrepreneurs who had visited Wellsbury and taken pity on the plight of the children. The school had been built within walking distance of the slum area, where most of the children lived. It was no longer a school, and children no longer lived in the slums.

Kate gazed up at the steep roof. Many of the slates were missing. The stone structure was in need of painting. The chimney stacks were tilting, waiting for a winter gale to bring them to the ground.

"Who lives here?" Kate's voice was filled with disbelief.

"Round the back."

"That's good to know. The vandals have been busy at the front."

Kate's sarcastic comment made Jasper cringe. He was beginning to regret bringing her.

Kate followed Jasper along a dark passage. A small, overweight man wearing an old, dirty neckerchief greeted them. Zak. His beady eyes immediately settled on Kate. He smiled, revealing missing teeth. His baggy trousers and collarless shirt belonged in the rag bin.

"Got somut for me?"

"Depends," Jasper replied.

"Haf yo bin to the Caymans?"

"No. I'm thinking of killing two birds with one stone."

They followed Zak along a poorly lit corridor into a windowless room. The smell of fried food, tobacco and whisky made Kate's stomach churn.

"Brought yo pussy." Zak's slimy voice and eyes made Kate shiver. "She's the talk of the place." He licked his lips.

Jasper slipped his hand into his inside pocket. A small velvet bag fell onto the desk. Zak's face lit up. He switched on a desk lamp and fixed a magnifying lens to his eye.

Kate was no expert, but she recognised uncut diamonds.

"Yo fucking bastard—yo had them all along." Zak's grubby fingers touched each diamond in turn. "This ain't all of 'em."

"How much?"

"Depends."

"Can you cut and polish?"

"No prob. They'll be unrecognisable when I've finished."

"I will need all of them cut and polished. These will do for now."

Zak's small beady eyes had suddenly grown in size with excitement.

"We'll talk money when we're done. You cut these"—Jasper pointed to the uncut diamonds—"and I'll bring your diamonds back. Deal."

Zak nodded.

They left him drooling over two of Colin Carmichael's diamonds.

"You trust him?" asked Kate when they were back in the Range Rover.

"Not really. Zak and I go back. We've something in common: he's a Cohen bastard and I'm a Carmichael bastard."

"Cohen?"

"Yes. Old family, Cohen. They came over during the war. Colin and the Cohens were friends."

"You're not a bastard."

"Colin was. I'm told his dad visited once when I was a baby." He paused. "Colin made his own way, but he was head and shoulders above the other members of the Families. Carmichael is a common name. I have no idea if Carmichael is my name, or if the woman I called mother was my mother. I'm nothing like Richard. He's supposed to be like my mother, but there's none of her in me."

Kate lay her hand on his knee.

"Colin was involved with saving the Dutch diamonds—he did have an uncanny knowledge about diamonds. He became a master diamond thief, as well as other valuables. But he double-crossed his partners. Lawson hated him and, with help, put him inside. Colin didn't live with us; he would just appear. Make a fuss of me and fuck her."

Jasper had stopped the Range Rover at Kate's favourite spot: the confluence of the rivers Wells and Bury.

"Come on, let's go for a stroll."

Jasper's arm was looped around Kate's shoulder.

"I don't trust Zak." Her voice was barely above a whisper.

"I'm not Colin. I don't cross my partners and Zak knows it. We've been in some tight spots, but we never grassed on each other."

Silence.

"You have the diamonds?" asked Kate.

"You've read Colin's records," Jasper answered.

She nodded.

"It was Colin that told me to leave. Go my own way. Be my own man. He didn't like Jack. But I wasn't confident back then." Jasper paused, deciding how much to tell Kate. "He left me everything. Money, diamonds, property. He told me to let everything lie. I would know when the time is right."

"Is that now?"

"Things are going to get rough." His voice was barely audible. "The Wilsons and the Families are bad news. I've never been a member of the Families, but Colin was. The Carmichael line ends with me. That's how it should be."

"What do you mean?"

"The old ways are over. The Families weren't big in the criminal world, but they made good money. It's different now. Gangs from abroad are taking over. Drugs, sex trade."

"But you're not into that."

"No. I've gone down a different route. But that won't stop them muscling in."

Silence lingered as Kate processed Jasper's words.

"You're leaving." Her voice quivered.

"I want you safe. I wish things could have been different. Trouble's going to follow me—I don't want you hurt."

"I can look after myself. How long have we got?"

"A month. Maybe two. After the Caymans. You have to be ready. Pack the stuff you need."

***

"He's here," Matt Wilson breathed into his phone. "Lovey-dovey by the river."

"Leave 'im alone. Watch," Charlie Wilson forcibly instructed.

Chapter Twenty-Five

Kate sat at her desk, searching the internet for the cottage that had caught her eye on their trip to Alwyn's boatyard.

"I'm going to spend the day with Zak. Wanna come?" Jasper's voice startled her.

She flushed and managed a half smile. "No."

"Our enemies have gone to London. So you'll be safe." He smiled.

***

Kate found herself driving around Wellsbury trying to lose one of the Wilsons' goons. It was proving difficult.

She swerved into the multi-storey carpark and hid the Evoque between two white vans. She waited until her tail had driven by and ran into the town. She dodged through the back streets until she reached Jasper's lockup. Inside was an old Land Rover Defender. Jasper had introduced her to her getaway car when they'd returned from Mitchem. She didn't like the old boneshaker, but Jasper was right when he said no one would dream of looking for an old Defender; they would be looking for the Evoque.

Kate had arranged to meet the agent at the cottage. It was difficult to see from the road, and the driveway looked like a track, but that didn't matter to Kate. It was love at first sight.

A smiling young agent was waiting with an

enthusiastic sales pitch. Kate smiled; his boss had probably told him to use the hard sell technique.

The cottage had obviously been on the market for some time. The "For Sale" board lay on the ground, and there was a degree of neglect about the place.

The exterior of the cottage looked sound, but the inside required a lot of attention: kitchen, bathroom, central heating. It would give her a project to occupy her after Jasper left.

Jasper... Would he be the love of her life? She couldn't bear to think of life without him. But she had to face reality. They had to go their separate ways.

A local builder stopped by, and she doubted it was a coincidence. However, she didn't mind, as she needed to have this cottage liveable as soon as possible and it was obvious that the agent needed a sale and the builder needed work.

The builder promised an urgent quote and although the agent had the usual checks to go through, Kate knew the cottage was hers.

***

Kate was in bed when Jasper returned. She suspected that he hadn't been with Zak but had been doing whatever it was he secretly did.

Jasper congratulated himself for not lying to Kate; he had gone to see Zak but that hadn't taken long. Zak needed cash and Jasper had a safe full. He'd spent the rest of the day preparing his yacht for a quick getaway. After buying supplies, he'd moved the yacht along the coast to a deeper mooring. The remaining money from his safe he'd hidden behind the food cupboard.

***

Jasper had an uneasy feeling about Alwyn. Before he could leave the boatyard, he had to put his mind to rest.

He left the Range Rover at the boatyard. Alwyn was nowhere to be seen, but his old battered van was parked at the pub. Jasper shook his head, recalling how Alwyn bragged about the van not being taxed, insured or MOT-ed.

The workshop was unlocked and the old wood-burning stove stone cold. Again, that was odd. The place looked as if Alwyn hadn't been there for days.

He flicked through the papers that covered Alwyn's desk. There was too much information about Miles Phillips. He hastily collected the papers and slipped them into his satchel. He kicked over a stack of newspapers and poured a can of used oil over them.

The old safe was easy to open. Jasper was shocked to find neatly piled stacks of new twenty-pound notes. Alwyn had another client. The thought set off alarm bells in Jasper's head. Alwyn had crossed him. He put the money next to the papers in his satchel. He left the satchel in the Range Rover and walked to Alwyn's cottage.

He slipped a credit card between the lock and the front door of Alwyn's cottage.

Alwyn isn't much of a housekeeper, he thought, shining his iPhone light so he could sidestep old coats that had fallen from hooks and shoes and boots left where they were easy to trip over. He silently walked up the stairs. The bedroom door creaked. An unsavoury smell filled his nostrils and he looked to the rumpled bed, expecting the worst, but it was empty. He quickly turned to leave, but a discarded book caught his eye.

The Carmichael Gang.

Jasper shuddered. The book had been out of print for years. The one and only book written about his father's reign as head of the gang referred to as the Families.

He remembered reading it. It depicted Colin as a murderer. A man that people in the community were frightened of. Colin had told him it was lies, but there were too many details on how Colin had tortured men that crossed him. Jasper thought his dad had been more than a little disingenuous. However, Jasper couldn't judge Colin, considering how he had dealt with men who had crossed him.

For a long moment he ran his fingers over the well-worn front cover, mulling over why Alwyn was reading about the Carmichaels and, above all, how he'd come by a copy of the book.

A little preoccupied, he stumbled into another bedroom. He stopped dead in his tracks as his iPhone lit up a wall devoted to him.

A photo of him and Kate had pride of place. Underneath were photos of Beth, Jack, Richard, Lawson, his mother and father, Charlie Wilson, Max, Matt and Don. In the top right-hand corner was a large question mark with an arrow leading to Don.

Alwyn had scrawled *Don's boss.*

In anger, Jasper opened his iPhone camera and took a photo before ripping the pictures off the wall.

Lying on the floor was a small notebook that would easily fit in a pocket. He quickly flicked through the pages and stuffed it in his pocket along with the photos.

Who is this man?

Blackmail shot into Jasper's mind. But he

hadn't time to analyse Alwyn's actions; he had to get back to Wellsbury before he was missed.

Another unsavoury smell wafted from the kitchen. Black bin-liners filled with rubbish were stacked against the back door. Unwashed pots filled the sink. Uneaten food was left on plates; whisky bottles cluttered the draining board.

Jasper crammed newspaper into the toaster and switched it on. When he closed the front door, the toaster was well alight.

Chapter Twenty-Six

Jasper was eating well-buttered toast and sipping an espresso when his burner phone blipped.

"Mr Phillips?" said a gruff voice.

"Yes," Jasper tentatively replied.

"Owner of Alwyn's yard?"

"Yes." Jasper hesitated. "He's refitting a yacht."

"This is PC Watkins. I've got some bad news: Alwyn's been in a fatal accident." He waited for the news to sink in. "He was on the motorway— no idea where he was going. Hit the central reservation. Van flipped and caught fire. We think a tyre burst, but we 'ave no way of knowing."

Jasper gasped. "Is he...?"

"Dead? Aye. You were with him yesterday?"

"No."

"But you were at the yard?"

"Yes."

"You moved your yacht."

"I did. I've paid for it to be moored in deeper water."

"Aye."

Jasper waited for PC Watkins to continue.

"I don't suppose you 'ave any idea where he was going?"

"No," Jasper lied. He had a good idea.

"He'd had a lot to drink and that old van was a death trap. No tax, insurance or MOT."

Watkins waited for Jasper to reply and sighed when he remained silent.

"The thing is, his cottage caught fire last night."

"Shit, what happened?"

"Fire chief reckons it started in the kitchen. Place was a fire waiting to happen. We suspect he went home after the pub and left somot on and it overheated."

"If there's anything I can do..."

"We'd appreciate it if you could copy the sale documents and send them to his solicitor."

"I'm perplexed; Alwyn had copies."

"Maybe, but the place was gutted. It's a shell."

"Of course. I'll do anything to help."

"Thanks for your time."

The phone went dead.

"Who was that?" asked Kate, pouring tea.

"Police. Alwyn's dead. Car accident."

"What?"

"His cottage was burnt down. Apparently, he was so drunk he left something on in the kitchen and the place burnt down."

Kate was only half listening as the sound of a car stopping outside caught her attention.

She peeped out of the window. "It's Don. What does he want?"

"I can guess," commented Jasper.

***

Don sat in one of the over-stuffed chairs, cradling a mug of tea, his eyes fixed on Kate.

"She stays," commented Jasper, preferring a very large malt to either coffee or tea.

"Not a good idea." Don fixed Jasper with a hard look. "Your dad couldn't leave your mother alone and look where that got him."

"I'm not him."

"You sure?"

"Spit it out, Don."

"They... *We* want you to run things."

"Because?"

"If you don't, blood will flow. The Wilsons are throwing their weight around."

"You mean Charlie is."

"The Families don't do drugs. Lost too many to heroin, and now sex slaves."

"What do you want from me?"

"You have a duty. You're the last of the Carmichaels. We need another Carmichael to carry on."

Don's eyes moved to Kate. Without any words, he said it all: she can't have children.

"Anything else?"

"Get rid of the Wilsons. Run the clubs, gambling, protection. Leave drugs to the other gangs."

A tense silence filled the room.

Jasper's eyes moved to Kate. She didn't return his gaze. Her eyes had filled, and her cheeks had reddened. She stood and walked towards the window. She didn't want them to see the single tear trickle down her cheek. Her stomach fluttered. Their relationship had come to an end. Jasper would fulfil his family obligation. And she couldn't give him children.

"We'll listen to any of your ideas," Don continued, not caring about Kate. "Look at the shopping centre. Run properly, it's a winner. How many of those could you develop?"

Silence.

"We need leadership, Jasper," he persisted.

"I've got a few problems of my own."

Don's eyes moved to Kate, who had her back towards them.

"We could offer her protection," added Don. Kate's headstrong ways would attract the wrong sort.

The confident, independent Kate turned and faced the two men. "No need to concern yourselves about me. I'll be gone: a new life away from Wellsbury. I won't cause trouble."

Jasper knew she was putting on a brave face. But could he live without her? She was his weakness, his strength, his comfort. And loyal.

"Let me think about it," Jasper added. "I wouldn't want to go south—new premises. I need people who I can trust. No double dealing with Lawson."

"Not a problem." Don grinned. *He's interested,* he thought. "I hear you had a problem with Matt. He won't rest until—"

"He's my problem," Jasper interrupted. He stood next to Kate and tentatively slipped an arm around her shoulder.

"Jack can't be trusted," Don warned. "Or Richard and Beth. You'll 'ave to put your own house in order."

Jasper turned and met Don's eyes with a hard stare. It was the Colin Carmichael stare Don remembered.

"I know that." Jasper's tone was sharp.

"Of course, you should marry 'er. That way, no one will dare touch 'er," Don commented, trying to goad Jasper into showing his true feelings.

A loud gasp escaped Kate's mouth, putting an end to the conversation.

***

Kate watched Jasper and Don talking by Don's Audi. Don was doing all the talking and Jasper occasionally nodded.

With each nod of Jasper's head, Kate's temper rose a notch. She needed to be calm before he returned. She wanted them to part as friends.

She watched Don slowly drive away and waited for Jasper.

She could feel his stare piercing her back.

Kate's upset, he thought as he watched her sip a malt. That in itself alerted him to her mood; whisky wasn't her tipple.

She had obviously guessed Don's meaning. As far as Jasper knew, he was the last of his father's line. He needed a son. And Kate couldn't give him that.

He didn't want to argue. He wanted her in his bed. He wanted her by his side when he took on Jack and the Wilsons. He didn't want to lose her to some meaningless argument.

He wondered if she could be persuaded to remain his lover if he got married and had a son with someone else.

Kate's strained, emotional voice broke the heavy silence. "Have you agreed to Don's request?" Her eyes were fixed on the amber liquid.

"Look at me."

"I agreed to check files. Keep house. For a few months." Her voice quivered as she fought to control her emotions.

"And satisfy my sexual needs."

"But I don't. And never will... I can't have a Carmichael."

She turned to face him. He was surprised to see tears waiting to cover her red cheeks. He took a step towards her, but she held up her hand.

"And I'm not a criminal. I don't live in that world." He was taken aback by the intensity of her emotions.

"Kate." He took another step towards her.

She flared. "Don't *Kate* me!"

"What did you expect?" His voice was firm.

"It's more like: what didn't I expect?"

He raised his eyebrows.

"To be drawn into Jasper's web." Her voice faltered.

Her guard had momentarily slipped. He seized his opportunity; his large hands gripped her shoulders. Before words were uttered, he caressed her face as their mouths mutually collided.

***

She was asleep, on her side, her back towards him. She had resisted, but it was futile. He knew her weaknesses, and slow, emotional sex was one.

Kate knew too much about his business, his money and, above all, where it was salted away. One day he might have to deal with her. But she was special. He felt responsible; he had ruined her life. He loved her.

But the present pressed heavily on his mind.

He switched on the coffee maker. He had Alwyn and a phone call to South America to deal with.

But Alwyn was dead, killed in a car accident. He'd obviously been on his way to Wellsbury, but Jasper wasn't responsible for his death.

Alwyn's collection of photographs and notes indicated that someone who knew Jasper very well had been talking. On his iPhone, Jasper studied Alwyn's collection of photos. They were all there: Jasper, Kate, Jack, Richard, Beth, Lawson, his mother and father, the Wilsons and Don. Alwyn had left a space with a question mark: Don's boss. Was Alwyn correct that Don had another boss?

Jasper's call to the South Americans was

late, and they hated that. He had to use all his persuasive powers for them to agree to meet in the Caymans. He didn't like involving the South Americans—they were not to be trusted—but needs must. He had to sell all his properties. He needed cash.

Chapter Twenty-Seven

Inspector Lawson impatiently paced Jasper's office. Amanda had told him Jasper was running late, but Jasper had no intention at being at the office; he was thirty thousand feet in the air, flying to the Caymans.

Kate hadn't wanted to join him, but he'd coaxed her. It was the promise of a day of mind-blowing sex that had finally clinched her decision.

The mattress dipped as he slid in next to her. Her eyes were closed, but she wasn't sleeping. A soft kiss caressed her forehead.

"Forgive me," he murmured.

She opened her eyes and her lips turned to a half smile.

"We'll be landing shortly and there are things you need to know."

Their eyes locked.

"These are in no particular order," he began. "We'll be staying in the penthouse suite." Her eyes widened. "I'm part owner of a hotel. The smallest part, so I've got the smallest suite." He grinned. "One bedroom, but a massive living space overlooking the Caribbean. And a jacuzzi." He hesitated. "I've never had a woman in the suite. There'll be questions and interest in our relationship. So, you're my assistant with benefits." He grinned again. "But you mustn't get any ideas."

"Ideas?" she repeated.

"This doesn't alter our understanding," he

continued, diverting his focus to the wall behind her.

"I'm perfectly aware of our understanding, Jasper. I'm not expecting anything." Her stern tone surprised him.

"You've got the money from the shop and your salary in a Swiss bank. All intact."

"I know."

He raised his eyebrows; her tone hadn't changed.

He slipped two cards in her bra. "One will open the suite; the other is for clothes, et cetera." She looked surprised. "A business suit, cocktail dress, lace lingerie. You know the stuff."

"I'm not one of your floozies," she retorted.

He didn't react to her comment. "Use the spa, pool, beach. But you must have this with you all the time." He pushed a phone into her hand.

***

A little unsteady, Kate followed Jasper down the steps of the private jet. She was thankful that the jet had taxied into a cool hangar, although the temperature had nothing to do with her uneasy feeling.

A large man in a black uniform with a cap pulled over his eyes opened the rear driver's-side door of the waiting limousine.

Jasper turned away from Kate while he talked in a hushed tone to the pilot.

An uncomfortable silence floated between them as they sat looking out of the rear windows of the limousine, each locked in their own thoughts.

Jasper had no intention of discussing all his plans with Kate. And Kate had no intention of telling Jasper her trust in him was rapidly diminishing.

The car slowed and turned into the circular entrance of the hotel. A man dressed in the same uniform as the driver raced from the entrance to open Kate's door.

"Welcome," he said, giving Kate a beaming smile. She didn't return it.

Jasper scowled and firmly gripped her hand, pulling her into his side.

"Take that worried expression off your face," he firmly whispered into her hair. "You're my assistant—act like it."

A forced smile appeared on his face as he gripped her elbow and confidently strode towards the reception desk.

The surroundings were luxurious, with a marble floor and chandeliers hanging from the arched ceiling, but Kate paid them no attention. Instead, her focus was on the glamorous receptionist who was eye-fucking Jasper. Her tongue slowly traced the outline of her lips as he returned her smile.

"Chloe." Her name softly dripped from Jasper's mouth.

"Your suite awaits you." Her sexy voice made people stare.

Jasper smiled and made a big show of signing the register as she leaned across the narrow desk, her dress top straining to keep her breasts contained. He grinned and dropped the pen into her cleavage.

"Later," he whispered, low enough that Kate could barely hear.

Kate's stomach flipped. Jasper was a cad. He had lied to her. Any thoughts she'd had that he only wanted her flew out of her mind.

"Mr Carmichael." All eyes turned to the glamorous concierge. "Everything is ready, sir."

"Thank you for accommodating my assistant at such short notice. I'm afraid she wasn't expecting this trip. It was her day off." His business smile crept across his lips. "Urgent business cropped up. Kate was the only one that could assist me."

Kate wasn't paying attention. Her mind was consumed with how many women in this hotel had dropped their expensive knickers for him.

The concierge smiled and nodded, clearly unsurprised.

She smiled at Kate, the sort of smile that was an instruction. Kate followed her, thankful to be out of Jasper's company. Kate guessed that she was to be restyled to fit in with her surroundings and Jasper's requirements.

With her hair styled to frame her face, a light covering of makeup and a casual outfit of white linen trousers and an oversized blouse, Kate felt like a different woman.

The concierge waved to a porter, who picked up Kate's new clothes and toiletries.

"Mr Carmichael is unable to meet for dinner. He suggested..." The concierge's words drifted as Kate cut across her.

"That's fine. I have work to do," she lied.

Kate waited for the porter to place her bags on the thick carpet. "I'm sorry. I haven't any money," she mumbled, going through her handbag.

"No worries. Mr Carmichael has."

Kate smiled at him and nodded.

The door closed, and Kate suddenly felt very alone. She kicked off her shoes and opened the balcony doors. A gentle breeze wafted through the net curtains, giving her some relief from the hot sun. Her eyes feasted on expensive yachts glistening in the sunlight. Happy voices drifted upwards, compounding her loneliness. She felt very sad. She wandered inside and slumped on the bed. Sleep came easy.

It was dark when she woke. She had no idea how long she had slept. There was no sign of Jasper. His case hadn't been unpacked.

***

"All alone? Jasper should take better care of you."

Kate looked up. Lawson was pulling a chair up to her table. *Where's he come from?* she angrily thought.

"Sea front café, and tea." Their eyes briefly met. "Be adventurous. A cocktail. Pina Colada," he cheerfully commented, raising his eyebrows.

"What do you want?"

"Where's Jasper?"

"I don't know."

A waiter placed a coffee in front of Lawson.

"Plain coffee." Kate's sarcastic tone made Lawson smile.

"What do you know about Jasper?" Lawson asked, stirring sugar into his coffee.

"Enough."

"You do know that he's killed for you?"

Kate's eyes widened.

"Don't know how he did it. Max roughed you up."

"It was a little more than that."

"Colin's more interesting. No trace of him." Lawson had an agenda and he was sticking to it.

"What do you mean?"

"No birth certificate, National Insurance number, death certificate. Et cetera, et cetera."

"There must be."

"I 'ad my people look into it. What I'm sure of,

though: he appeared at the Lord Nelson. Picked up the best fuck in the bar. Set 'er up in a terraced house to look after a baby."

"But he died in prison."

"Now, what prison would that be?"

"Jasper visited him."

"Ask 'im where he visited. Colin was involved with the war." Lawson returned to his agenda. "I reckon he was about sixteen when he brought the first consignment of diamonds back. He was fluent in many languages. Good education. Intelligent." Lawson paused. "He was a master thief. The brains behind many a heist. But he was a double-crosser. Colin Carmichael was only interested in Colin. He would appear at the Nelson, organise the men. Day later, the haul was split up: money, diamonds. Colin always 'ad diamonds. The last lot of diamonds 'as never surfaced. Jasper's sitting on 'em."

"You make him sound legendary." Kate's voice had a tinge of disbelief.

"I've told you the truth. The community loved him. He brought stability and hope where there was despair. It didn't matter to them what he did. Some thought of him as a godfather. Whatever else you've 'eard is myth. Then Colin Carmichael just disappeared.

"Jasper is Colin's bastard. People who knew Colin look to Jasper; they thought he would eventually fill Colin's shoes. But Jasper has disappointed many. Things started to fall apart when Colin was put inside. Money ran out. Jasper and 'is mother had to learn to survive."

"I thought you fucked her?"

Lawson nodded. "Best fuck I ever 'ad."

"What about Richard?"

"Big mistake... Jasper runs rings around the

lot of 'em. He's certainly Colin's son."

"And you want him in prison."

"Jasper Carmichael is a murderer. At least twice. The newsagent and Max. He's going to prison, so you better dump 'im."

"My job is temporary. I have a new life waiting."

"That's just as well." Lawson paused and took a few moments to enjoy his coffee. "He changed after Beth… He likes a different fuck every night."

Kate tried to hide the unexpected hurt that filled her. She didn't want to hear this.

"The doorman told me Jasper didn't return last night. Chloe 'asn't turned up this morning. Some big business dinner last night. Jasper was there with Chloe."

Kate's eyes filled.

"I need the inside dirt on Jasper. His associates. His money, his deals… and where the diamonds are."

"Diamonds?" Kate tried to sound surprised as the meeting with Zak flashed through her mind.

"Colin's diamonds. The ones he double-crossed his associates for." Lawson stared at Kate's watery green eyes, which stared into space. "You can do better than 'im. He really is no good."

Chapter Twenty-Eight

It took Jasper longer than he expected to conclude the deal with Anton. He didn't like doing business with Anton, but he was a powerful man with many friends. Friends that Jasper might need. He had smiled at the well-rounded South American, but Jasper knew he'd flinched too many times when Anton talked about Kate. Anton's dark, piercing eyes never missed a Carmichael flinch.

Anton had laughed when he reminded Jasper that he had fucked Chloe the night before, leaving Kate alone. Jasper didn't need reminding. There had been too many questions about him and Kate; he'd had to hide his feelings for Kate and draw attention from her. And so, he had fucked Chloe. He came away feeling empty.

Anton insisted that he paid Jasper cash. At first Jasper objected but soon realised that he'd open a new account at the same bank that held Zak's diamonds. *Two birds with one stone,* he mused.

Jasper was thinking about leaving when Anton turned the conversation to diamonds.

"I could pay you in diamonds," he said mischievously.

"Diamonds?" repeated Jasper, somewhat surprised.

Anton turned a small velvet pouch upside down. Six uncut diamonds spilled across the table. Jasper stared at them, not daring to lift his eyes towards Anton. He knew they weren't real just by looking at them.

"Use this to examine them." A diamond tester skidded towards Jasper.

He's testing my diamond knowledge, thought Jasper.

"I had a friend—I thought he was my friend—who was very knowledgeable about diamonds," said Anton.

"I've never been interested in diamonds. I stick to cash," Jasper said convincingly.

"Pick them up, feel them. Tell me what you think. Colin was an expert."

Jasper dropped the fake diamonds back into the velvet pouch without bothering to test them.

"I'm not Colin."

***

It was late when Jasper arrived back at the hotel. He was too preoccupied with trying to second-guess Anton's diamond game to notice the stares from the hotel staff.

The penthouse suite was unusually quiet. No Kate. On the central glass coffee table were her new clothes, still in the hotel bags. Door card, credit card and phone lay next to the bags.

Kate had gone. She hadn't left a note.

Jasper slumped onto the white, over-stuffed couch, head in his hands. Kate had left him. She must have heard about last night.

The hotel phone rang.

"Yes," snapped Jasper.

"Watched her get on a plane," Lawson sniggered.

Jasper recognised the voice. "You bastard. What poison did you spread?"

"No poison. Just the truth."

The phone went dead. Jasper slung the phone across the penthouse, hitting the far wall.

Four Years Later

Chapter Twenty-Nine

Jasper slowly guided his small yacht towards his boatyard. He had changed the yard beyond all recognition since Alwyn's day.

After Kate had disappeared, sailing had become his solace. He'd loved her—he'd finally realised it—and now she was gone. He couldn't find her. But what had he expected? He had made the rules; her appointment was only ever temporary. And he had behaved badly in the Caymans. He knew Kate had been in love with him, and he'd wanted to show her that she meant nothing to him, but he hadn't expected her to leave. He'd thought he would have more time with her, but Kate was proud, strong willed. He had messed up big time.

He slowly walked towards his Range Rover, his head tucked into his chest as if he had the world upon his shoulders. He was unrecognisable. His salt-and-pepper hair lay in his neck, his stubble had grown into a small beard, his blue eyes were dead. His T-shirt and shorts needed a wash.

"Back early, Mr Carmichael. Everything alright?" shouted the latest apprentice his yard manager had employed.

Jasper smiled and carried on walking past the boy.

"Mr Carmichael," shouted the young receptionist. "You have an urgent message."

Jasper kept walking as if he hadn't heard her.

"One word," she continued. "Kate."

Jasper stopped in his tracks. His stomach fluttered. The holdall he was carrying fell from his grip. He raced towards the young girl, snatching the slip of paper from her small hand. He groped into the deep pocket of his shorts, searching for his mobile that he'd had switched off—he hadn't wanted to be disturbed when he was thinking about Kate. It instantly rang.

"Where the fuck 'ave you been?" bellowed an angry voice he hadn't heard since Kate disappeared. John, Jasper's investigator, who'd failed to find her. "Your bloody phone switched off—what're you fucking playing at?"

"Kate," Jasper nervously answered.

"She's in Wellsbury with a kid." He left a long pause, letting Jasper digest what he had just said. "The fucking Preservation Society persuaded her to help." Another pause. "Ken 'as somot to do with it. He's been looking after that old Defender."

"Is she there now?"

"Presentation at the town hall."

Jasper threw the mobile onto the passenger seat and gunned the Range Rover. His drive back to Wellsbury was fraught with what-ifs. Would she still be there? Would she be happy to see him? Was the child his?

***

A small boy sat on the town hall wall, singing and swinging his legs. Jasper abruptly stopped and stared at his mass of blond hair and shining blue eyes. He flashed a smile at Jasper. The Carmichael smile.

"We're going for ice cream," the boy said cheerfully. "Chocolate. By the river." The boy carried on swinging his legs. "I've been good."

"Who're you waiting for?" Jasper said calmly.

The boy gave Jasper a curious look. "Mummy, of course."

"Can I join you?"

The boy nodded.

"Your legs are brown," commented the boy, gazing at Jasper's bare, hairy legs.

"Where's your daddy?"

The boy shrugged.

"What's your name?"

"Harry Reynolds."

"Is that your daddy's name?"

The boy shook his head. "Carmichael."

Jasper's eyes filled, the contents of his stomach churned. *Could he be my son?*

"How do you know?"

"Harry!" shouted a familiar female voice. Harry jumped up and raced towards the voice.

Although Kate didn't recognise the scruffy man talking to Harry, she did know the watery blue eyes. Jasper nervously waited for Kate to smile, but no smile came. However, he had no need to be anxious. Her dull green eyes suddenly came alive.

A small hand tugged at her jeans. She looked down at two expectant blue eyes and smiled. The small boy jumped up and down.

"Yippee! Ice cream!" he shouted, breaking into a skip. He didn't seem to notice Jasper swiftly walking towards his mother.

In a well-thought-out move, Jasper cupped her face and carefully planted a soft kiss on her dry lips. He was prepared for her to push him away. But she stretched her hand into his long hair.

"Kate," he murmured, his expression softening. His fingertips trailed her cheeks. She slowly sloped her head towards his touch.

"Kate." His voice was soft and low.

Their watery eyes locked. Blue on green.

Their mouths hesitantly met, tongues hesitantly touched and danced. Her fingers threaded through his hair; he swallowed her sighs.

She broke the kiss and settled into Jasper's shoulder.

"Mummy," a small voice nervously stuttered.

"Let's walk." Kate's voice was soft and calm as she ruffled Harry's hair.

Jasper walked beside her, and Harry walked on her other side, happily singing about ice cream.

"We have to talk. I have a lot of explaining to do." Jasper's voice was so low Kate could barely hear.

"Don't. Let's just walk."

Kate's stomach nervously churned. Jasper had taken her by surprise. She couldn't think straight. Jasper always had that effect on her. She needed time to think, but her body didn't. It knew what it wanted: Jasper Carmichael.

When the Riverside Café came into view, Harry sprinted ahead.

By the time Kate and Jasper arrived at the café, Harry was sitting at an outside table, grinning and licking chocolate ice cream.

"Knew you were on your way." Molly's cheerful voice echoed around the small café.

Jasper stood at the counter. "Kate will have tea."

Molly's gaze followed Jasper's. His eyes were transfixed by Kate. Molly smiled; she was happy that Kate and Jasper had found each other again.

"She's moved back," Molly said. "But she'll tell you that. Harry needs a better school. He's very bright. She's been worried."

"Worried?" said a concerned Jasper, picking up two teas.

"Wants the best for Harry," Molly commented to Jasper's back.

***

"He's back."

Don's boss could hardly hear him. But Don heard the South American curse.

"With her?"

"They're at the Riverside Café. Can't hear what they're saying."

"Is he still a mess?"

"Worse."

"I was convinced he would involve the Families."

"What about his hidden millions?" asked Don.

"Nothing."

Silence.

"Is Joanne pregnant?" asked the South American.

"No. Jasper's too careful."

"Get her bloody pregnant."

"Too late. He hasn't fucked her for some time."

"Make life difficult for them," snapped the South American. "I'll get back."

***

"What's wrong?" Kate said quietly.

Harry had moved to the water's edge, throwing stones.

"I've missed you. More than..." His hand stretched across the table so he could touch her fingers. His stomach settled when she didn't snatch her hand away. "I'm a mess, Kate."

She smiled and nodded. "Life's not the same for me. Harry needs routine: eating, sleeping, school." She paused. "The cottage isn't much, but I'll change it when Harry's more settled."

Kate couldn't think about Jasper. She turned her mind to her new life with Harry.

"What?"

She looked surprised. "Hasn't Don told you? I'm renting the cottage just up from Kenny's Garage."

"You can't live there." Their eyes met. Green on blue.

"I don't work for you anymore."

"I don't want you to work for me... I want you to be with me."

Kate stared into his deep blue eyes, Harry's eyes. She saw hope.

"You seem to forget Harry."

They both turned and watched him throwing stones into the river.

"He'll do that for hours. When we go to the beach, I sit painting and he paddles and throws stones."

"I'd like to join you both."

"Any time, Jasper. You're welcome." Kate had prepared herself for Jasper wanting to spend time with his son.

They turned and faced one another. A smile crept across her face.

"I've missed you." Her voice was low, as if she didn't want him to hear.

"That makes two of us," he said thoughtfully as his fingers caressed her knuckles. "Move into the penthouse with me."

Her eyes widened in surprise. "What about Harry?"

"He'll have his own room... We'll have a room," he tentatively added, waiting for her to object.

"There's a massive living room, state of the art kitchen. Both bedrooms are en suite."

"Jasper, I'm not looking to buy it," she teased.

"Private underground carpark. Security."

"Why?" she said.

"I want you back. I can't think straight without you. The business is falling apart, I don't know who to trust, and that creep Anton appeared. How the hell he knew where to find me, I don't know."

"Anton! What did he want?"

"I was drowning my sorrows in my favourite bar, and he just appeared, pretending to be my friend. He said if they knew he was with me, there would be big trouble. I have no idea who 'they' are. He knew I was struggling with the business. He told me to invest more, but that would mean borrowing, and I don't want to do that. He suggested I involve the Families; he had it on good authority that they would only be too willing to invest in my shopping centre. When he mentioned in a matter-of-fact way that I might want to use some of my hidden millions, he laughed—that false laugh that he has. My gut told me to be careful, he had an ulterior motive. He changed the subject and talked about you and that builder who wanted you to be a mother to his three boys."

"How strange," Kate interjected. "Kenny told me you and Joanne were thinking of getting married and starting a family."

Jasper's face stiffened as he tried to control his temper. Too many people were trying to get him and Joanne together. She was just a fuck— and not a very good one at that.

"Anton knew about Harry. Even said he was a Carmichael."

"He is a Carmichael, Jasper."

"Anton knew about your beach walks and painting. Is it true you sell to Americans?"

"Yes, that's true. My paintings are original and relatively cheap. They like to go home with the story that they met the artist." Her smile quickly faded, replaced with a frown. "How does he know all this?"

Jasper's hand cupped Kate's face, and to his surprise, his eyes filled. "I thought you couldn't have kids."

"So did I. I didn't know I was pregnant until Harry decided to come into the world. Doctors are not always right. Love finds a way." She smiled, turning into his hand.

"You'll tell me everything?" he tentatively asked.

Jasper's mind flicked to their last lovemaking. He couldn't remember how many times he had filled her. What he would give for her to be in his bed, waiting. What he would give for her comfort.

"I want you back, Kate."

"As...?"

"My lover, friend, confidant... Life's been a living hell without you."

"Harry?"

"He'll be loved. Want for nothing."

"No secrets, Jasper."

"No secrets, Kate."

Suddenly, Harry shouted as if he was in danger. Kate turned fast, just in time to see Don reaching for him. But Harry was too quick and dodged him, racing back to Kate.

"What the fuck are you doing?" shouted an angry Jasper.

"She can't stay here. She's not welcome." Don glared at Kate as he strode towards them.

Jasper stood, tightly clenching his fists. Jack,

Richard, Beth and Joanne were following in Don's wake.

Harry clung to Kate's leg. She knelt, putting a reassuring arm around him.

"Is he yours?" snapped Joanne.

All eyes moved to Harry, who began to sob.

Kate cradled Harry's head. She looked up at Jasper. "We'll go."

"No." Jasper knelt and slipped an arm around them, his head resting on Kate's. He stood and glared at the others. "Fuck off out of my private life."

"She wants your millions," snarled Jack.

Jasper's temper flared; he took a step towards Jack. Jack took two steps back.

"Look at you, Jasper," Beth snipped. "Hair needs washing and cutting, haven't shaved for days, and your clothes, well..."

"The Families won't like her being back." Don's voice took a hostile tone.

"Fuck the Families. Fuck you. Now get out of my fucking life."

***

"What's a penthouse?" Harry's enquiring tones filled the Defender.

"A large apartment on the top of a building."

"Is Jasper my dad?"

"Why all the questions?"

"You look at each other funny."

Kate's neck suddenly became very warm.

"Look, Harry!" said Kate, trying to distract her inquisitive young son.

"Where?"

"Over there."

"I can't see!" said Harry, craning his neck.

Jasper's new headquarters appeared. It was the tallest building in Wellsbury, much bigger than the Carmichael office of old.

Harry's eyes widened. "We're going to live there?"

"We'll see."

Kate turned into the drive that led up to the main entrance and turned to the side of the office where Jasper was waiting.

"You look at Mum funny," piped up a cheerful Harry as he followed Jasper towards the lift. "I've never been in a lift." Harry smiled, looking up into Kate's eyes.

The lift doors opened into a large open-plan room. The large, state-of-the-art kitchen caught Kate's eye while Harry ran the whole length of the room.

"Come back," Jasper whispered into Kate's ear.

"I don't know," she said nervously. "Don was very hostile. So were the others."

"Don intended to make you uncomfortable. He knows you." Jasper paused thoughtfully. "He's been a bit off lately, as if he..." Jasper hesitated. "Has a hidden agenda."

"Is this my room?" asked Harry, pushing open the door of the second bedroom. "Wow!" echoed from the room.

Kate raised her eyebrows with a smile. "It looks as if we're staying, at least for a while."

Chapter Thirty

"She's still sleeping," Harry quietly said so as not to wake Kate. He jumped on the breakfast stool next to Jasper and continued drinking his milk.

"You look different," Harry said between sips of milk.

"Business clothes," answered Jasper, flicking through his emails. He was clean shaven and dressed in a crisp white shirt, tie pulled away from his neck, and his customary Armani suit.

At the sound of sheets rustling, Harry made as if he was about to jump from the stool. Jasper, lightning quick, grabbed his arm.

"Leave her."

"She's awake," protested a struggling four-year-old.

"She needs rest."

Harry turned and stared at Jasper. "Are you really my father?"

"Yes." Jasper's reply was somewhat impatient.

"You left her," Harry said accusingly.

"A misunderstanding."

"You'll leave us?"

Jasper looked Harry in the eye. "Can you keep a secret?"

Harry nodded, smiling. He liked secrets.

"Life without Kate is not worth living." Harry's eyes widened. "I found out the hard way. I'm going to do everything to keep her and you."

Jasper was taken by surprise as Harry jumped onto his lap, putting his small arms around his neck and planting a wet kiss on his smooth cheek.

"Am I interrupting?" Kate's happy voice greeted them.

"Man talk," said a beaming Harry.

Jasper couldn't control his smile.

To see father and son sharing a kiss warmed Kate's heart. But she did wonder what had caused Harry to be so affectionate.

Kate wandered over to the warm kettle and gently touched it. Jasper felt a surge of contentment. He had missed Kate's morning tea ritual.

"I've organised a van and a couple of men to help empty your cottage," Jasper tentatively said, not wanting to annoy Kate. He was well aware of how independent she was.

Their eyes met over a cup of steaming tea.

"Bruce?" she asked with a glint in her eyes. It was Bruce who had moved her out of the flower shop.

"How did you guess?" Jasper returned her smile. "Use the underground parking to sort through your stuff."

His phone buzzed. "Amanda!"

"She still works for you?" Kate asked, somewhat surprised.

"Keeps me in check." He winked. "Have a good day!" he shouted as he picked up his laptop and strode out of the door that led to the office.

***

Jasper's good day was shattered when Amanda burst into his office.

"Jasper! Look."

Kate and Harry were being frogmarched

through the open-plan office towards his. The head of security had a worried look on his face, whereas Don looked very smug.

Jasper left his office and hurried towards them. Kate was angry and Harry had been crying. As soon as Harry saw Jasper, he let go of Kate's hand and raced towards him, jumping into Jasper's arms. Looping his arms around Jasper's neck, his legs wrapped around his waist, he sobbed onto Jasper's white shirt.

"Keep your bitch and bastard under control!" bellowed an angry Don.

"I did nothing," murmured Harry into Jasper's shoulder.

"Picking on women and children, now?" Jasper retorted in a calm voice.

"Kid's out of control. Running round, skipping, shouting."

"He," Harry whispered into Jasper's ear, "pushed her to the floor." Harry's gaze fixed firmly on Don. "She was only—"

Jasper had heard enough. He put Harry onto the floor and Kate took his hand. Jasper marched towards Don.

"You interfere with what's mine, you—the Families—will pay." Jasper's voice was calm, but his intent was obvious.

"You won't be so confident when Charlie and Matt arrive. The Families aren't happy."

"Fuck the Families. If you think the Wilsons bother me, think again." Jasper's calm demeanour had abruptly changed. His anger had surfaced. "Choose your side, Don."

"You're risking everything you've worked for—for a bitch and bastard."

Jasper suddenly turned and gripped Don by the collar. "Tell your master: mess with my wife and son, he'll regret it and so will the Families." Jasper let go of Don's collar and pushed him away. He turned to his head of security. "Escort him off the premises."

***

"Harry just bumped into Don. That's all." Kate was checking the temperature of a cottage pie. "Harry's favourite," she added.

"Where is he?"

"Washing for dinner." She smiled. "It'll take him forever."

Jasper swiftly moved towards her and claimed her mouth. Her hand stretched into his hair as he deepened the kiss.

"Marry me," he whispered into her hair.

Her hand pushed against his shoulder.

"You'll be safe. The Wilsons won't dare touch you or Harry." Their eyes met, hers full of questions. "You'll be a Carmichael. They think I'm like Colin." She still looked uncertain. "I have a reputation." He smiled, trying to reassure her.

She pushed him away and walked towards the floor-to-ceiling windows that overlooked the shopping centre she had initially been involved with.

"I've been married, Jasper. It didn't go well."

"I'm not Eric."

"No. But you're a serial womaniser. I don't think I could cope with that."

Jasper reddened. He was a sexual man and that would never change.

"At the very least, Harry needs a say."

"He's four years old. What does he know?" Jasper retorted.

"He knows I love him. He trusts me."

"That's a no." Jasper couldn't hide his disappointment.

"No, it means I'm going to discuss it with Harry."

"You haven't time. The Wilsons must be on their way."

"I'm hungry," said Harry's small voice.

Kate turned. Harry was holding his hands ready for inspection. Jasper turned and stormed towards the door that led to the garage.

"Where's he going?" asked Harry, looking after Jasper.

"Food's ready," said a concerned Kate. Jasper's reaction had taken her by surprise.

Dinner passed in silence while Kate mulled over Jasper's proposal. Harry's tearful eyes caught every flicker of emotion on Kate's face. She didn't notice.

"Tell me," Harry said nervously.

Kate sat on the bed and put her arm around her son. How could she tell a four-year-old that his dad wanted to marry her?

"Jasper wants us to be together."

"Here?"

"Yes."

"Live together?"

Kate nodded.

"Like Scott's dad wants."

Her eyes filled as she nodded. Her mind flicked to Scott's dad, Bob, who wanted her to marry him and look after his three boys.

"Would you like to live with Jasper?" Kate asked.

Kate watched Harry finger his bedtime book.

"I don't want to live with Scott's dad. He has dirty hands and clothes."

"He's a builder. They get dirty."

"Do you want to live with him?"

"No."

"I like just the two of us."

"You're growing up. You need a school."

"I can read, write, count."

"That's not enough. You need to grow, Harry, into the wonderful boy and man that's Harry Carmichael."

"You called me Carmichael."

"That's who you are."

"Will we still go to the beach?"

Kate pulled Harry into her. "You bet."

"Okay. I vote we stay here."

Kate kissed his head. "You make me so proud. I love you."

Harry grinned and slipped down the bed, his eyes closing.

Kate switched off the light and left Harry's bedroom door slightly open.

Kate abruptly stopped; her stomach churned when a voice she knew well came from behind.

"You're still fuckable, even skinny." Matt Wilson's words were full of intent.

Chapter Thirty-One

"Jasper's getting sloppy. The security let us in the main door, even switched the lights off. The place is in darkness." Charlie Wilson laughed.

"What do you want?" Kate uttered.

"He wants to fuck," said Charlie, pointing at Matt. "I wouldn't mind. There's something gratifying about fucking Jasper's woman."

"He won't be back. He's at Joanne's. Fucking as we speak."

Kate tried to hide her dismay. Her heart skipped a beat. Jasper appeared to have changed, but he hadn't. The Caymans flashed into her mind, when Jasper virtually ignored her, preferring Chloe.

"We 'ave a score to settle. Jasper killed Max."

***

The Wilsons had slipped out of Joanne's back door as soon as Jasper arrived. Jasper had a wild look about him, a look Joanne hadn't seen for some time.

Jasper had snatched a bottle of malt from the bar and settled in his usual corner seat. Joanne made a beeline for him and snuggled up to him. She draped her large breasts over his chest. Her hand gripped his crotch. He was familiar with Joanne's foreplay, but he wasn't interested. He brushed her hand away.

An uncomfortable silence hung over Joanne's bar. The clientele stared at him as if they knew something he didn't. Some of Joanne's girls wouldn't look him in the eye. Jasper's gut told him something was wrong, and it involved him. His mind flicked to Kate and Harry alone in the penthouse. He stood and hurried towards his Range Rover, which he'd parked away from Joanne's so it wouldn't be seen.

Carmichael House was in darkness, except for the penthouse. A Rolls Royce Phantom was parked across the entrance.

The Wilsons, he thought. *They have Kate.*

He gazed into the darkened reception. No security. Without thinking, he slipped from his pocket the penknife he always carried. *I knew this would be useful one day,* he thought, as he sprung the corkscrew from its closed position.

He took the stairs two at a time until he reached the open-plan office and stopped. He hadn't time to dwell on the chaotic state of the office.

He quickly moved to the stairs that led to the penthouse. The stairwell was in complete darkness, hindering his progress. The door into the penthouse was open. *Fucking security.*

He eased the door open and silently cursed as he watched Kate trying to shield Harry from Matt Wilson.

"It's me you want." Tears were running down her face as she tried to control her fear. "Let Harry go back to his room."

"No chance. The Carmichael bastard is going to watch," snarled Matt, grinning and stroking his crotch in such a manner that his intentions were obvious.

"I suggest you do as she says." Jasper's calm voice echoed in the silent penthouse. All eyes watched as he prowled slowly around the edge of the room.

"You don't frighten us," sneered a cocky Matt. "There's two of us."

Jasper moved to Harry's side and gently touched his head.

"You're getting sloppy, leaving Kate and the boy alone."

"It won't happen again."

Jasper slowly dropped his Armani jacket onto the carpet. His Cartier watch and Carmichael ring followed.

Charlie cringed. He knew that Jasper was belittling them, flaunting his wealth and power. Showing them who was in charge.

Matt took a step towards Jasper, fists clenched.

"Matt," Charlie commanded.

Matt turned and glared at his brother. "Why? There's two of us. Let's take him out, once and for all." His angry voice echoed.

Charlie walked to his brother and touched his arm. "Later. He'll let his guard down; she'll be alone. You'll get your revenge."

Matt shrugged his brother's hand off his arm and stormed out of the penthouse.

"Later, Carmichael," shouted Charlie as he followed his brother.

Jasper followed Charlie and Matt out of the building. The tyres of the Phantom squealed in the night air as Charlie floored the accelerator.

With competent ease, Jasper changed the security settings of Carmichael House to administrator only.

Chapter Thirty-Two

"What's going on here?" Kate's voice made Jasper turn away from the chaotic open-plan office. She and Harry had followed him.

Jasper prided himself on running a tidy ship. But the office was far from tidy. Computers were left on, files open on desks, just as if they were about to be read. His accountant Johnson's office was even worse. The filing cabinet, which should have been locked, was open. Momentarily, his mind flicked back to when he'd caught Joanne in Johnson's office. Johnson hadn't been aware of Jasper's presence, his eyes glued to Joanne's more than ample breasts.

A red-eyed Harry was gripping Kate's hand so tightly that his little knuckles were white.

"He wouldn't settle," said Kate as a way of answering Jasper's gaze.

"I don't know."

"Don't lie," sobbed Harry. "Tell us."

"I really don't know. The office shouldn't be like this. The Wilsons shouldn't have been here."

"And you shouldn't have been at Joanne's. Enjoying her delights."

Jasper and Kate's eyes met. Was that a tinge of jealousy in her voice?

"The place is locked down." He moved towards Harry, picking him up. "No one's going to hurt you or your mother," he said into Harry's hair. "Now let's get you to sleep."

Once Harry was settled, Kate found Jasper in

the lounge. A glass of red wine stood on the glass coffee table.

"Brunello," Jasper said while he gazed into the night sky. "Asleep?"

"Yes," answered Kate as she joined him, gazing into the darkness. "I haven't had this since..."

"We were in the mansion apartment then." His words were low and soft. "Kate, you have to marry me." He felt her tense. "That's the only way I can keep you and Harry safe."

She didn't offer a reply.

"If I hadn't turned up when I did, I fear I would've found two dead bodies."

"I know."

"You know what I want. But I can wait. Till you trust me."

"Harry?"

"We'll all go and have a medical check-up, including DNA."

"You doubt me?"

"No. But to make you and Harry my heirs, a solicitor will. And I need you to be sure I'm clean." He paused and looked at her. "I need to know that you're well. You're too thin."

"My money's been blocked," she blurted.

"What?"

"That's why I sell my paintings."

"Why didn't you come to me?"

"You were with Joanne. I didn't want to." Her words faded as an unexpected tear trickled down her cheek.

Two strong arms wrapped around her waist as his mouth found her neck. "Marry me. We fit, Kate. I missed you and I know you missed me."

"You make it sound so easy. But what about the Wilsons? The Families? Anton?"

"Let me deal with them. Remember, no

questions. You and Harry won't have to worry about anything, including your bank account. My IT man will sort it."

"Look!" said Kate.

In the distance, on the dark roads out of Wellsbury, a fireball lit up the night. Sirens and blue flashing lights broke the night's stillness.

"Accident," said Kate, trying to explain the fire.

I hope so, thought Jasper. He'd expected the Wilsons' Rolls to have left the road ages ago.

Chapter Thirty-Three

"You're up early," Kate said to Jasper as she waited for her morning tea to brew.

Jasper planted a soft kiss on her cheek. *I could get used to this,* she thought.

"Malcolm and Clare have agreed to increase their hours. Malcolm will be your driver, and Clare will be our housekeeper." Jasper took a step back and waited.

"I'm quite capable of housekeeping and driving." Her voice was curt.

"Not with the Wilsons about. And I need you in the office."

She raised her eyebrows in disbelief.

"Something's going on, I just can't figure out what," he said. "And Harry will be at St Martin's."

"You've decided, then?"

"Don't take that tone. Harry's bright for his age; he needs a good school. St Martin's is the best, thanks to my donations."

"Sir!" A well-built man dressed in a fitted grey suit appeared at the internal door. Kate caught his eye and he nodded. *Malcolm,* she thought. "The police are here."

A tall man barged past Malcolm, followed by Lawson and Don.

"Inspector Watts."

Jasper stared disapprovingly at the inspector's ill-fitting suit, tie pulled away from his collar, dirty shoes and greasy hair.

"Interrupting, am I? Good." His eyes settled on

Kate. "You 'ad visitors last night? Matt and Charlie Wilson?"

"Yes." Kate's voice was soft and low.

"What did they want?"

"To fuck me in front of Harry." Kate's sudden change of tone surprised the inspector.

He turned his attention to Jasper. "You were at Joanne's. What time did you leave?"

"Ask Joanne."

"Why did you leave?"

Jasper was becoming irritated by this line of questioning, and it showed. Lawson and Don smirked.

"Charlie's Rolls was parked across the entrance. The place was in darkness and there was no security. I was more than a little concerned. Kate and Harry were alone."

"You threatened them?"

That was the opening Jasper had been waiting for. "I don't know what you've been told, but I didn't threaten them."

The inspector was taken aback by Jasper's honesty. Lawson had told him Jasper knew about the accident, but it was obvious that he didn't.

"The Wilsons are dead. Killed in a car accident last night."

"Oh!" exclaimed Kate.

"They were drinking in the George till past closing time. They hit a tree on the lane to the old airfield. Ring any bells?"

"I don't know what you mean," answered Jasper, his mind racing. What had they been doing on that road?

"What do you know about the airfield, Kate?"

"Nothing much. It was the Ministry that developed it during the war. There was talk of it being redeveloped, but nothing came of it."

"Who owns it?"

"Council," interjected Jasper. "I wanted to buy. They refused." Jasper gazed at the surprised faces. "I thought I'd get it cheap. And when the time was right, sell it or develop it."

"Make a tidy penny," commented the inspector.

"I'm hungry," said a small voice. Harry was walking from his bedroom and rubbing his eyes.

Kate was by his side in a flash. He looped his small arms around his mother's neck and kissed her cheek.

"Have those nasty men gone?" he whispered in her ear.

The inspector wandered over, not believing his eyes. He was looking at Jasper's blue eyes.

"Who're you?" asked Harry.

"A policeman."

Harry began to cry.

"Let's get you dressed," Kate said. "I think we have Coco Pops for breakfast."

Harry stopped crying and grinned, running into his bedroom.

"You don't deserve her," the inspector said to Jasper.

"I know."

"I've seen enough. I'm satisfied that the Wilsons meant her and the boy harm. You're not off the hook." He glared at Jasper. "My gut tells me you're involved."

"I was here. Kate and Harry needed me."

"I've got too many loose ends." The inspector hesitated. "You bother me, Carmichael. There's just something that makes my gut churn. These two would have you down the station. I make my own decisions. I've no evidence; a hotshot solicitor would make mincemeat of any charge."

"He's fucking guilty," snarled Lawson. "He's

got away with murdering the Wilson brothers. The Families will 'ave revenge."

"Shut up," said Don.

"'ave you searched this place for Charlie's briefcase?"

"Warrant," said Jasper as he watched Malcolm escorting them towards the lift.

The briefcase was in Jasper's Range Rover, which was locked up in the underground garage. The inspector's gut might be churning, but Jasper's was working overtime. Time wasn't on his side, and there were unknown forces working against him. So, after the late-afternoon appointment at the clinic, Jasper was going to do some snooping. Jack, Richard and Beth had moved back into the mansion. That was his first stop.

Chapter Thirty-Four

Kate sat in the passenger seat of Jasper's Range Rover. He had called in a few favours for the urgent medical appointment.

She felt his hand stroke hers.

"Everything's going to be alright." His soft tone did nothing to reassure her.

Kate's gazed into space as she recalled the time Eric pushed her down the stairs and killed her baby. At the time, the doctors had advised against hysterectomy; they wanted her to have time to recover. She'd been a mental and physical mess.

She'd had no idea she was pregnant with Harry. She'd just felt unwell.

When the doctor finished this latest examination, she handed Kate a packet of pills and a prescription. There was no doubt that she could become pregnant again. Sex with Jasper was just days away.

"Kate, you haven't heard a word."

Jasper had stopped in a driveway of a very large house.

Kate's gazed out of the front windscreen. She recognised the house. "The Isaacs House," she murmured.

Harry was already out of the car, running towards the front door.

"Let me look after you," Jasper said. "I know it's hard for you to accept." He watched Harry skipping around. "He's healthy, happy and a credit to you. Be thankful."

He lifted her from the passenger seat and looped his arm around her shoulders.

"I bought it not long after Mrs Isaac died. Everything is as she left it. I haven't got around to knocking it down."

"You can't do that; it's beautiful, full of character. It just needs—"

"—Kate Carmichael, to bring it back to its former glory," Jasper interjected.

Kate looked admiringly at the bay windows that extended over the doorway, the stone columns that supported the windows, the leaded panes that looked original.

Jasper took her hand. "Let's go inside."

The front doors opened into a square hallway with a central staircase. There was a spacious living room with a large inglenook fireplace. French doors opened onto a patio, overgrown flowerbeds and a lawn that appeared to go on forever.

When they walked into the library with another inglenook fireplace and bookshelves that reached the ceiling with the customary ladder, Kate turned and planted a kiss on Jasper's lips. She was smiling, the trauma of the medical examination forgotten.

"It's yours, Mrs Carmichael," he whispered into her hair.

There were four bedrooms. Harry had already picked his.

"A complete remodel up here," she said, still smiling.

"You haven't mentioned the kitchen," he commented as they walked into the rear garden.

"Needs gutting and redesigning."

"We could extend. Plenty of room out here."

He took her hand and pulled her to the bottom

of the garden. Harry was having the time of his life running in and out of overgrown bushes.

They stopped and looked back at the house.

Jasper pointed. "Kitchen."

"Yes. In the stable block, with the dining room adjoining," Kate excitedly added.

"I need an office," said Jasper. "Extend into the garden." After a thoughtful pause, he added, "I'll find an architect. It'll be a big project. Planning permission may be a problem."

"Is it too much?" She gazed into his eyes.

"If it makes you happy, nothing is too much."

***

Jasper waited till Harry was asleep before he told Kate he had to go out. *Something's afoot*, he told her. And it involved Don, Lawson, Jack, Richard and Beth.

Dressed in his stealthy black outfit, Jasper drove to the mansion. He parked his Range Rover in the lane that ran to the mansion's side and slipped through the wall gate.

The mansion was in darkness, giving the appearance of being empty. He skirted the garden, only stopping when he reached the mansion.

He stood still, listening and watching. Something didn't feel right. He was about to retrace his steps when headlights lit up the front of the mansion.

The front door opened just as a bald, blurry man opened the rear door of the Range Rover that had just pulled up.

Even in the shadows, Jasper recognised the smallish round man who slipped out of the rear seat and stood staring at the mansion.

Jasper pressed himself against the mansion

wall. He turned his head to see a figure walk towards the Range Rover. "I didn't think you'd come." The unmistakeable dull tones of Jack's voice pierced the still night air.

Small, light footsteps crunched on the gravel drive.

For a brief moment, images of the small round man dressed in an immaculately fitting dark grey Armani suit and Italian leather shoes, swishing a brandy, flashed into Jasper's mind.

Catlike, Jasper circled the house to the living room where he guessed they would be meeting. The curtains of the sash window were only partially closed and the window was slightly open.

"I told you the last time we met that I would be here when the time was right." The South American accent echoed through the room.

Anton gazed around the gathering; he knew them all.

He peered at them each in turn. Eye contact was important to him; he wanted to read the vultures' eyes, of Jack, Richard, Beth and Lawson. They were just pawns that he would dispose of. They had failed him, and they would all pay.

"Where's Don?" he demanded.

"Can't trust him," Lawson replied.

"Get him here. How can I manipulate Jasper without him?"

Richard walked to the window and made a phone call. Jasper slid to the ground, hoping Richard wouldn't look out or hear his racing heart that was trying to escape his chest.

Lawson waved to a seat by the fire, but Anton preferred to stand.

"Drink?"

"I don't want your fucking hospitality. I'm here

to put this fucking mess right. I want revenge. I want Jasper's business. I want his woman. And I want the fucking diamonds. I want Carmichael to grovel, beg." Anton's angry voice dominated the room. "You're nothing without him. You're all fucking nothing without him. Relieving Jasper of his empire was going to be so easy, but you fucking idiots have changed that. I shall have to take care of people I like."

A cold shiver slipped down Jasper's spine.

"Where's Joanne?" Anton angrily barked.

Joanne moved out from the shadows, so Anton could see her. His dark eyes wandered up and down her form. He liked what he saw. For a brief moment, he imagined fucking her.

"Your instructions were to get pregnant. Jasper likes fucking. It shouldn't have been difficult."

"He's changed," Joanne sputtered. "He wears a condom."

Anton raised his eyebrows.

"He would withdraw before completion." Joanne's voice nervously quivered.

"Before he knew about his bastard?" said Anton.

"Yes. He virtually stopped drinking. He would stare into the glass for hours."

Anton had experienced Jasper doing just that.

"The kid might not be his," offered Jack.

"Open your eyes, Jack. It's mini-Jasper," Anton snapped.

The furious beat of Anton's footsteps brought the room to silence.

Only Don knew of Anton's obsession to own everything Carmichael. When Colin Carmichael died, Anton had expected to fill Colin's shoes and control the Families. But not even Lawson could have prevented the police from clamping down on the gangs. Men were imprisoned, gangs broken up; if it hadn't been for the Cohens, the Families would have disappeared.

Anton became a wanted man and left the country. He could do nothing but wait. Carmichael and Swain grew, and so did Jasper.

It was important to Anton that the Carmichael line ended with Jasper. Beth had always taken precautions, but when Kate had Jasper's son, everything had changed. He wouldn't let Jasper's family reach old age.

Anton suddenly turned his anger on Lawson. "This is the last fucking time I'm clearing up your mess. I give you the simple task of bribing Jasper's staff, and you fuck it up. Those stupid guards left the doors open. The Wilsons walked in and so did Jasper. The Wilsons are dead. It has Jasper's hallmark all over it." He paused. "If I was Jasper, I would sack Johnson and put Kate in charge."

"Jasper acted out of character." Jack meekly offered.

"I will give you that his departure from Joanne's was unexpected. But you should have captured Kate and the kid. If we had them locked up, it would be easy to control Jasper. He's in love with her, for Christ's sake."

"Boss," said the gruff voice of Anton's driver.

Don pushed past Anton's driver.

"What the fuck are you doing here?" Don exclaimed.

"That's no way to greet an old friend." Anton grinned.

"Those days are long gone. Let it lie." Don's tone was harsh.

Anton stood by the open window, looking out into the night sky. He dismissed Don's words, but he knew their meaning: he should let his obsession with Colin Carmichael go.

Anton had been young and naïve when Colin had double-crossed him, and he'd become consumed by hatred and revenge. So he'd manipulated Lawson, a new recruit in the police force who wanted to show his worth. Anton grassed on Carmichael, and with the help of Lawson, Colin Carmichael was jailed. If Jasper found out, Anton would be history.

Anton began pacing.

"He's got the box," blurted Don.

Anton abruptly turned away from the window and stared at Don.

"The box?" he asked, his tone suddenly nervous.

"He fetched it out the office safe. It was Colin's."

"Where is it now?"

"I don't know."

Silence fell as Anton resumed pacing.

"That explains why he destroyed the archives." Anton's South American accent was suddenly thoughtful.

"I suspect all Colin's records are transferred onto a card or stick," added Don.

"Not all. Colin Carmichael kept detailed books and records. Names, accounts, banks, all lying dormant until the right time. Jasper's decided the time is up."

Anton's mind was whirling. If Jasper read those books, their days were numbered.

"You're telling me Jasper has had access to the Carmichael fortune, all this fucking time?" Jack shouted. "How long?"

"Since Colin died."

"All this fucking time!" shouted Jack, kicking over a chair.

"What's interesting is he's destroyed the archives." Anton laughed. "Oh, Jasper's better than his old man! Who would have thought he was sitting on the Carmichael money?" Anton paused. "He's waiting for revenge, or is it a reckoning?"

A low murmur moved around the group.

"Jasper is Colin's son." Anton looked at Don. "When the police handcuffed Colin, he shouted that Jasper would seek revenge."

You could have heard a pin drop as they waited for Anton to reveal his next move.

His evil eyes were fixed on Don. "You'll spy on Jasper. Gain his trust. Watch over Kate and the kid. I want to know what he thinks before he thinks it. And get this fucking lot out of his house."

"He doesn't seem to care," said Richard.

"Fools. Jasper must have this place bugged. He'll know everything before you lot sleep."

Jasper bit on his hand as a gasp tried to escape from his mouth.

"He'll be seeking revenge," said Jack.

"Leave him to me," Anton said.

"He's outmanoeuvred you before," commented Don. "Remember when he sold the Miami portfolio to your enemies." Don's words were measured. "No one traced the money. He moved the money before those goons even opened their laptop."

Don watched Anton's body stiffen. He remembered. He'd thought he had their tightly knit property consortium eating out of his hand, but Jasper had been one step ahead selling to his South American rivals.

"But the goons are dead," commented Anton, not wishing to be reminded. "Don. Walk with me." He walked towards the front door. "Jasper's injured. He will be after revenge." Anton's voice was low so only Don could hear.

"It's not going to be easy," Don said, turning, looking into the darkness. "He's changed. Difficult to anticipate."

"That's the Kate effect. He's calmer. Not relying on his gut. I want him relying on his gut. I want him vulnerable."

"Remove Kate?" Don's surprised voice made Anton stop and walk back towards the house.

"Not yet. I want her and the kid threatened. Make him protective. Make sure his sleep is interrupted. That kid seems to have too many dreams. Get my meaning?"

Don nodded, but his gut had an uneasy feeling. Someone was watching.

Anton slipped into his Range Rover.

"I was young when I finished Colin, but he'd anticipated it was over and planned ahead. Jasper moved and you with him. I haven't fathered a Jasper. And by God, I've tried," Anton confessed. "That boy of his is already showing signs of potential."

"What do you mean?" asked a puzzled Don.

"He's punching above his academic age."

"That's Kate's doing."

"Some of it. But he's a Carmichael. If Colin was alive, he would be preparing him to take over the Carmichael empire."

"There's no Carmichael empire," retorted Don.

Anton smiled. *Of course there's a Carmichael empire,* he thought. *Jasper's just loaded it onto a memory card.*

"I will contact you. No calls to me."

Again, Don nodded, but his eyes were scanning the darkness. His gut told him they were being watched. Was it Jasper's men or Jasper himself?

Anton's Range Rover sped along the gravel drive as Jasper slipped through the gate in the garden wall. He sprinted up the lane to his waiting Range Rover.

Anton wouldn't stay in the country long. His ruthless leadership of his cartel had killed too many; gangsters and the security service alike wanted Anton dead and his cartel split.

Jasper floored the Range Rover, gambling that Anton was heading for the small disused airfield. That was where the Wilsons had been heading.

The back roads brought him to the woods above the airfield. The moon peeked from behind a cloud, revealing a small light aircraft. Anton's Range Rover skidded to a halt by the plane's open door. He hurried into the aircraft while his driver parked the car in the hangar at the far end of the airfield.

Jasper watched and waited until the plane taxied and disappeared into the night sky. Anton had made a mistake by coming to Wellsbury. He had showed his hand. The news of his visit would be spreading. Jasper would have to prepare for visits from Anton's enemies and the security service.

Jasper had started to walk back to his Range Rover, milling over his next move, when the roar of motorbike engines surprised him. Three men sped from the hangar at the end of the airfield. But a black Audi pulled in front of them. Don.

Don did most of the talking. His arms moved towards the woods, pointing. Jasper knew that they had spotted him. He didn't wait for Don to scan the darkness with night-vision glasses. He slowly moved further into the woods, towards his hidden Range Rover. He would return another day.

Jasper had just reached his Range Rover when the motorbikes slowly crawled along the lane. He was confident that his black Range Rover wouldn't be seen from the roadside, but Don wouldn't be looking from the road; he would be on foot.

Jasper slid into his Range Rover and waited and listened for the Audi. He anticipated that Don would coast by and leave the Audi at the far end of the wood.

The woods were still and the silence heavy when the moon made a welcome appearance, just as the Audi with no lights sped by Jasper. Don was leaning on the window, talking into a phone.

After a long moment, Jasper made his escape.

Chapter Thirty-Five

"Why are you here?" asked a small voice.

Harry peered at a dozing Jasper, his shoes and socks discarded on the carpet, his black jeans undone, black shirt open to his waist. Jasper opened one eye; he hadn't had any sleep.

"You can sleep with Mummy. I don't mind," said Harry in his mature voice.

Jasper stared at his son who was old beyond his years.

"Where's she hidden the Coco Pops?"

"Where you can't find them." Kate's words rescued a very tired Jasper.

Harry's face fell as he realised Kate had caught him trying to hoodwink Jasper. He gave Kate a weak smile and raced back to his bedroom.

Jasper sat up and pulled Kate to his side so her head rested on his naked chest.

"I don't like you in PJs," he whispered.

"I can't walk about naked in front of Harry."

"Silk, satin, lace nightdress, then."

She momentarily studied his stern expression. "What's wrong?"

"Anton is what's wrong. He's using the old airfield. He was Colin's last partner; he's out for revenge. He knows I have Colin's diamonds. He wants them."

"This is ridiculous. You can't be held responsible for Colin. It happened years ago."

"You don't know these people. They have long, long memories. Revenge is embedded in their DNA."

"First step?"

"First step: I bury myself deep inside you. Second: breakfast. Third: take Harry to school. Fourth: I sack Johnson. Fifth: you take over the accounts. Sixth: with a bit of luck, I fuck you again before Harry returns."

In a trice, she was in his arms, being carried to the bedroom. This was the old Jasper, the one who knew what he wanted and took it. The one she had fallen in love with.

Jasper slowly removed her PJs, taking in her form.

"Too thin," he remarked.

Can't say the same about you, she thought as she admired his muscular body.

"I've missed this." Her hands wandered over his chest.

But Jasper was in a hurry. He needed Kate's particular unique therapy to give him the strength to fight Anton.

"I'll be gentle," he murmured as he slowly entered her.

He gasped at the sudden surge of sensations. Sensations that had eluded him while they had been separated. Kate's therapy, warm, wet and tight, as he swallowed both of their ecstatic cries.

***

"Where's Mum?" said a small voice from behind Jasper.

"Sleeping," came Jasper's dismissive reply.

He was preparing breakfast. Toast for them, and Coco Pops for Harry.

"I'm hungry." Harry moved to the bedroom and a sleeping Kate.

Jasper caught his arm.

"Let go of me!" demanded Harry.

In a swift move Jasper lifted Harry and marched back to the kitchen. Harry's legs were trying to kick Jasper, unsuccessfully.

Jasper unceremoniously plonked Harry onto a breakfast stool.

"Let go of me!" Harry's small voice was unusually loud.

Kate stirred.

"Listen to me, you selfish brat." Jasper's voice suddenly became stern.

Harry's fists flailed at Jasper, but Jasper caught his wrists.

"Your mother's sleeping."

"She never sleeps."

"She is this time."

"You're not my father," said Harry, wiggling, trying to get away from Jasper.

Kate stirred again, but she was too exhausted to go to Harry's aid. Sex with Jasper was better than any sleeping pill.

***

When Jasper returned from the school run, Kate was in Johnson's office, cold toast and steaming tea beside her.

"Harry okay?" she asked without taking her eyes from the computer screen.

"We had disagreements. I won."

"It's what he needs. I'm too soft with him."

Their eyes met. They were both smiling.

Amanda, who was keenly watching the two, opened her mouth in surprise. They were lovers. It was written all over their faces. *No going back now,* Amanda thought as she walked back to her desk and picked up the phone.

"You were asking about Jasper and Kate?"

"Yes," answered the gruff voice.

"Whatever you had in mind, forget it. Jasper's back to his old self."

"He's fucked her?"

"Oh! Yes."

"But the doctor said—"

"Forget that. I would say Kate will be back to her old self in record time."

Amanda was curious. Jasper hadn't left Johnson's office where Kate was working. He appeared a little hesitant. That wasn't like him.

Jasper put a new MacBook on Kate's desk.

"I've installed your bank account details. The old passwords are still valid."

Kate raised her eyebrows.

"For some reason I never deleted them. I've given your old laptop to the IT tech to sort."

Kate's mouth opened and closed.

"I'll be out of the office for a while." He hesitated. "I wanted you to have this."

He opened a small velvet ring box. Kate gasped. She knew nothing about diamonds, but this was clearly expensive. He slipped it onto her ring finger.

"Jasper, I can't. It's…." Her words faded.

"It's beautiful. Like you," he said. "The cut is round brilliant. Fifty-seven perfectly aligned facets. The cut is perfect."

"This is too much…"

He put a finger over her lips. "I want you to wear it this afternoon when we go shopping. You have no clothes to speak of." Jasper turned to leave.

"Jasper!"

He turned to face her just as her mouth consumed his. Jasper took charge of the kiss, wrapping Kate in his arms and deepening the kiss.

A red-faced Kate watched Jasper stride towards the exit. She caught Amanda studying her—or was it the ring? Amanda was talking into the phone; Kate felt sure that she was describing her ring.

Kate sat for a while, admiring the ring. She hadn't had many presents—the usual childhood presents; Nigel had brought flowers once or twice. But the ring was special; it meant a lot to her that Jasper had given it to her. She began to wonder where Jasper had got it from. Suddenly, it didn't matter. What mattered was that he had given it her.

***

Harry was overjoyed that Kate and Jasper were waiting for him, his morning disagreement forgotten. Kate expected him to be full of stories from his first day at school, and he was, but also surprised her by asking if she was feeling better.

In his way, Harry was concerned for his mother. Jasper had called him selfish, and after asking the school librarian what that meant, Harry had realised Jasper was right.

Kate cupped Harry's face and kissed his forehead. Harry smiled and slung his arms around his mother's neck.

She was quite relived when Jasper announced that he was going out after Harry was in bed. She didn't ask where; he would tell her when she needed to know.

Chapter Thirty-Six

The moon was bright as Jasper slowly drove to the wood above the old airfield. He switched off the Range Rover's lights and engine and coasted to a halt behind a row of bushes.

Dressed in his black outfit, he walked the short distance to the edge of the trees. He had a good view of the airfield from this elevated position. He lay on his stomach and pulled binoculars and a pocket camera from his jacket and hung them around his neck.

The doors of the hangar nearest the wood were open and lights blazed. It was a hive of activity, with men carrying boxes towards the back of the hangar. If Jasper wasn't mistaken, Don was giving instructions.

The sound of an aircraft filled the night air. Jasper's eyes moved skyward. Suddenly out of the darkness, the outline of a small aircraft appeared. The pilot skilfully landed on the dimly lit runway and taxied close to hangar. The steps were lowered, and Anton struggled down them.

Jasper switched his camera into night mode and began to click away.

Anton stopped the men moving boxes and instructed one box to be opened. He reached inside and pulled out a rifle. He immediately put his eye to the scope and pointed to the tree line.

Jasper immediately crawled backwards into the dense undergrowth. *What the fuck is going on?* he thought as he gunned the Range Rover back to Wellsbury.

Don's goons were parked across the road from Carmichael House. Jasper calmly walked up to their BMW and knocked on the driver's window. The goons were more interested in their Chinese takeaway than the man knocking on the window. Jasper took the driver by surprise when he wrenched open the door and cracked him across his head with the gun that had been carelessly left on the dash. The passenger was equally surprised; he was all fingers and thumbs as the takeaway flew from his hands. Jasper slammed the butt of the gun into the goon's head. Jasper returned the gun to the dash, pushed the driver back into the car, closed the door and calmly walked back to the Range Rover.

***

Jasper sat in his office, flicking through last night's photographs of Don and Anton.

He'd waited till the school run, when he knew he'd be alone. He didn't want to arouse Kate's curiosity.

The first thing that struck him was that Anton was not his usual dapper self. His suit was creased, his hair wasn't trimmed to his exacting standards. Jasper suspected that Anton was under pressure.

Anton and Don walked away from the camera, but Anton's body language clearly showed he didn't like what Don was saying. The last photograph was of Anton swinging a rifle towards the wood.

Jasper was unsure what to do, but he had to do something before Anton organised himself.

Kate was still his priority. His first call was to his director of security, demanding a bodyguard for Kate. He knew she would object, but he would take the flack. Once they were married, things would be different.

He opened his desk drawer and placed two old velvet ring-boxes on the desk blotter. He took each ring from their box and stared at them.

They were obviously family heirlooms. He had no idea why Colin had left them to him, but he was going to put them both to good use.

The main office door slowly opened, and Don's bulky figure approached.

"To what do I owe this pleasure?" Jasper said bitterly.

Don pulled up a chair and sat staring into space.

"I've been a Carmichael man all my life. I was there for you when Colin died and then your mother. You have the Carmichael temper. You're so like Colin; you can't forgive betrayal and you seek revenge. That was Colin's undoing. He took on someone who was far more ruthless than he ever was." Don eyed the drinks tray and poured himself a large malt in one of Jasper's crystal glasses. He stared into it.

"Anton's angry. Since Kate's been back, you're more like the old Jasper. Anton wants revenge. He's going to get it, one way or another." Don paused, taking long swigs of malt. "He thought he had you eating out of his hand. He would have your business and the diamonds."

Jasper eyes widened. *Diamonds again.*

"Kate comes along with your son. That was unexpected. And now you have something to fight for. She scuppered Anton without doing anything except fucking you."

Jasper's mouth opened, but Don waved his hand.

"He'll regroup. He wants revenge. He doesn't like losing."

"Have you come to change sides?" Jasper checked.

"It's too late for that. You should leave. Take her with you."

"Do you think that would stop him?"

"Not really. Nothing will."

Don placed his empty glass on the drinks table.

"He's using outsiders. I would guess Latins, but I could be wrong." Don stood by the door. "This is goodbye, my old friend. Watch your back, and especially Kate's. You see, he wants you to suffer. No better way than to hurt her. You're in love, Jasper. He knows your weakness."

His eyes rested on the rings. "Colin even gave you the Carmichaels' rings. I'd 'eard about them but never seen 'em. Colin must 'ave been his dad's favourite to 'ave those. Enjoy 'er while you can."

"Don! Anton and Colin were partners?" Jasper asked.

Don stood with his hand on the doorknob.

"Last heist. Colin gave Anton paste. I thought he'd 'ad his revenge when he and Lawson put Colin inside, but he'll only be satisfied when you give him the diamonds and you beg."

"Beg! What for?"

"Kate's life."

Jasper watched the last of Colin's trusted men leave. Don no longer walked with a confident stride. He was a beaten man.

Jasper couldn't ponder on the past, he had work to do. He strolled into the IT department. His new team were still working.

"How easy is it to hack?"

The young man looked up. "Anything can be hacked."

"Not good enough. I'm paying for the latest and

best system." Jasper's voice was a little angry. The young man was taken by surprise. "No one comes in here except me and Kate. Do I make myself clear?"

"Yes, sir," was the meek reply.

The head of security was waiting for Jasper.

"Trouble?" he growled.

"I want security doubled. Patrols at night. Kate will have a bodyguard. Every night you'll search the offices. Once you're satisfied, the office will be in lockdown until seven. Do I make myself clear?"

"Yes, sir," said the security guard.

"Post men in and outside the underground car park. First thing tomorrow we'll start work on a perimeter fence."

Jasper strode towards the elevator. He could feel the tension rising in his body. He needed to fuck her.

***

"I've been looking everywhere for you," he said calmly, slipping his arms around Kate. "I've got to go out. Don't know how long. The penthouse must be in lockdown."

He devoured her mouth as he lifted her on to the work surface.

"I need this before I go."

Her oversized tracksuit bottoms were on the floor and her legs around his waist.

"Hold on," he softly said.

His thrusts were deep and hard, his release quick.

"Thank you," he breathlessly murmured as he pulled out of her. "I thought love was a myth. Until you."

"Jasper, what is it? Why are you dressed like

that?" Kate had just noticed he had changed into his black outfit.

"Maximum security, my love."

He left the penthouse by the fire escape to the underground car park. He waited in the shadows, watching and listening. He was about to move when he saw the red glow from a cigarette and heard whispers.

He had anticipated Anton would make a move, but not this soon. He didn't hear the man that floored him then kicked him in the ribs, winding him. But the man was surprised when Jasper swept his legs out from beneath him. In an instant Jasper was up and jumping on the man's leg. The crack was deafening. Another man was watching Jasper and fumbling with his jacket, trying to find his gun. Jasper didn't hesitate. A kick in his balls and the man was on the concrete floor. A knee in the chin and the man lay dazed. But Jasper wasn't dazed; he had his hands around the man's neck. One quick twist and he was dead.

"Carmichael," mumbled the other man. Even though his fibula had broken the skin, he was still trying to crawl away from Jasper. But he received the same treatment as his friend.

Jasper emptied their pockets and dragged and heaved the dead bodies into an almost-full industrial waste bin.

He began to feel a little light-headed as he pushed the bin outside to the collection point. He threw more rubbish bags on top of the dead bodies.

Chapter Thirty-Seven

Kate looked out over a dark Wellsbury. She could never understand why the street lighting switched off at midnight. It acted like a curfew. She wondered if it was dark where Jasper was. He had increased security for her and Harry; the place was in lockdown. Something had happened—he wouldn't say what.

***

While Kate was gazing at the Wellsbury night sky, Jasper was running through the long grass surrounding the airfield. He'd hidden the Range Rover in an unused farm gateway, finding one of the few that hadn't been barricaded to stop travellers invading the fields.

He jogged towards the hangar that contained the boxes of rifles, stopping and kneeling at the edge of the long grass. It was open ground between him and the hanger; the grass had been destroyed.

He took a long moment to catch his breath and survey his surroundings through his night glasses. There were no obvious signs of an alarm system or human activity. Jasper inwardly smiled; Anton didn't want to bring unwanted attention to the place. That didn't surprise him, considering the number of boxes he'd seen being carried into the hanger.

He sprinted to the hangar, finding the doors

secured by a padlock that was easy to pick.

He opened the doors and slipped through the narrowest of gaps. With light from his iPhone, he carefully made his way to the boxes. A rifle lay across an open box. Jasper had a quick look inside—more rifles covered with wax paper.

Jasper wandered into the small office. It was very clean and tidy—*Don,* he thought—but the computer was left on. Jasper found the USB stick he had tucked away in his top pocket and slotted it into the computer. While files were being copied to the USB stick, Jasper wandered back to the boxes of guns, mulling over his next move. At the back of the hangar he found barrels of petrol and aviation fluid.

Uppermost in his mind was preventing Anton from selling guns, if that was what he intended. Jasper couldn't contemplate what else Anton could use them for. He briefly wondered what a young Anton had been like. Was Colin responsible for this cruel monster?

Without fully thinking his plan through, Jasper tipped one of the barrels so petrol trickled towards the boxes of guns. He returned to the office and collected his USB stick.

On his way out, he helped himself to a rifle and ammunition. By the time he'd reached the hangar door, the petrol was trickling through it. He threw a match into the petrol and watched the flame race towards its source.

He'd begun to jog back to the field when the blast from the hangar hit him in the back, knocking him face first onto the ground. He looked back to see the heavy hangar doors blown away and flames leaping out towards the night sky.

Men ran out of the far hangar, shouting at one another.

Jasper crawled his way back to the cover of the field and darkness.

Wellsbury was a hive of activity. Blue lights and sirens sped towards the airfield. Jasper stopped in a side street, waiting for the sudden surge of activity to die down.

He checked on Kate and Harry before collapsing onto the couch.

***

Jasper woke to the sound of a small voice.

"I'm the only one in my class with one mummy," said Harry, moving his Coco Pops around his bowl. "How many mummies should you have?"

"Let me see," answered Kate. "Mummy and daddy, mummy and mummy, daddy and daddy."

Harry's eyes widened and settled on Kate. "Only have you." His small voice quivered as his eyes filled.

This was Jasper's opportunity. He opened his eyes. Kate was embarrassed—she had turned away from Harry; she didn't know what to tell him.

Jasper walked up behind Harry and put his arms around him.

"Can you keep a secret?" His voice was low, but Kate could hear.

Harry nodded, eager to hear what Jasper had to say.

"Very soon, you'll have a mummy and daddy."

Harry dropped his spoon into his Coco Pops, eyes firmly on Kate. She turned, smiled, and Harry's face glowed. Jasper picked Harry up and walked towards Kate, who cupped his face, planting a kiss on his smooth cheek.

"Does that mean you'll sleep with Mummy and wear PJs?"

Happy laughter filled the penthouse. But Kate noticed a slight cringe from Jasper as he held Harry. He was unusually quick returning Harry to his breakfast, and with his back towards them, he hurried into the bedroom.

***

Jasper stood staring out of his office. He knew Kate had seen the bruises from Don's goons. He was waiting to tell her about them when she returned from the school run.

Jasper didn't like who he had become. He longed to be with Kate, to know she was waiting for him, ready to share his problems.

That newsagent had swindled him, but he'd been a nasty piece of work, hated by the community. He had done them all a favour. Max Wilson had abused Kate to get at him; he deserved to die. The other two Wilsons had broken into the penthouse with the intention of raping Kate. Anyway, he'd owed Matt after that beating he gave him. He hadn't intended to kill them, just put them in hospital; it wasn't his fault they'd stopped by the George and drank too much.

"Carmichael!" bellowed Inspector Watts.

Jasper abruptly turned to face Watts and Lawson.

"Lawson here told me that you're trouble," said Watts.

"What do you want?" was Jasper's terse reply.

"Two men are missing," blurted Lawson. The sudden change in Watts's face told Jasper that Lawson shouldn't have said that.

Jasper shrugged in a 'so what?' manner.

"My men!" bellowed Don from behind Lawson.

Watts visibly cringed.

"Two good Family members. Don't know how you bettered them, but you'll pay for it." Jasper had never seen Don so angry. "And then there's the airfield."

"What's this to do with me?" Jasper said.

"There was a fire in one of the hangars," said Watts, trying to defuse the situation.

"I thought that place was derelict?"

"No matter. There was a fire and explosion. Hangar is a shell," said Watts.

Jasper thought it was best to stay quiet, particularly as he had just eyed Kate walking towards his office carrying two mugs of tea. He couldn't hide his admiring glance as she handed him a mug. His blue eyes jumped to life as he admired her white fitted blouse and Carmichael grey trousers.

While Kate's clothes had Jasper's attention, her ring was being scrutinised by Don and Lawson.

"Does that rock mean what I think?" snarled Don.

"Kate and I are to be married." Jasper slipped his arm around her waist and planted a soft kiss in her hair.

"Is it true you bought the Isaacs' house?" asked Lawson.

"Yes. I was going to knock it down, but Kate's persuaded me not to."

Watts noted that Jasper had become more relaxed now Kate had appeared. And that he hadn't taken his arm from her waist. *Powerful woman,* he thought.

"Any plans for the Isaacs?" asked Don.

"We're going to live there," answered Kate, looking over her mug of tea.

"You can't do that."

"We're getting off track," said Watts. "What do

you know about the two men and the fire at the airfield?"

Kate looked at Jasper with that 'what's going on?' look.

"Don's missing two men, and there was a fire at the airfield."

"What's that to do with us?" asked Kate.

"I'll tell you what it has to do with Jasper." Don's venomous voice took them all by surprise. "My two men were watching the penthouse."

"Why?" interjected a slightly angry Kate. "To take over from the Wilsons?"

Don's face reddened and he gave Kate a deep look.

"Don't even think about it, Don." For a brief moment, Jasper's harsh words got to Don and their eyes locked.

"Like I was saying," Don said. "Two men have gone missing. And a hangar has been destroyed."

"I don't see the link. Do you, Inspector?" Kate answered. Watts reddened. "Or is there something I'm not being told?"

"We're done here," snarled Don, pulling on Lawson's sleeve.

"Till next time, Mr Carmichael," said Watts.

Chapter Thirty-Eight

"Let's walk," said a subdued Jasper.

The Range Rover was filled with a heavy silence as they drove to Kate's favourite place, the confluence of the Wells and Bury.

"It's confession time, Kate. You can't marry me without knowing some of my past."

"I know the worst. Newsagent. Max."

"I have the diamonds and Colin's book. Anton will kill for them both."

"I know."

He looped his arm around her neck and pulled her into him. "Anton appears to have been Colin's protégé. But then he double-crossed him. And gave the diamonds to me."

"You're blood, Jasper."

"Sometimes I feel that he isn't dead. He sent me here for some reason."

"To meet me," she said, trying to lighten his mood.

"Finding the Wilsons ostentatious Rolls parked at Carmichael House made my blood boil. The tyres were old, weak."

"What're you saying?"

"I helped the Rolls crash. I never intended for them to die. Alcohol did that. Anyway, they were going to harm you."

"Jasper..." She laid her head on his shoulder.

"When I left the other night, Don's men were waiting. One gave me a right going over."

"I know."

"But I got the better of them."

"Where are they?"

"Landfill or incinerator."

"Jasper!"

"I had no choice; it was them or me. The airfield fire was me. I knew Anton had something going on. Weapons. Boxes of them."

Kate was silent, gazing out over the river as she processed what she was hearing.

"Anton will want me dead, and you and Harry."

Kate gulped.

"I see it this way: I'm the second Carmichael to scupper his game."

"What do you think he wanted the weapons for?"

"To sell. Can't think why he stashed them at the airfield unless he intended to sell them here."

"England?"

"Gang warfare. He's always fancied being top dog in London."

"This is England, not the Wild West."

"Anton lives on a super yacht. He's not welcome in many countries, including this one."

"Well, grass on him."

"Kate, if only it was that simple."

"I don't like the idea of you going after him."

"This has got to end, one way or another."

Kate put her hand on Jasper's arm and looked into his eyes. She smiled and he smiled back.

Suddenly four large buzz-cut men stood in front of them. Jasper and Kate had had no idea they were being followed. The men were dressed in black suits a size too small, emphasising their size. The inner two men parted, revealing a small round man.

Kate shivered as his dark, piercing eyes settled on her.

"You have cost me a lot of money."

"Me?" Kate stuttered.

Jasper slipped a comforting arm around her. "It's me you want."

"I should have fucking killed you when I had the chance. You went to pieces pining for her. But no, I was greedy." He kicked the gravel in frustration. "I wanted your business. The Families would have followed—they're nothing without a Carmichael. But you"—he stopped and pointed his small, chubby index finger at Jasper—"have what's mine. Colin's diamonds." He took a step towards Jasper.

From out of nowhere, Don appeared.

"Anton, we've got to go. Watts knows you're here." Don's eyes settled on Jasper.

"I know the diamonds are hidden," Anton said. "You will give me them. Bring them to me."

"Anton!" Don was becoming anxious.

"Don will tell you where." Anton's attention turned to Kate. "My dear. If Jasper fails me, I will have the delightful pleasure of fucking you and then giving you to my men."

The four bodyguards surrounded Anton and pushed him along the riverside path, away from Kate and Jasper.

Kate's head fell against Jasper's chest and she sobbed.

"Come. Let's go and pick Harry up."

***

Harry came skipping out of school carrying two large pieces of paper. His beaming smile filled his face when he saw Kate. He was still jumping up and down when Jasper joined them.

"Look!" he said. "I've drawn a mummy and daddy." He waved the drawing of his mummy and daddy in front of them. "The first one's rubbish but the second is cool."

"Harry, I've asked you not to use that word."

He climbed into the rear of the Range Rover, turned and put his arms around Kate's neck and kissed her. Kate's heart jumped and she smiled. How could she be angry when he flashed her the Carmichael smile?

Chapter Thirty-Nine

Anton cursed, knocking his breakfast onto the plush carpet. The steward rushed to clean it up. A kick to the ribs, and the steward stumbled into the breakfast.

"You imbecile. Get me the fucking captain."

The steward lifted himself and scurried towards the bridge.

"Sir." The captain's loud voice announced his presence.

"Radio for my plane."

"The storm—"

"I don't want fucking excuses. I need to get off this godforsaken place."

"Sir, the jet can't land at Vagor Airport."

"Then take me to where the jet can land."

"Kirkwall."

The captain rushed back to the control room. If Anton had listened to him, they would be sailing across the Atlantic, away from this hurricane-force storm. He had managed to avoid the worst of the storm by heading to the Faeroes. However, when they arrived, the authorities had been waiting.

Anton may have escaped the UK police, but they had been one step ahead and contacted the Faeroe police. The Faeroe police had boarded the yacht with the intention of taking Anton into custody, but Anton had turned on his persuasive charm, and the police were letting him stay on the yacht until the UK police arrived.

But Anton had other ideas.

"We're slipping anchor in the early hours," the captain informed the crew.

The crew looked from one to another, not too happy with Anton's orders.

"With a bit of luck, we'll drop the boss off in Kirkwall, hopefully before the authorities realise he's there."

A heavy silence filled the control room.

"We can do this. I've never let you down. You all know what you have to do. It's a good yacht. Just rig for hurricane. Double check the safety lines."

***

While the captain was giving his crew instructions, Don marched into Jasper's office.

"Get the fuck out, Don. I have work to do."

"You owe us."

"Owe?! I owe fucking nothing."

"You owe us a cut of the diamonds."

"Us?!"

"Me, Jack, Richard, Beth."

"Beth! I owe her nothing. She had everything until she wanted Jack and Richard."

"She's pregnant."

"That's nothing to do with me."

"The money's gone."

Jasper pushed his chair away from his desk and stepped towards the window.

"If they've squandered the money from Carmichael and Swain that's their problem."

"They want back in."

"No fucking chance."

"It's that fucking bitch. It was all going well until she turned up."

Jasper stared at Don; he couldn't read his eyes or expression.

"You've backed the wrong horse," Jasper said.

"Milly warned me."

"You should have listened to her."

"Anton's been delayed. Just 'ave the diamonds waiting for him."

"Or?"

"You know what'll happen."

"And you know what'll happen if he so much as touches Kate or Harry."

"The Families aren't happy with you."

"Oh, for fuck's sake! Do you think I give a flying fuck what they think?"

"Old Man Cohen wants to see you."

"There's the door, Don. Use it."

Jasper watched as Don marched confidently through the open-plan office. Jasper waited until he was out of hearing range before kicking over his chair in a temper-ridden fit. He swiped every piece of paper off his desk.

These fucking people are fucking with my life, he thought. He was desperate to get his office back to normal. He had dismissed Johnson and his support staff. Kate had found what he had long suspected: Johnson was fiddling the finances. He needed a new accountant, at least one bookkeeper and a couple of office general dogsbodies.

He would have preferred Kate to look after his finances, but he wanted her to project manage the Isaacs alterations. And there was the small matter of another child. She had no idea he wanted another child. He wondered what her reaction would be if she knew that he'd had a meeting with her doctor. Her prognosis had been encouraging. Kate had neglected herself—she needed rest and good food—but the doctor had noted that she had seen an improvement in her general health.

Kate, he thought. He looked at the clock; she would be on the school run. He needed to be inside her. He closed his eyes and imagined her delightful moans as she gave herself to him, her fingers threading through his hair. If he stopped, she would open her green, sparkling eyes and smile. Kate, his Kate. A deep thrust, another thrust, and he was hers. Sensations sped through him, going deep into his core, piercing the tension that was lying waiting for relief.

And now he had to deal with fucking Anton. Colin should have dealt with him all those years ago after the diamond heist, but for some reason he hadn't.

Jasper considered his fledgling revenge plan and its many flaws. He was no marksman, let alone an assassin. He had pondered that the best spot for a shot was from the edge of the wood, from where he'd watched the boxes being carried into the hanger, but he suspected that Anton's goons had already sussed that out.

So, Plan B was to leave the Range Rover in that disused farm gateway and walk to the edge of the long grass surrounding the airfield. The chances of him being seen were greater with this plan; he was relying on Anton's men not paying attention to the field.

Plan B was a long shot, but Jasper had no choice but to play.

Don had inadvertently given Jasper a vital piece of information: Anton had been delayed. He was out of the country. Jasper suspected that his yacht had been forced to sail into international waters, giving him an extra day or two to finalise his plan.

Chapter Forty

It was Kate's fourth night alone. Jasper was convinced Anton would return to the airfield under the cover of darkness.

He had told her his plan was far from complete and it relied heavily on surprise. She had questioned him about the rifle he had taken when he set fire to the hangar. He had convinced her that all was well—he had adjusted the rifle and his aim was good. A white lie, but one he was prepared to live with.

Kate would have felt much happier if he'd been using Plan A. Her heart was hammering, knowing he'd only have the long grass for cover.

***

Jasper switched off the Range Rover lights and coasted to the disused farm gateway. He sat for a long moment, adjusting to his surroundings, listening and scanning the field. Under heavy clouds, he set out for the airfield. Long before he reached the edge of the field, he heard loud voices. He lay on his stomach and slowly separated the long sheaths of grass. The jet was at the far end of the field, pushed into the bushes. They had tried to camouflage it, but they hadn't made a very good job of it.

Through his night-vision glasses, he watched two men run towards the Range Rover. Jasper had to guess which hangar Anton was in, but he didn't have to wait long, as Don pushed open the doors of the hangar that the bikers used.

Anton strutted outside, waving for his Range Rover.

One shot, thought Jasper. *One chance.* He aimed his rifle at his target and, without hesitation, pulled the trigger. He just saw Anton fall as he collected his rifle and crawled away as fast as he could, jumping to his feet as soon as he was out of sight and running back to his own Range Rover.

Behind him, he heard loud angry voices and every available light was switched on.

***

"A shooting last night." Watts's voice echoed in Jasper's office.

Jasper wasn't thinking about the shooting; he was thinking about Kate's lovemaking. She'd been waiting for him and ran into his arms.

"Shooting." Jasper just managed to get the word out.

"Asked for a warrant to search the penthouse and swab your body for gunshot residue."

Jasper tried hard not to show any emotion.

"Judge refused. Not enough evidence. But that'll all change when the big boys get here."

"Big boys?" Jasper repeated; his thoughts hadn't cleared from Kate.

"A bit slow, they are. Anton flew in sometime yesterday. Shot early hours. His men put his body on the jet. Didn't get very far though—pilot misjudged the trees, crash landed in the field. Set fire to the grass, whole field went up. All evidence of the shooter up in smoke. The gateway where the getaway car must have been parked was churned up as if a herd of cows had gone through it."

"I don't see what this has got to do with me."

"You look tired, like you've been at it all night. Kate looks well-fucked."

Jasper clenched his fists; his temper was rising.

"You're not making any sense."

"For once I agree with Don. You shot Anton. He threatened you. More to the point, Kate."

"I'm inclined to say, 'prove it.' But really, Inspector, I'm no assassin."

"What I'm saying is that you got lucky. You sussed out when Anton was likely to land and then you waited for the right moment." The inspector mimed shooting a gun. "Nasty piece of work, Anton, by all accounts. I lost count of how many countries wanted him dead. But he was murdered on my patch. Whoever shot him is guilty of murder and should be put behind bars."

Silence.

"Don's singing like a bird, and so's Lawson. Some story going back to the war. Jack, Richard and Beth want to give statements."

Silence.

"Something about diamonds that Colin, your old man, swindled Anton out of. My men have been looking into Colin Carmichael, and the diamonds from his last heist were never recovered. Don and Lawson say you've got them."

Silence.

"They want revenge, Carmichael."

"Who?"

"Don, Lawson, Jack, Richard and Beth."

"Lawson's wanted revenge since I was a kid. Ask him who Richard's father is. Ask him who got Richard out of prison. Don and Jack have had a good life out of me—ask Don's wife. I gave Beth everything, until she decided she preferred Jack and Richard." Jasper paused. "If you're not going to arrest me, leave. And next time, bring a warrant."

"Don and Lawson swear someone has got your back. You've always had a charmed life. If you fell into a barrel of muck, Carmichael, you'd come out smelling of roses."

The office door slammed closed.

***

Jasper didn't hear his office door open. He was gazing out over the shopping centre, which was well behind schedule. But he wasn't thinking about the shopping centre; Inspector Watts's visit occupied his mind.

"I waited till he'd gone." Jasper recognised Zak's gravelly voice, indicative of too much booze and cigarettes.

Jasper spun round. Zak had cleaned himself up: clean white shirt, open at the collar, tweed sports jacket and grey trousers.

"Not now, Zak. I've too much on my plate."

"That's as may be—got a message from Cohen."

Jasper's eyes widened. "You've been talking to Cohen?"

"Bastard I may be, but a Cohen all the same."

"What's he want?"

"Wants nothin'. He's pleased Anton is no more."

"Christ. News travel fast."

"He's very displeased with Don."

Jasper raised his eyebrows.

"Don, Jack and Lawson been throwing their

weight around. Making life difficult for Cohen. Taking away his authority. With the Wilsons gone, Don and Jack see an opportunity." He paused and waited for Jasper to grasp what he was saying. "It's going to be taken care of the old way."

Jasper was deep in thought as Zak poured himself a more than generous measure of malt. Was Zak saying the Families were going to take care of Don, Jack and Lawson?

"Just a matter of time before heroin takes Richard," Zak resumed, staring admiringly at the amber liquid. "You keep a good malt, Jasper." He sipped his drink "Beth's pregnant by Jack, Nigel or Cohen's son, but he's dead—heroin. Feel sorry for Old Man Cohen. Jack doesn't want to know. So, bet Beth hangs around Wellsbury."

"Another bastard," commented Jasper.

Zak nodded. "Cohens take care of family. Just like Carmichaels. He knows you 'ave Colin's diamonds. Who else would Colin look after? I'm guessing, but the old man wants a truce. He doesn't want to fight you, Jasper. More like business partners."

"What's he want from me?" Jasper's voice was a little edgy.

"The council's kicking me out of me 'ome. New development. Shame—that old school 'as a lot of history. Vicar's got an action group. Wouldn't be surprised if he enrols Kate." He grinned as Jasper's expression morphed.

"What do you want?"

"A deal on that corner unit. The one that'll be next to the entertainment block."

"I have plans for that," Jasper retorted. "Going to cater for moneyed people."

"You sayin' a Cohen ain't got money?"

Jasper stared deeply into Zak's eyes. *The*

crafty bastard, he thought. *Old Man Cohen's foothold in a Carmichael empire.* Cohens look after family.

"The whole unit?"

"Retail outlet. High-end jewellery. Workshop shop. Strong room. Solid construction. Don't want any would-be thieves helping themselves. Good idea for your architect to submit new plans."

Jasper remained silent, preferring not to give anything away.

Zak broke the silence. "I'm thinking us bastards could make a pact. Diamonds are my business. Good at it. You, on the other hand, are an exceptional fence."

"I've finished with that."

"You 'ave Colin's diamonds to get rid of. You've seen what I can do—it's on Kate's finger. You need the money to finish this and expand. You're not a partner man, neither am I. A business pact—you scratch my back and I'll scratch yours." Zak paused. "You're not a double-crosser like Colin. If you were, I'd have been inside years ago, and that's good enough for me."

"Leave it with me. I have a few problems to deal with."

"If you mean Watts, he's being dealt with as we speak."

The office door shut and Jasper slumped into his office chair. He felt deflated. For years he'd thought he'd outmanoeuvred Old Man Cohen, but the old fox had waited until the right time. In exchange for a foothold in Jasper's new enterprises, he would rid Jasper of his enemies, Jack and Don. Jasper had heard Lawson had had a mild stroke, drugs would finish Richard, and Beth was pregnant.

He thought of a new life with Kate, living in the

Isaacs House. There was Harry, and hopefully another Carmichael.

He had big ideas: Carmichael Shopping, Carmichael Food, Carmichael Entertainment, Carmichael Clothes, Carmichael Construction. And it was all going to start here, in Wellsbury. It'd take time and money, lots of money. He'd need support during the rough times, and there would be many.

Kate, he thought. Behind every great man is a woman. And in his case, there certainly was.

Chapter Forty-One

Jasper thought he was blessed. He had everything he'd ever dreamed of: a wife that loved him, a growing successful business—the Carmichael brand was going from strength to strength—and two sons. Harry was six going on seven, and Oliver a growing baby.

Jasper loved them all, but his love for Kate went to his very core. When the demons of the past tried to surface, Kate quelled them with her love. Jasper was happy.

"I'm bloody pregnant again." Kate dropped a clear blue strip into his lap. "How the fuck did that happen?" She paused and glared at him. "I've been so bloody careful. Oliver isn't one."

Jasper had a golden rule: when Kate used the f word, you kept your mouth shut.

"Say something." Her face reddened and eyes filled.

"Let's see what the doctor says. There's always abortion."

Just the word abortion ignited another tirade from Kate.

That was how Jasper found himself waiting for Kate in his private clinic. He cast his eyes admiringly around the opulent surroundings of the birthing suite.

He'd bought the bankrupt private health company not long after Kate had given birth to their second son. Never again would Kate be subjected to the degrading conditions of

Wellsbury Hospital.

He had decided there and then to convert the mansion into a private health clinic. He congratulated himself on the quality of the conversion. He had employed many local builders who were desperate for work, bringing them under the umbrella of Carmichael Construction.

Carmichael Health Clinic was state of the art, staffed by dedicated doctors, nurses, midwives and other health workers he had poached from the best hospitals in the country. Excellent working conditions and a good remuneration package was all it took. He hadn't needed to advertise posts; he'd had many young, newly qualified doctors eager to work for Carmichael Health.

Jasper was particularly proud of the birthing suite with its relaxing, soothing, soft background music, very comfortable sofas and neutral décor.

The suite had four birthing rooms and a four-bed bay, along with a birthing pool. Jasper wasn't convinced about the birthing pool, but the experts had insisted. However, it was Jasper who had insisted on two private rooms for mother and baby. He'd had Kate in mind, only the best for her.

The doctor confirmed Kate's pregnancy. He didn't like her being pregnant so soon after Oliver's birth. He had quietly suggested termination, but Kate had point-blank refused, even though she felt physically weak.

Harry had suddenly become demanding; he didn't like her spending so much time with Oliver.

"A baby needs its mother," she had told Harry, hoping that would console him. It didn't.

In actual fact, Kate would never admit it, but she couldn't have coped if it wasn't for Clare, who had become cook, housekeeper and nanny.

Kate was pleased when Clare and Malcolm

had decided to move into the top floor of the Isaacs House; they had become part of the family.

The doctor had given in to Kate, but he wasn't happy, telling her that, in his opinion, a termination was inevitable. He had insisted that she started a daily regimen of rest if she wanted to have this baby.

An uncomfortable silence filled the Range Rover as they drove back to the Isaacs House. Even cheerful, talkative Harry read Kate's mood and soon after dinner retired to bed.

After Kate had checked that Harry and Oliver were fast asleep, she went in search of Jasper. He was in his study, catching up on work.

"Boys asleep?" he tentatively asked as Kate lowered herself into the chair opposite his desk.

Again, an uncomfortable silence hung between them.

"Look, I'm sorry you're pregnant. But it takes two to tango." His words were hurried and a little harsh.

"I can't work out when it happened," she said.

"Does it matter when it happened? All that matters is your health."

Silence.

He stood and walked over to where she slouched in the chair. "I can promise you this: if you become unwell, the baby will be terminated."

Before she could respond, he unexpectedly lifted her from the chair and carried her into the bedroom.

"You need this more than me," he whispered before devouring her mouth.

Jasper had grown to cherish the moments after they made love. He was relaxed, all the tension of the day gone. He was at peace with the world. Kate's head rested on his naked chest, sleeping after three orgasms, their legs entwined. She was his and he was hers and that was all that mattered. He gave thanks every day for his good fortune. He didn't deserve her, but thanks to her he was a different man. His violent past was behind him, but sometimes he worried that if she died because of him, he would react in a manner she wouldn't want. She had given him hope, a second chance to prove he could be better than his father and the woman he called mother. Kate had guided him onto a redemptive path.

***

His mind drifted to his life before Kate. The criminal gang called the Families and how Colin had told him to cut his ties with them and start afresh in Wellsbury. But they'd turned up like a bad penny.

Security had alerted him to a traffic jam outside Carmichael House. He had gazed out of the window to find a convoy of old Rolls Royce cars turning into Carmichael House.

Jasper took a moment to admire the four cars, one representing each member of the Families: Miller, Cohen, Brown and Johnson. The small group of families shared similar values, experienced similar struggles, had survived the Blitz, rationing and various gang turf wars. They had stuck together through thick and thin.

It had been Colin's idea to start the gang and call it the Families. At first, the gang lacked confidence, enabling Colin to take control. By the time he died, they were a confident group capable of any crime. However, all had changed since the old ones had passed and the next generation had taken over.

This generation wanted to go where the big

money was: the drugs trade. The steady income from protection, clubs, buying and selling goods, and the occasional heist was dropped in favour of dealing drugs with the big boys. But the big boys wanted total control, and the fight back had begun.

His musings were interrupted as the head of each family stepped out of the cars and gazed at Jasper's headquarters. They were all a lot older than Jasper, including some of their sons, the current members that favoured the drug trade.

Jasper was against drugs. He had seen what they had done to Richard. Violence followed drugs, turf wars between rival gangs.

At their last meeting, only the heads of each family had been present. It had been made perfectly clear that the old ways were over. There was no interest in the opportunities offered by Jasper's plan of owning numerous shopping and leisure centres. They argued that it would take too long for their investment to make money in the quantities they wanted. Jasper retorted that they would own everything from construction companies to casinos to theatres, but they wouldn't listen.

Jasper left feeling dejected, but that hadn't prevented him from expanding the Carmichael brand. Since Kate had returned, the Carmichael brand had grown beyond all expectations.

And now the same men that had said the old ways were over stood by their Rolls Royces, dressed like something from *The Godfather*, in dark overcoats and homburgs, waiting for their sons to join them before they walked into Carmichael House reception.

A half smile formed on his mouth.

A child caught Jasper's attention; she was a

similar age to Harry. She stood close to Mr Cohen. He looked down at her with loving eyes and gave her a smile of reassurance.

Jasper pressed the intercom.

"Security here, sir. We have—"

"Show them to the conference room," Jasper interrupted. "Help Amanda with refreshments and find Kate."

Jasper confidently strolled across the open-plan office to welcome the entourage. Mr Cohen shuffled towards him with his arms open, and Jasper reciprocated. The old way of greeting.

"Jasper." His rough croak was just above a whisper, totally different from how he'd sounded on the telephone.

"Mr Cohen." Jasper took the old man's elbow and slowly walked to the conference room.
Mr Cohen handed his homburg and wool overcoat to Amanda and lowered himself into the seat opposite Jasper's.

Moments passed while the Families organised themselves and indulged in small talk while Jasper's staff served refreshments. *The old ways,* thought Jasper.

The hum of small talk dwindled when Kate confidently walked into the conference room. Jasper smiled admiringly at his wife, approving of her choice of formal dress: grey suit, crisp white shirt with the top two buttons open, showing her cleavage to best effect, and heels that emphasised her shapely legs. He slipped his arm around her, their eyes momentarily locked before he planted a soft kiss on her cheek.

"Introduce me," croaked a smiling Cohen.

"Kate. My wife."

Kate felt herself blush. That was the first time Jasper had introduced her as his wife.

Cohen put his arms on her shoulders, pulling her into an unexpected hug.

"You're a lucky man, Jasper," Mr Cohen croaked as he slumped back into his chair. "Colin died before his time. You're the spit of him." Cohen spoke his thoughts aloud as he glanced at Jasper's and Kate's wedding bands. "I see you collected the Carmichael rings. I saved them for you in our pawnshop."

Jasper had had no idea it was Mr Cohen who had saved his family rings.

"Your mother was useless without Colin. She had no thought of the importance of family. She pawned Colin's rings." He shook his head in disgust.

"You must be tired," Jasper said in his caring tone. "We could have met on neutral ground."

"I wanted to see for myself what you've made of yourself."

The young girl Jasper had spotted earlier leaned on Cohen's shoulder and he slipped his arm around her waist.

"This is my granddaughter." Cohen's arm tightened around her waist. "We all agreed that the next in line would be here."

A puzzled look spread over Jasper's face, although Zak had told him of the Cohen family tragedy.

"She's the last of my line." Cohen's voice quivered. "Daughter, son, dead."

Jasper's heartstrings tightened as tears trickled down Cohen's wrinkled cheek. Jasper couldn't imagine life without Kate, Harry and Oliver.

"Both lost to drugs. He got in with your stepbrother and your cast-off. You made a good decision; she's expecting. Played the Cohen card for all it was worth. But she's not carrying a Cohen." He paused as if debating what to say next. "She's living with that Nigel."

"I had no idea," mumbled Jasper as his mind whirled with Beth and Nigel making difficulties for him and Kate.

"My mind wanders, and my thinking's slow," Cohen continued. "I'm here to settle our differences."

Silence fell as Jasper slowly gazed into the eyes of each family head.

Cohen laughed. "Colin did exactly that." He paused again, taking his time to form his words. "No good getting in bed with the Devil." He suddenly lifted his head and stared at Jasper. "The Devil in this case was Anton."

"Colin played with the Devil," said Johnson aggressively, eyes piercing Jasper.

"So I'm told. I don't remember; I was too young."

"Nothing to do with it. Colin and Anton were partners," Johnson said.

"So you say."

Old Man Cohen waved his hand at Johnson, indicating for him to stop. "Anton came to us with Don, offering a get rich quick scheme," croaked Cohen. "They convinced the majority of the Families the old ways were over. Drugs were the new way. Anton supplied drugs; we sold. Now he's gone, the drugs have dried up. We can't fill orders without money up front—our word is no longer trusted. We need money, Jasper."

"I haven't got the amount of money you want."

"Diamonds!" snarled Johnson.

"I don't have any bloody diamonds."

"You just bought the Isaacs place."

Jasper's head whipped round to face Johnson.

"Shut the fuck up." Cohen's croaky voice went up an octave.

A hostile tension descended.

"You've made a lot of money, Jasper," Cohen said.

Jasper nodded. "When I dissolved Carmichael and Swain, I paid Jack and Richard off. It cost a lot more than I expected. No one would lend me money." Jasper stared into Old Man Cohen's eyes. "Remember?"

"We hadn't cash at the time," said Cohen.

"Remember the old ways: if one family was in trouble, the others helped out. No questions."

Jasper took a long moment reflecting on Mr Cohen's words. His eyes wandered to each family member, but none would meet his eyes. He wasn't surprised.

"You forgot. All of you made it perfectly clear you didn't want a Carmichael in your exclusive group." Jasper stood. "And now, suddenly, when the going gets tough, you want a Carmichael to bail you out." His temper was rising.

Old Man Cohen looked at each of the members in turn with an 'I told you so' look on his face.

"Diamonds!" yelled Miller. "I've never liked you, Carmichael. You owe us."

"I owe you nothing. Particularly after you threw my loyalty in my face."

"These are dangerous people, Jasper. Do you want me to beg?" Cohen's voice quivered.

"No need to beg. This lot are using you."

"This is the end of the Families. You'll be responsible," Cohen said.

"The Families were finished when you got rid of the last Carmichael."

"There will be blood."

"Not on my part."

At that moment the office doors bounced open. Harry had pushed past his security. Kate jumped up, kicked off her shoes and ran to meet him.

Harry's school bag fell to the floor as Kate knelt and Harry leapt into her arms.

"That nasty Nigel," he cried, burying his head into Kate's shoulder.

Jasper glared at Harry's security.

"Nigel followed Harry into his maths lesson. Dragged him out, saying he didn't want his son mixing with the likes of Harry."

Kate and Jasper's eyes met.

"I'll deal with this." Her voice was harsh.

"Not a good idea," said Jasper. "I'll sort it."

"That's what Nigel and his cronies expect. It's time Nigel and I had a reckoning."

"You should listen to her, Jasper," interjected Cohen.

The croaky voice made Harry peer over Kate's shoulder.

"Who're you?" Harry asked, looking at Cohen's granddaughter.

"Helena!"

"I'm Harry."

"Why don't you and Helena go and sit at that empty desk, and Amanda will bring you milk and chocolate biscuits?" said Kate.

Harry's face lit up. "Come on," he said to Helena.

Old Man Cohen smiled and nodded at his granddaughter.

Kate strode back into the conference room and settled into her chair.

The room went silent, waiting for Kate to return.

"No blood," said Kate in an authoritative voice. "It's obvious that there is a consensus that the old ways are over." Her eyes moved from one family to another. "Let's not drag up the past—no one knows the truth. We could argue about Colin and Anton, but not even Don knows what went off. No one knows what Colin did with the diamonds."

"He gave them to his son," snarled Johnson.

"I'll tell you what I do know," croaked Cohen. "Colin appeared one night with a baby. Mary was flirting with every man in the pub until Colin looked at her. They just left. The next thing you know, Colin set Mary up in a terrace to look after baby Jasper." He paused to regain his breath. "I had men follow Colin. He met a posh-looking man in a dingy old café. Another time, Colin went into one of those toff clubs—came out looking like a rich geezer. Another time..." He paused and stared at Jasper. "Your grandfather—big tall man, head of silver hair, very distinguished—visited. Colin changed after that. He was seen going into a Freemason Lodge. He did one last heist, then prison—or so we were led to believe."

"What're you saying—he never went to prison?"

"I don't expect you'll believe me. If you want to know, you must dig. But be prepared—you might not like what you find."

Kate rested her hands on Jasper's shoulders. He leaned back in his chair and smiled at his wife, but she read his expression: he was confused. He didn't know what to believe.

"There should be a new understanding between the Families and Carmichael," offered Kate.

"There'll be no Families when I've gone. This lot will join the drug gangs."

It was Old Man Cohen's turn to smile. Kate had offered an olive branch, but it was too late for that.

"As a gesture of good faith, Zak Cohen's new

premises have got the go ahead."

"No!" shouted Johnson.

Jasper didn't let him finish. "I haven't got the money."

"You've seen Zak," croaked Cohen.

"I've got men working on the strong room. Shop fitters start tomorrow," Jasper said.

"Zak's a diamond man," said Old Man Cohen.

"It's a long-term project."

"You're funding it?"

"What's the deal?" snapped Johnson.

"Zak needs new premises to expand his jewellery business. He's branching out. If you're thinking 'What's in it for me?'—at the moment, nothing. But one never knows what the future holds." Jasper paused. "Think of it as repaying past kindnesses."

The old ways, thought Old Man Cohen. He sensed Jasper wasn't being completely genuine, but he couldn't blame him. He suspected that Zak Cohen and Jasper had some sort of understanding with diamonds. Colin's diamonds.

"You haven't mentioned the airfield," said Cohen. "How did you know it's ours?"

Jasper was taken aback. He'd had no idea that Cohen owned the airfield.

He thought on his feet. "Anton wouldn't have been foolish enough to own anything in this country. Someone would have purchased the airfield. At first, I thought of Don," he lied, "but Anton used you, Mr Cohen. I don't know if he blackmailed you into doing it or if you were a willing partner."

Mr Cohen stood and stared at his granddaughter and Harry talking and smiling as if they were brother and sister. He pulled his phone from his trouser pocket.

There was a pause as he dialled a number. "Email those airfield documents to Carmichael."

"Anton wanted the airfield for bringing in drugs and weapons, whatever. And to be near you. He wanted those diamonds. He was so close to finishing you and gaining Carmichael Enterprises and the diamonds when Kate appeared with a Carmichael heir. The change in you was immediate. Anton lost all sense; there was no reasoning with him." Cohen paused, his old, tired eyes gazing at his granddaughter.

"I ask one thing, Jasper. Helena is everything to me. Helena has nobody but me. I haven't long. She needs the love and support of a family. Take her in, look after her as if she was your own." Tears were running down Cohen's cheeks. "I was envious of Kate's reaction to her son and him to her—love. I want Helena to have that."

Jasper turned and looked at Kate, but she was moving towards Mr Cohen. Her arms settled on his shoulders and her cheek against his.

"We'll look after her. Don't worry."

Tears were dripping off Old Man's Cohen chin. After a long moment, he stood and faced Johnson, Miller and Brown.

"Diamonds!" snarled Johnson.

"It was reported that the diamonds were uncut. A third party is needed. Sooner or later, the police will find them. Those diamonds are bad luck—let them rest." The tone of Old Man Cohen's voice said that the topic was closed, but his old mind was chewing over the unlikely arrangement of a Cohen and a Carmichael and Colin's diamonds.

After a little while longer of mingling, eating, drinking and small talk, the entourage left.

"Goodbye, Jasper Carmichael," Cohen whispered in Jasper's ear. "We won't meet again in this life. And keep that wife of yours."

As they hugged for the last time, Jasper had an overwhelming feeling of sadness. His eyes filled as he watched the old man shuffle out of the office.

Chapter Forty-Two

It was six thirty when Zak caught up with Jasper.

"Zak."

"You're a creature of habit, Jasper. A reporter from the *Wellsbury News* told me about your early morning inspections."

"What do you want?"

"Went to Old Man Cohen's birthday party."

"And?"

"Relatives there I'd never seen. They complained about you being Helena's guardian."

Jasper stopped by the coffee vender, who handed him his early morning coffee.

"It was his decision," said Jasper, taking his first sip. He nodded in appreciation to the vender.

"Nothing to do with it. You're a Carmichael."

"How's trade?"

"I haven't finished: the old man asked if you 'ad looked into Colin's past."

"Not yet. I don't know if I'm going to."

"Plenty are."

"What do you mean?"

"Colin's diamonds have become newsworthy."

Jasper stopped and dropped his empty coffee cup in the recycling.

"Beth and Lawson are feeding Nigel James. He's a score to settle with Kate." Zak took a sudden step back. He hadn't seen that retributive look for some time. "They're the only two left."

"Richard?"

"Lying in some gutter waiting for his next fix.

Don and Jack disappeared. Crossed too many."

So, the Families had got rid of Don and Jack. *Poor Milly,* Jasper thought.

"How's business?"

"Good. Retail could be better. Wholesale makes up for it." Zak turned away from the security cameras and pulled a velvet bag from his coat pocket. "My latest."

Jasper stared admiringly at Zak's creation: a diamond pendant.

"Beautiful," Jasper murmured.

"A Kate gift. Birthday, anniversary, number three."

Jasper slipped the pendant back into the velvet pouch.

"The design is unique. One off."

Zak waited for Jasper.

"She's worth it."

"Kate's worth can't be measured by money or jewellery."

Relief spread through Zak when Jasper slid the pouch into his inside pocket and started to walk.

"You want more diamonds."

"I wouldn't mind, but it's best if we wait. These reporters are getting too close."

"Why can't they leave me alone?"

"You're a Carmichael, and..." Zak hesitated, staring into Jasper blue eyes, mentally debating. "You've upset a lot of people. You owe people."

"I've paid my debts."

"They don't see it that way. Your past is catching up with you." Zak waited for Jasper to say something, then sighed heavily. "Newsagent. Max. Wilsons. Anton. Lawson's got it written down. Says he's got proof."

They had reached the luxury apartment building.

"Who's your source?"

"Lawson. He drinks too much. Brags in the George." Zak was on edge; he didn't like morose Jasper.

"You like it here?"

Zak nodded. "Went to a fair. You'd be surprised by the interest." He smiled.

"I'm thinking of developing into a jewellery quarter. Carmichael's Jewellery Quarter."

"Our understanding still stands?" Zak was a little nervous.

"We bastards must stick together." Jasper offered Zak a half smile.

***

The walk back to Jasper's office would take some time. He could have called for his car, but he preferred to walk and mull over the conversation with Zak.

He had to have a plan for Nigel, Beth and Lawson. He needed more information. He didn't feel inclined to dig into Colin Carmichael, but he would investigate the Freemason angle.

He hadn't used a burner phone for some time, but for some reason he had slipped one into his jacket pocket.

"I was just thinking about you," the investigator said. "How you doing, you old rogue?"

"I'm in need of your special skills."

"Let me guess: Nigel, Beth, Lawson."

***

To his surprise, Kate was waiting when he arrived at his office. She smiled that 'I love you' smile that made his heart jump.

She had already told him how she had angered

Nigel when she'd reminded him that she knew all about his and Michelle's sexual encounters that went back to when they were teenagers. Jasper was beginning to dread what she was going to tell him next.

She put her arms around his neck and kissed him.

"As much as I like your kisses... What's wrong?"

"I just wanted to see you."

"Kate."

"I think you're right about Harry," she hesitantly admitted.

Jasper raised his eyebrows. They had argued about Harry. Jasper recognised that if he was going to give Harry the best start in life, Harry needed his intellect stretched. He had asked the head teacher to put Harry in the year above his age as his peers were holding him back.

"He talked about nothing else but being moved up a year. He was so excited." Kate paused, holding back tears. "What have I become? How could I be so selfish? Harry needs to grow to be his self."

"Are you sure? He's exceptional. The head's suggested that we should consider moving him to a school that suits his intellect. It could mean him living away from home. I'm so proud, Kate, of you both."

She nodded and tears trickled down her cheek. He put his arms around her; he knew how difficult a decision it was. A deep, unconditional love had developed between them during Harry's early years. She had struggled both mentally and physically. She had sacrificed so much for Harry, and now she was going to make the ultimate sacrifice: letting him go.

"I'm going out to the old airfield. I could use some company."

She gazed into his blue eyes, knowing full well what he was doing. In his way, he was comforting and supporting her.

"I'll make a thermos. Biscuits or cake?"

"Both."

A smile stretched across his face. Kate hadn't stopped eating biscuits and cake so far in this pregnancy.

Chapter Forty-Three

"He is exceptional," Kate commented, staring through the Range Rover's windscreen.

"You made him, Kate. You read together every night, check his homework, even discuss a news item."

"He took to reading like a duck to water." She grinned as happy memories flashed through her mind. "He got into fights at the village school. When he admitted school bored him, I knew we had to move. Who do you think he takes after?"

They had stopped at the airfield's new security gates.

"I have no idea." Jasper's stomach nervously twitched; he was being somewhat disingenuous. His gut told him that Harry was a true Carmichael—not like him, but from Colin's paternal family. A family powerful enough to be Freemasons.

He sheepishly glanced at Kate, but she was staring into space.

"It's all so different from the last time I saw it. It was a teenage playground. We thought we were being defiant, breaking the rules. Nigel was the leader, with Michelle."

Jasper caught her hand and started to walk towards the far end of the runway.

"Did he fuck you?"

"Jealous?" she playfully replied.

He pulled her into him. "There's rumours that he, Beth and Lawson are out to make trouble. Nigel's targeting you."

"Me?!"

"He has a score to settle."

"And you think..."

"I think he'll make up any dirt to get at you. He won't mess with me; I can take it and dish it back. But you..."

"There's no dirt on me. I was a virgin when I left for uni. He was Dad's solicitor. He was a shoulder to cry on when I divorced. He's never fucked me." Her voice had lost its playfulness.

"Where're your dad's papers?"

"I have them, but Nigel will have copies. They're not relevant anyway."

Oh, my darling innocent Kate, Jasper thought. *Nigel is going to get his pound of flesh one way or another.*

"I'm going back to the car," she said. "Coffee and a bite to eat."

"Biscuit or cake?"

"Both." She grinned.

Jasper continued to the end of the runway. The fire had cleared bushes and trees, giving a clear view of Carmichael's Airfield. In his mind, he'd already named it. His aim was to make it a small, regional airport, offering flights to various UK cities and Europe.

It was going to be a big undertaking. He needed a specialist aviation consultancy firm, council approval. Above all, he wasn't confident that Wellsbury needed an airport—but he did. He was going to construct Carmichael's Shopping Centres in other towns, and he didn't want to waste time travelling by road between them. And he didn't want to leave Kate alone.

His mind moved to the possibility of a helicopter and employing a pilot. There was plenty of room to land at the Isaacs House.

Probably the best use of the airfield was for enthusiasts. A flying club.

He was deep in thought when he turned to the field that had given him the cover to use his rifle. There was no evidence of the long grass, either burnt or trampled on by the emergency services. He could just make out the gateway where he had hidden the Range Rover.

Just at that moment, a flash of light caught his eye. Jasper's head whipped to the most likely place the light could have come from: the wood. A reflection from binoculars came into his mind. He was being watched.

He delved into his jacket pocket and snatched out his burner phone.

"I'm quick, but that's bloody quick," snapped an irritated voice.

"Break into Nigel James's office. Paper copies of anything Reynolds, flower shop—also computer files. I'm being followed, or could be."

"The fair Kate," said the voice.

Before Jasper could reply, the phone went dead.

***

"You're back?" said Kate. "Coffee and cake? I've saved you some." She was reclining in the front passenger seat. She smiled. A smile that said 'kiss me.'

Jasper leaned over and kissed her. "Has Kate left anything for me?"

"There's always something for Jasper." Her voice was playful.

Their kiss deepened.

"I'd have you on the back seat." Jasper's voice was low and husky. "But we're being watched."

"Who's being watched. Me or you?"

"Not sure yet. Probably both."

"I've been thinking about Nigel. He does have an axe to grind: he wanted me to marry him, even though he was still fucking Michelle. She would never leave Dan. Dan's a good provider, totally old school; the kids are his responsibility. But they're not his. She married Dan because she was pregnant."

"You know too much."

"I could certainly outdo Nigel in mud-slinging."

***

Jasper welcomed the solitude of the terrace. He was happy here at Isaacs House with Kate, Harry and Oliver. But this evening, the boys had been more than a handful.

Harry wouldn't stop talking about his new class and friends. He threw a tantrum when Kate spent time with Oliver, who for some reason wouldn't stop crying. By the time she had settled Oliver and then Harry, she was exhausted.

Jasper was exhausted, and he hadn't done anything. He would have to employ a fulltime nanny. Kate needed rest and Clare had other duties.

His mind turned to getting his men to finish the conversion of the stable block. Clare and Malcolm could move in there, and the nanny could have their attic rooms.

Kate objected to the stable block being converted, but Jasper put his foot down, insisting they would have no horses. He hated them.

"Don't look around," said a voice he knew well from behind him.

"What're you doing here?" whispered Jasper.

"Employ more security. Kate's their target."
Jasper's temper simmered. "But the cops are after
you. Inspector Watts. I don't know what Nigel and
Beth have planned for Kate, but it won't be nice.
Is Kate pregnant?"

"Yes," choked Jasper.

"Could be something to do with that. There's a
brown envelope with Reynolds papers in, but most
were on the computer. USB on the windowsill. I'm
sticking around for a while."

"You don't have to."

"Kate doesn't deserve to be degraded by that
back-stabbing sneak. If you don't finish him, I will.
You married a lady. What she sees in a bastard
like you, heaven knows. You treat her well. Just
as well."

As quick as it had arrived, the voice was gone.

***

"What're you out here for?" Kate's voice seemed
unusually loud in the still night air.

"Recovering."

"I think I'll join you, but you'll have to keep me
warm."

Jasper couldn't see Kate's smile, but he felt it.
She slipped onto his lap, wiggling until she was
comfortable. Her head rested against his broad
shoulders as he wrapped his arms around her. He
planted a kiss into her hair.

"You smell nice."

"It's that expensive shower gel you insist I use."

"Worth every penny."

She giggled.

"You do know you're everything to me?"

A delightful sigh escaped her mouth.

Chapter Forty-Four

Jasper was leaning over the conference room table, gazing at his model of the airfield. He wasn't concentrating. He hadn't had much sleep, but a night on the terrace with Kate in his arms made it worthwhile.

"Where the fuck is he?" Nigel James boomed angrily as he marched through the open-plan office.

Nigel pushed Amanda out of the way when he saw Jasper.

"You fuckin' bastard!" Nigel shouted as he stormed into the conference room.

An out-of-breath Inspector Watts stood behind Nigel, eyes firmly fixed on Jasper, looking for any flinch of nervousness.

"Take that fuckin' surprised look off your fuckin' face."

"Mr Carmichael is trying to figure out what's going on," said Watts in an authoritative manner. "Mr James's office was broken into last night."

"What's that to do with me?" answered Jasper.

Nigel was about to go into another tirade when Watts caught his arm.

"Office wrecked. Papers on the floor, chairs turned over, computer smashed, safe open." Watts stared deep into Jasper's eyes. *He knows nothing about it,* thought the inspector. "Where were you last night?"

"I can answer that, Inspector." Kate's calm voice shook the three men. A concerned Jasper looked over towards Amanda, who was rocking Oliver. "We were both exhausted; the boys wanted our attention. When they were finally settled, I found Jasper on the terrace. We spent the night there."

"Fuckin' all night by the looks of him," snarled Nigel, pointing at Jasper.

"James, shut up. And for the record, Mrs Carmichael is telling the truth. My men watched her join her husband on the terrace."

"Your men?" uttered Kate.

"Yes, Mrs Carmichael. Your husband is a person of interest. As such, he's being watched."

"You're going inside, Carmichael. Just like your old man," taunted Nigel.

Kate looked at the inspector.

"Mrs Carmichael, you should know that Mr Carmichael is being investigated for the murder of Anton, the disappearance of Don and Jack, and the cold case of Max Wilson."

"You haven't asked about my office, Kate," interjected Nigel, trying to divert the conversation back to last night.

"Nigel thinks I broke into his office last night." Jasper moved towards Kate and slipped his arm around her.

"What for?"

"Whoever broke in was looking for something," said Nigel. "I suspect information on your dad."

"That's ridiculous. I have all the Reynolds documents. Why would I want yours?"

"The safe was emptied." Nigel paused and stared at Jasper. "Money gone, and all the documents."

"Just so I get this straight, Inspector." Kate was becoming impatient with what she thought was utter nonsense. "Have you got evidence linking Jasper with Anton?" The inspector reddened.

"I know the police tried to pin Max's death onto him. And as far as Don and Jack are concerned, they went to London along with Beth and Richard. Jasper hasn't been to London since they left."

"You seem very sure."

"I am. The Families made it perfectly clear that Jasper wasn't welcome in London. Jasper's been in Wellsbury, busy developing the shopping centre and the Carmichael brand. It might be a good idea to check his diary."

"What about my office?" Nigel glared at Kate.

"I'm sorry about the break in, but it's nothing to do with us."

"You cocky bitch. I remember the time—"

"Be careful, Nigel. *I* remember the time." Kate's temper flared.

Amanda strolled in, carrying a very alert Oliver. Kate took Oliver, who appeared more than a little interested in what was going on.

"He's a lovely lad, Mrs Carmichael," said the inspector as he manoeuvred past, smiling at Oliver. "You're a lucky man, Carmichael."

Nigel wasn't so considerate as the inspector, and jostled past them without saying a word.

"Oliver?" Jasper asked Kate when they were alone.

"Doctor's not sure, but it's probably teething."

Oliver grinned at Jasper as he lovingly cuddled his son. But Oliver was more taken with his father's face. Their eyes met and a beaming Jasper kissed his son's fingers.

"Let's go home."

***

"Jasper, what's wrong?" Kate's words were soft as she placed two coffees on the glass table.

Jasper was staring out into the garden. "I never realised that we had such a big garden."

Kate wrapped her fingers around her coffee cup and slowly sipped the hot liquid as she joined her husband.

"What do you think about a place for a helicopter?"

"Helicopter?"

"I'm forward planning." He took the cup from her and pulled her into his side. "You do smell good."

"You mean I don't smell of baby."

"The planning's approved for the side extension." He waited for her to comment, but nothing came. "The men are finishing off the stable block conversion." He paused again, but Kate remained silent. "Malcolm and Clare can have their own place." Still no response. "For goodness' sake, Kate, say something."

"I'm waiting for you to finish."

"I've asked an agency to find us a nanny," he blurted, waiting for an angry tirade.

"The boys are our responsibility." Her voice was curt.

"They're too demanding."

She tried to pull away from him, but he held her tight.

"Is this about last night?" she asked.

"You were in my arms all night. I'd sacrifice anything for that."

"Sex?"

"I'm talking sharing intimate time with the person I love."

Her hands circled his neck; she lightly brushed her lips against his. His hands cupped her buttocks as he claimed her open mouth, pushing his tongue inside. He sighed as her hands caressed his hair.

"I don't want to argue."

"Kate," he murmured as he kissed her ear.

Her head tilted back, exposing her neck. Soft gentle kisses trailed down her neck to her full breasts. Buttons flew from her blouse. Jasper sighed as his mouth nipped and sucked first one nipple and then the other. Her Carmichael grey trousers fell onto the carpet.

Her body had changed: the baby bump was pronounced, breasts bigger. He hesitated. Their eyes met, blue on green, and she smiled that 'I love you' smile. He couldn't resist.

She stretched out her hand; their fingertips touched. He eagerly followed her to the couch.

He lay atop her, stroking her blonde hair that now was peppered with grey.

"What's wrong?" she tentatively asked.

"I didn't realise how much your body's changed."

"I'm pregnant."

"But you're big."

Her hands cupped his face. Their mouths met.

"Don't make me wait," she whispered into his ear.

Her calves moved against his thighs as his erection eagerly waited. She delightfully gasped as his fullness filled her.

Her head tilted back; erotic moans filled the air. He felt her legs quiver. Sensations built inside him as his thrusts became erratic. In that brief moment, he lost control as he pulsed inside her.

They lay still, calm. Their warm bodies entwined. Jasper listened to Kate's regular breathing; she was resting.

He cast his mind back to their first time. That wasn't love. That was fucking. It had been about him relieving the anger and tension resting inside him. Now he felt connected to her. He smiled as he remembered when he first saw her unloading flowers. Her well-washed jeans, T-shirt and fleece. She'd been laughing and joking with the delivery man. Even then, he'd felt a little jealous that she wasn't smiling at him. But she had smiled at him when she flicked her long blonde hair back. His temper surfaced at the thought of Nigel James resting his hand on the small of her back, staking his claim.

He kissed her forehead and felt her smile.

He wanted to deepen their connection, if that was possible. Grow old with this woman, share happy times with their children.

I swear, he thought, *if those bastards try to get at her, they will wish they had never heard of Carmichael.*

Chapter Forty-Five

Clare walked into Jasper's study, nursing Oliver. Jasper looked up from his laptop, surprised to see her.

"Where's Kate?" he asked.

"She must still be asleep—Oliver was crying." Jasper stood.

"Haven't you noticed how tired she's become?" He nodded.

A loud scream came from Kate's bedroom, filling Jasper with dread. Harry was shouting, crying and screaming.

Tears began to run down Jasper's cheeks.

"Phone the clinic," he shouted. "Malcolm, get the car!"

He wrapped an unconscious Kate in the bloody sheets.

"Is she dead?" screamed Harry between sobs, racing down the stairs behind Jasper as he headed for the car.

Jasper didn't answer; his mind was concentrating on Kate and what had happened.

"I'm coming!" yelled Harry as he climbed into the passenger seat. Jasper hadn't time to argue.

The Range Rover was out of the security gates before they were fully open. Tyres screeching, Malcolm hit the gas.

***

A patrol car pulled out, following the speeding Range Rover.

"Sir!" the policeman said. "Carmichael's rushing towards the clinic."

A sleepy Inspector Watts feared the worst.

"Stay with 'em."

***

A team of doctors and nurses were waiting on the clinic steps. Before Jasper realised it, Kate was being rushed inside with a doctor barking instructions.

"Any news?" said Clare. She was still nursing Oliver.

Malcolm dropped a holdall on the floor. "Clothes for you and Harry."

Jasper looked at Harry's blood-stained pyjamas. Blood covered his legs, chest and boxers.

He took Harry's hand. "Come on, let's get you cleaned up."

Harry shook his head and stuck his bare heels into the carpet.

Jasper knelt so their eyes met. "Do you want Mummy to see you like that?"

Harry buried his chin in his neck. "She'll think I don't care."

"No, she won't. But you'll upset her dressed in dirty, blood-stained clothes."

"We'll stay here," said Clare. "If there's any change, we'll fetch you."

***

"Jasper!" A loud voice boomed in the small waiting room.

Jasper held a coffee between his hands and was staring at the carpet. Malcolm and Clare had been a godsend, fetching drinks and snacks and keeping Harry occupied. Oliver was as good as gold. He sat quietly in his pram, eyes wide, watching as if he knew what was going on.

Jasper was expecting the worse, and the doctor's grim face said it all.

"We couldn't save the baby. She was very small, and—"

Jasper didn't let him finish. "Kate?"

Harry had moved next to Jasper and held his hand.

"Weak. We can't move her. Lost a lot of blood. There's a problem with supply."

"You mean the hospital is dragging its heels."

"I didn't say that. It's a question of money we don't have." The doctor stared at an angry Jasper.

Jasper began to walk to the door with Harry running after him. "Fucking money. Tell whoever that Carmichael Enterprises will pay. Kate will have whatever she needs."

"Jasper, you must realise there's only so much we can do."

Jasper turned and marched to the doctor. "You'll send a minion to that fucking hospital and get whatever Kate needs. Do I make myself clear?"

He took a moment to calm before opening the door to Kate's room. A nurse appeared to be fitting a new blood transfusion bag. She blushed as if Jasper had caught her doing something she shouldn't. A syringe fell out of her hand and rolled under the bed.

Kate was as white as the bed sheets. She looked small in the bed.

Jasper's gaze rose to the beeping monitor.

Her blood pressure was low. Too low.

Harry raced to Kate's bedside and took her hand. Tears were streaming down his cheeks. He pulled up a chair. His wide blue eyes went from his mother to Jasper. He nervously began to swing his legs.

"What're you doing?" Jasper asked the nurse.

"Checking her fluids," she mumbled, somewhat embarrassed.

"What's this doing on the floor?" said Harry, holding up the syringe.

The nurse immediately sprinted towards the door, knocking Jasper off balance.

"Put that down, Harry."

The syringe fell to the floor.

Chapter Forty-Six

Jasper rolled over, extending his arm to cover Kate. His arm rested on empty sheets. He was half asleep when he realised Kate wasn't there.

He listened. He could have heard a pin drop. He staggered along the landing and carefully crept down the stairs, not wishing to wake Harry, who had become a light sleeper since Kate had returned from hospital. But Jasper's concern wasn't necessary. Harry had followed Jasper and his mother out of bed.

The kitchen was bathed in a warm glow from the work-surface lights. The kettle was still warm and Kate's favourite mug was missing.

Jasper hurried through the glass corridor that linked Kate's art studio to the house. She stood staring at the painting she was working on, holding the mug between her hands.

Jasper was concerned. It had only been five days since the doctor had reluctantly agreed that Kate could return, and that was on the proviso she had bed rest.

Kate had ignored that proviso. As soon as Harry went to school and Jasper to the office, Kate was up, either in the library reading the documents the previous owners of the house, the Isaacs, had left or painting. But more worryingly, Kate refused to talk about her miscarriage and subsequent hysterectomy.

"I know you're there." Her voice was soft and low.

"Kate. Talk to me," Jasper said, as he moved into the studio.

Unknown to Kate and Jasper, Harry had crept closer to the studio's glass door. It had one solid door, the rest were glass. Bulletproof glass. Jasper had explained to Harry that there were some nasty people who wished Kate harm.

Kate had been so happy when they had blindfolded her and marched her into the art studio. She had flung her arms round Jasper's neck and kissed him. Her happiness had been infectious; they had all laughed.

Tears rolled down Harry's cheeks. It had been the last time he'd seen his mother happy.

"There's nothing to talk about." Kate's words didn't appear to be coming from her.

"Tell me." Jasper's desperate words echoed in the still studio.

Kate walked to the bi-fold doors that led into the garden. She gazed into the night sky.

"You want me to spell it out?"

"Yes. Idiot's guide."

"I won't be enough now."

"What do you mean?" Jasper stepped further into the studio.

"I thought we'd have children until I couldn't have any more."

Jasper stood perfectly still, not daring to speak in case he said the wrong words. He had no idea how to handle this.

"I know Joanne was in your office. And then you went to visit. So, it follows, I'm not enough."

"Kate, this is not like you, jumping to conclusions. Joanne wants to expand her boutique business. The bank refused her a loan, so she asked me. I looked over the business plan, made a few suggestions. That's all." His words were rushed. He suspected they wouldn't reassure her.

Jasper waited for Kate to answer, but no answer came. He studied her reflection in the bi-fold doors. Tears were streaming down her cheeks and onto her night-robe.

"Hey," he said, placing his hands on her shoulders. He waited a long moment for her to react. "Joanne was just a fuck. Not a very good one. I haven't touched her since you came back." His hands slipped to her stomach and he nestled her into his bare chest. "I have quality in my arms. Why should I go looking for less?"

His lips caressed her neck.

"But I can't," she mumbled.

"If you're talking sex, there're other ways we can satisfy each other." He felt her lips soften into a half smile. "If you're talking children, you've given me two beautiful boys. I never thought I'd be a father. You did that for me." His voice had become loving, caring. "Have I told you how much you mean to me?"

"You've shown me many times."

It was Jasper's turn to smile.

"I'm not a man of many words, Kate. But my life wouldn't be worth living without you. You're the sun, moon and stars rolled into one. I want my Kate back. The Kate that had Wellsbury's great and good eating out of her hand. The Kate that had me when she smiled and flicked her hair back."

She turned, cupped his face and kissed him.

"For a man of not many words, you're doing pretty well." She paused, stomach churning. She had to ask, even if the answer would devastate her. "You don't mind that I can't have any more children?"

His lips brushed her ear and trailed along her

neck. He swallowed her delightful sighs as his mouth covered hers.

"I'm happy with two boys. I have no desire to see you in so much pain." Their eyes met; his fingers lightly caressed her forehead. "Bed?" he tentatively suggested.

She shook her head.

"Come." His voice was low and soft. He guided her to the chaise longue, which he had insisted on buying.

Her head was tucked into his shoulder. His fingers trailed up and down her back.

"You promised to tell me about Harry. When did you know you were pregnant?"

"I felt ill. I went to the doctors. A month later, Harry was born."

"You didn't know." Surprised, Jasper turned and stared at her.

"No morning sickness. Just a little bump. I was tired. I thought I was doing a lot of work on the cottage... I've struggled with my health since."

"Who looked after you?"

"The doctor and nurses were very supportive. They made sure I was well stocked with baby supplies. The local mums' group was very helpful. There's a lot of good second-hand stuff out there."

"Why didn't you come to me?"

She stopped and met his eyes. "I did. Your car was outside Joanne's... Kenny said you were there a lot... I just..."

"Just what?"

"Joanne was a good fit."

An uneasy silence settled between them. Jasper was thinking about how many times he'd fucked Joanne when he needed Kate.

"I must have driven past your cottage many times." His thoughts became words.

"I had no idea you had become an expert sailor," she said, trying to change the subject.

"It kept me away from Joanne. She had designs on becoming Mrs Carmichael."

A surprised look flashed across Kate's face.

"I looked for you," he said thoughtfully.

"We were meant to be apart. And then find one another."

"Don't go psychic on me. You know I don't believe in that crap."

Kate smiled. "One day, Jasper."

Their eyes melted with mutual desire. He pulled her into his arms. Mouths eagerly met, full of desire and promise.

"You know what I want?" he whispered. "I'll wait. Your call." Their foreheads touched. "When did you tell him I was his father?"

"I think he guessed the day you met."

"He's worried about you."

"I've never been ill. Just always there for him."

"He doesn't want to lose you."

"Does he know I care?" Jasper asked.

"I explained that I'd made a lot of bad choices and you weren't one. He knows you care, want the best for all of us. You will look after him, I mean, if anything happens to me."

Jasper stopped rubbing her back. A lump formed in his throat. He was holding back tears.

"He'll need you," Kate continued in a soft calm voice. "He'll need a strong hand to guide him." Her voice faulted.

Jasper felt a tear fall onto his bare chest. Deep sobs echoed through the studio.

"Harry!"

Harry, who had been sat on the floor of the glass corridor, listening, raced to his mother, squeezing himself onto the chaise longue.

"Are you going to die?" Harry choked. "I don't want you to die."

"No. She's not going to die." Jasper's voice was calm but firm. "We're going to make sure she does as the doctor says."

Harry looked into Jasper's eyes and nodded.

"I'll do the school run. And Mum will rest."

"Ok." Harry kissed Kate's cheek. "Love you." He stretched his small arms around both of them.

"Now let's get you back to bed," said Jasper, taking Harry into his arms.

"Do I still tell Mummy about school?" asked Harry, as Jasper was tucking him in.

"Might be a good idea to tell me while she's resting," Jasper answered, pausing as he turned to switch off the light.

"Harry, is there a problem at school?"

"Not really. It's just that nasty Nigel."

Jasper knelt by Harry's bed.

"He's saying things about Mum. About her losing the baby. 'Serves her right.' He pulled my arm."

Jasper's temper churned deep inside him. He'd have to deal with Nigel James.

He stroked Harry's head. "Leave Nigel to me. I'll sort it."

Chapter Forty-Seven

While Jasper was comforting Kate and Harry, Meredith Spencer was hitting golf balls into the night sky.

Meredith Spencer was no longer considered young. His sons had taken over the business and put him out to graze. But Meredith was spritely for his age. His tall frame was still straight, and his hips, back and legs could swing a golf club like a man half his age. He was practising his golf swing from the library balcony while Higgins, his trusted butler, sighed in despair as balls flew from the balcony, landing somewhere on the immaculate lawn. Someone would have to collect those balls before the gardener cut the grass; he feared it would be him.

"Sir," Higgins nervously uttered.

"Not now, Higgins. I'm busy."

Higgins stood statue-like just inside the balcony doors.

"If it's my sons, they can go to hell."

"Carmichael," Higgins stuttered.

The golf club slipped from Meredith's hand, hitting the stone balcony with a clatter.

"What did you say?"

"Carmichael, sir." Higgins took a step further inside the library, dropping a large brown envelope onto the small table next to Meredith's favourite chair.

"Carmichael, you say?"

The Carmichaels were a major client for

the Meredith Spencer Law Firm. Meredith had personal responsibility for the Carmichael trust fund.

"Tragic family, the Carmichaels," he mumbled as Higgins handed him a very large brandy. "Rich beyond all comprehension. Powerful enough to influence government policy."

He opened the envelope, emptying the contents onto his table. He sipped his brandy, and to Higgins' surprise, his hands were shaking. He stared at the photograph of Jasper Carmichael.

"Jasper Carmichael," he said in a shaky voice. "They all have the same features: a head full of thick black hair—though Jasper's seems to be greying already—staring blue eyes and a smile you never say no too." His aged, thin fingers touched the photograph.

"He," he continued, pointing to Jasper, "he is a bastard. And his dad, Colin, had the audacity to name him Jasper." Meredith's voice rose in disgust. "Only the firstborn son should have the privilege of that name. Colin was the youngest son of my friend Jasper. Colin was wild, confident, handsome, charismatic, clever, spoke several languages. His siblings envied him and hated him. He was just sixteen when he went to Holland to rescue diamonds."

Meredith held his glass out for Higgins to refill. "Married money. He didn't love her. Not enough excitement in married life for Colin. All changed after his mother died. He blamed his dad, who was fucking a younger woman, Alice—good-looking woman." Meredith paused to sip his brandy. "Rumour has it that Colin fucked her the day she married his dad." Meredith's finger hit the photograph. "This Jasper is their love child."

He swished his brandy around the brandy

bowl, wondering if Jasper had inherited any of Colin's dark side. The police had tried to bring a number of murder cases against Colin, but Meredith had always managed to get rid of vital evidence. Until Colin double-crossed that South American, Anton.

"Stepmother and stepson," mumbled Higgins in disgust as he busied himself dusting the crystal wine glasses.

"Jasper Senior had business in America, and Alice didn't want to join him. It was while he was away that she gave birth. Colin was supposed to get rid of the baby, but as usual, he had other ideas. His son was brought up by one of his whores." Meredith paused thoughtfully. "Colin was a cad, but above all he was a master diamond thief."

Higgins spluttered, not believing his ears. In all the years he had worked for Meredith, he had never heard such a story.

"What's happened?" Meredith glared at Higgins.

"You know he's married?"

Meredith scoffed as he flicked through the photographs of Kate, Harry and Oliver. He took a long moment staring at the Isaacs House. "The Isaacs watched over Jasper like guardian angels. They contacted Colin when Jasper got in trouble. He kept a close eye on his favourite son."

"Do you think this is the reason?" Higgins held a photo of Kate's ring.

Meredith was spellbound.

"Apparently the work of Zak Cohen," Higgins added. "He has orders to replicate the design."

"It's not the design but the diamond. Even in a photograph you can see how it reflects the light." Meredith considered the photo. "Colin was a diamond expert."

Meredith moved his thoughtful gaze to Higgins. "No wonder Colin was so interested in his bloody son. He has the diamonds."

He walked to the balcony doors. "I'm betting he's in league with Zak Cohen—he's a bastard as well. The Cohens kicked him out years ago."

"He has a jeweller's in Jasper's shopping centre. Doing very well by all accounts."

"You're well informed, Higgins."

"I've been making a few enquiries. Renewing old acquaintances."

"I wonder if he has Colin's black book?"

"It's highly likely, I'd say."

"Is he fucking around?"

"No, my contact tells me."

"Jasper Carmichael is already a rich man."

"When are you going to tell him he's the last heir to the Carmichael fortune?" asked Higgins.

Meredith shook his head. He couldn't contemplate giving control of the Carmichael trust fund to a Carmichael bastard.

"What about the diamonds? Are you going to the police?" Higgins' interest was piqued.

"Not on your life. The Carmichaels owe me for all the dirty secrets I've buried. I've waited too many years for Colin's diamonds to turn up. There's only Lawson alive who knew about the diamonds, and he has Jasper firmly in his sights."

It was Higgins' turn to shake his head.

"Weekly reports, Higgins. Only to me. I don't want my sons knowing about this." Meredith walked over to his desk and pulled open the top drawer. A wad of notes skidded across the desk. "This should tide you over. Let me know when it's gone. Remember: money talks, Higgins."

Higgins walked back to his little office and slid the wad of notes into the bottom drawer of his desk.

In all the years he had worked for Meredith Spencer, he had never seen this side of him. The Carmichael trust fund had given Meredith and his family a good life, and he had no intention of giving it up. The knowledge that he was swindling Jasper out of his inheritance and a considerable amount of money didn't sit well with Higgins.

And then there was the question of the diamonds. Meredith Spencer had succumbed to greed.

***

Zak Cohen strolled through Carmichael's open-plan office with an air of authority. He stopped at Jasper's office. A concerned expression fixed upon his face as he looked at Jasper with his head in his hands.

It must be Kate, Zak thought.

Jasper looked up. "What do you want Zak? Have we got a problem?"

Zak dropped a card on his desk.

Meredith Spencer Law.

Contact: Nigel James.

"They're all over the place. Do you know Meredith?" Zak said.

"Should I?"

"Nigel's revelling—a top-notch lawyer making enquiries about Jasper Carmichael, using him as a go between."

"He's a pain in the arse. Upsetting Harry. Daren't tell Kate."

"How is she?"

"Not good. She should still be in hospital. But it's the kids."

"You mean Harry?"

Jasper gave Zak a very deep stare.

Zak poured himself a coffee and settled into the chair opposite Jasper. "Meredith Spencer was, and still is, a Carmichael lawyer. He and your grandfather were great buddies. Your grandfather had four sons—Colin was the youngest. You're the love child of Colin and his second wife, Alice."

Jasper leaned back into his chair. Could this day get any worse?

"Colin fucked his stepmother and I'm the result." His uninterested tone surprised Zak.

"Colin agreed to get rid of you, but instead you were brought up by one of his whores. He even named you Jasper Carmichael. Only the eldest son of the family has the name Jasper. When Meredith found out what Colin had done, your grandfather was hopping mad."

"Hang on. I remember Colin bringing an old gentleman to see me."

Zak nodded. "Colin's brothers were all dead: accident, drugs, suicide. Colin was the only son alive. Whatever life Colin had abruptly ended. When the old man died, Colin became head of the Carmichaels and their fortune. Moved into the ancestral home, took the Carmichael's place in the Freemasons and was active on various political committees. But Meredith was in charge of the money. No one trusted Colin with money. Your grandfather made a trust and many of your cousins live off it. I bet you're included."

"Meredith Spencer runs a Carmichael trust fund." Zak had finally got through to Jasper. "I've got cousins. Ancestral home," commented Jasper in a surprisingly uncaring tone.

"The Carmichael Trust runs the house. There's a farm but that's run separately as a business. I'm guessing you're the Carmichael that should be living in the ancestral home, overseeing the trust fund and farm."

"Is Colin dead?"

"Yes. Not sure about Alice. When your grandfather died, she went to America. She wasn't mentioned in his will—revenge for fucking Colin. But she's done well for herself. Married into oil."

"How do you know all this?"

"Old Man Cohen rang me. Decided it was time to reconcile, said he doesn't have long left. He wanted you to know about Meredith and your inheritance before he dies."

"I'm not interested in Meredith or the Carmichael inheritance," Jasper snapped.

"You should be. Meredith is a cunning, ruthless character. He won't let go of the Carmichael trust fund without a fight. Using Nigel as a go-between complicates matters."

"He better lay off Kate."

"You can't solve this problem like you used to. It's time to fight them at their own game." Zak searched his inside pocket. "Give Kate these. They match her ring."

Jasper cradled a pair of diamond earrings. He smiled. "Come round Sunday. Join us for lunch."

Chapter Forty-Eight

Jasper was having trouble sleeping. He had tried to hide his concern about the story Zak had told him. He had no idea if it was true, but he had no inclination to dig into Colin's past. What's more he was reluctant to share Zak's story with Kate; he had no idea how she would react, but he was confident she suspected something was wrong. However, he couldn't go on like this; he needed sleep—his work was suffering. So after another sleepless night, he told her Zak's story.

"What are you going to do?" she tentatively asked.

"Nothing."

She raised her eyebrows, but after a few moments of consideration, she agreed that nothing was the best policy. However, she added that there was more to the Carmichael saga. He smiled at her use of the word 'saga'.

He rolled over, needing to touch her. But she wasn't there. He hadn't felt her leave the bed; he must have dropped off.

He pulled on a T-shirt and boxers and went in search. The kitchen work-surface lights were on, the kettle warm and Kate's favourite mug missing.

He stopped in his tracks when he saw a light shining under his study door. Kate was at his desk, hunched over his laptop.

Their eyes met.

"I didn't want to wake you," she said. "I can't

get the relationship between Meredith Spencer and Nigel out of my mind."

"Kate, come to bed."

"It was always a mystery to me why we left the house and moved to the shop. It was like World War Two when I tried to talk about it."

"You're not making sense."

Jasper picked up the laptop and stared at the page she was reading: Meredith Spencer Law.

"I've come across that name before," she said. "Who did you buy the house from?"

"Kate, that was a long time ago. I can't remember."

"I never came across the house sale when I was going through your files. I would have remembered."

"I bought it not long after we moved here. Don and Milly needed somewhere to live."

"And the house was on the market?" she asked.

Jasper put the laptop back on his desk and sat opposite Kate. "No. I believe it was a private sale. I was buying properties that needed refurbishment. Buy cheap, sell at top price. We made money very quickly."

"Did they go through the books?"

"Not all of them. I was having cash-flow problems. Any profit went into buying more houses. Some cash sales never went through the books." Jasper stared at her, his mind going back to his first few months at Wellsbury. "I remember I bought the mansion with cash."

"What about my family home?"

"I think it was Don who said the owner had money problems." Jasper's words were slow and thoughtful.

"Did you meet the owner?"

"No. Don dealt with it. I gave him the cash."

"You made that much money?" Kate said incredulously.

"Wellsbury was a town in decline. You must remember—no jobs. I had builders, plumbers, electricians fighting over jobs."

"All I remember is that I was desperate to leave the place," Kate said. "Nothing was the same after Mother died. My father didn't care for her or me."

"Did Reynolds gamble?"

"I don't know. He went out a lot... They never talked about anything in front of me. We pretended to be a happy family."

"Tell me about Nigel," Jasper said, opening his safe and lifting out a wad of papers.

"Not much to tell. James Solicitors looked after Dad's business. When Nigel's father died, he took over."

Kate stared at Jasper as he flicked through the papers. He pulled a brown envelope from the wad. *Last Will and Testament of Laura Reynolds nee Spencer. Solicitor: Meredith Spencer Law.*

Kate's mouth opened. Jasper moved close to her so they both could read it.

Kate couldn't believe what she was reading. "Mother left the house to me."

"And that bastard sold it to me."

Jasper returned to the papers.

"What're you looking for?"

"The fucking deeds."

The last entry: *Sold to Jasper Carmichael.*

"The house was built by John Stanley. Heard of him?"

"A rich Victorian. He had a hand in building the old school and the slum houses."

Sold to Meredith Spencer.

"It was in the Stanley family until Meredith Spencer bought it."

"Where have those papers come from?"

"Nigel's safe."

Kate made no comment. As far as she was concerned, Nigel deserved everything Jasper gave him.

"Do you think I'm related to Meredith Spencer?"

***

Sleep had evaded Meredith Spencer since he'd seen Kate's photo, the one he was holding in his hand. Kate was smiling, her head to one side, her blonde hair free. The smile, the hair—she was a mirror image of Laura.

"Golf today, sir?" asked a stern-voiced Higgins.

"Do you know who this is?" Meredith's despondent gaze remained on the photo.

Higgins looked at the photo. "Kate Carmichael, sir."

"My granddaughter."

Higgins' old legs buckled, and he sought a chair to steady himself.

"Laura, her mother, was my dirty secret. I supported her and her mother until Laura went off to college. She was something—beautiful, smart. I wanted her to join the firm; she would have run rings around my sons. But she met Reynolds. Put her in the family way. I refused her the security she deserved. Called her a whore. She was far from that. I did make sure she had a roof over her head. He turned out to be the evil bastard I suspected."

Higgins was now sitting in a chair as his employer rambled on.

"I've kept a distant eye on Kate. I thought

history was repeating when that scum fucked her, but she lost the child. She seemed to be attracted to the rough type when she got involved with Jasper Carmichael, Colin's bastard son. She has two sons and is recovering from a nasty miscarriage. I'm regretting contacting Nigel James—his reports are full of hatred for Kate and she doesn't deserve it."

"What about Carmichael?" Higgins muttered, trying to regain his composure.

"He's in love with her. There's no greater force than love."

"But his reputation..."

"He was heading to jail. Rightly so—he's done some bad crimes. But Kate's turned him. Her gentleness, love, loyalty have rescued the Carmichael good qualities."

"What about the diamonds?"

"There's no doubt in my mind that Jasper has Colin's diamonds and he has some sort of understanding with Zak Cohen."

Meredith dropped Kate's photo onto the side table.

"May I make a suggestion, sir?"

Meredith glared at Higgins. How dare an employee make suggestions to him!

But Higgins wasn't deterred. "Go and see her."

Chapter Forty-Nine

Jasper stood gazing out of the floor-to-ceiling window. He wasn't looking at anything in particular. His mind was somewhat fussed. The report on Meredith Spencer had disturbed him. How was he going to tell Kate that Meredith Spencer was her grandfather?

The doctors had given her the all-clear to restart her life, starting today. Her spontaneous morning kiss had stirred him. She had leapt out of bed giggling, excited. He caught her hand. She stopped and their eyes danced. She smiled.

"Kiss me," she said seriously.

It was a passionate, slow kiss, full of desire and promise. Her mouth was warm and soft.

"We shouldn't," he'd whispered.

"We should," she'd answered, pulling him back to bed.

He felt his designer trousers become uncomfortably tight. Just the thought of being inside her did this.

Jasper was late for his morning walk to the shopping centre. He didn't care about being late and reorganising his day. He had renewed his lovemaking with Kate after losing their daughter. She had missed him, and she showed him by how much.

He was smiling as he approached the unit that no one was interested in. It was a large corner unit opposite Zak's jeweller's and a coffee shop that had just opened. A golf buggy caught his eye; it was heading straight for him. It was Kate. She leapt off the buggy and raced towards him, planting a soft kiss on his cheek. His heart skipped a beat. *What does she want?* he thought. *Whatever it is, she's got it.*

He was putty in her hands as they walked towards the unit.

"You know the council shut the library," she said.

Jasper remembered Kate had been incensed by the closure.

"Well, I have an idea! I could open a book shop." Her excitement was infectious. "Part of which would be for people to borrow books and another section to sell books."

Jasper took a long moment thinking about Kate's proposition; he thought it an impossible scheme. But Kate had always managed the impossible.

"What do you want from me?"

She planted another kiss on his cheek, but she lingered with this one. A kiss full of promise.

"Any more kisses and we'll christen the unit," he said.

***

Meredith Spencer sat outside the coffee shop opposite Kate's latest enterprise. Higgins had explained it was being converted into a book shop and gallery. The shop would sell and loan books, and the gallery was for Kate's paintings. Meredith was keen to view Kate's paintings as by all accounts she was talented, having sold a number of her works to Americans. However, Meredith considered the book project doomed.

He continued to sip his excellent cappuccino

and recalled Jasper's luxurious hotel. He inwardly congratulated the man on a job well done. No expense had been spared: marble floors, chandeliers, immaculate staff, but above all, excellent food.

And then he recalled those awful men talking about his granddaughter. He had been lounging in one of the many overstuffed white leather chairs, enjoying the cigar and brandy that were included with his meal. His attention was piqued when he heard her name.

"Kate Reynolds has always been well thought of," said a man with his back towards Meredith. "She takes after her mother, not that bastard of a father."

"She married Carmichael," said the other, with so much venom in his voice Meredith shivered.

"You're angry that she chose Carmichael. Get over it."

"Have you got over him?"

"I'll see Carmichael gets his just desserts."

Meredith was itching to turn around, but he had guessed the two men were Nigel James and Lawson.

"She'll be at that empty unit that Carmichael can't get rid of," mentioned Lawson matter-of-factly. "Apparently he's given it to her to do as she pleases. Book shop. My source told me that she had a humdinger with the council when they shut the library."

"She's on a mission, then."

"Bitten off more than she can chew," remarked Lawson.

"Not Kate. That's why she's well liked: she makes the impossible possible. Look what she did with the flower shop! When she came back, it was ready for closing. I had my eyes on the property, but she turned the fucker round."

And that's how Meredith Spencer found himself sipping coffee opposite the empty unit. Nigel and Lawson had taken a seat just in front of him, but he wasn't interested in them; the group of workmen that had collected outside the unit had his complete attention. A golf buggy stopped, and Kate threw a bunch of keys to a bear of a man who caught them, grinning. He walked to the buggy and lifted her out with one arm. She smiled and looped her arm around his neck.

"Boys," he said, "this is our boss, Kate Carmichael."

He placed her on the ground, and she walked over to the crew, taking her time shaking every workman's hand.

"She looks well fucked," said Lawson so everyone could hear.

"Shut your foul mouth," shouted Nigel.

Kate diverted her gaze, but the bear of a man was by her side, whispering so only she could hear.

Meredith was starting to feel a little anxious. Lawson's comment had served only one purpose: to anger Nigel. Meredith's stomach calmed when Jasper appeared. He was tall, his full head of dark hair showing signs of greying. Meredith had no need to see his eyes when he flashed the Carmichael smile at Kate—he knew they were blue.

"I've ordered some materials," said the bear of a man, walking towards Jasper, who had his arm around Kate.

"She told you about the arch linking the books to the gallery?"

The bear smiled.

"Glass dividing door?"

"Aye, she's been thorough," said the bear.

"Gallery walls smooth, an off-white colour? Kidney-shaped counter?" Jasper continued.

"What should I do first?"

Jasper, quick as lightning, put a finger over Kate's mouth. "Gallery. Mrs Carmichael has an exhibition to organise."

The bear of a man laughed when Jasper claimed Kate's mouth.

By this time, a crowd had gathered outside the coffee shop, including the local press. Jasper and Kate hadn't noticed. They had only eyes for each other while Jasper stroked her hair.

Jealousy consumed Nigel as he glared at Jasper's hand stroking Kate's hair. He went to stand up, but Lawson's arm shot across the table, gripping Nigel's.

"Not now. Our revenge will come soon enough."

Nigel glared at Lawson, temper flaring, eyes bulging. He threw Lawson's arm to one side.

"She's mine. I've waited too long. I should have fucked her while Old Man Reynolds was alive."

"Don't find excuses. You were too busy fucking Michelle. And you weren't interested until she inherited the shop." Lawson grinned. "She's aged better than Michelle," he added.

Lawson hadn't noticed Nigel push his chair to one side and run towards Kate. His punch hit Kate's cheek with such force it momently knocked Kate and Jasper off balance.

"You fuckin' whore!" Nigel shouted at the top of his voice.

Lawson pushed through the gathering crowd and stood between Jasper and Nigel.

"You deserve everything you get, Carmichael," he snarled, gripping Nigel's arm.

The bear of a man appeared with a wet towel

and placed it on Kate's red cheek.

"Hold on to Kate for me." Jasper's voice was unusually calm.

"No. I'll deal with a woman hitter," growled the bear. "Like hitting women, do you?"

"What's it to do with you?" Nigel's voice echoed towards the crowd. "You fuckin' her as well?"

"Bruce!" Jasper shouted. "I need you here, not in jail."

Unbeknown to Bruce, Inspector Watts, accompanied by six officers was hurrying towards the crowd.

Meredith Spencer found this sort of behaviour unseemly and distasteful. He would have to do something; this man had hit his granddaughter. He heaved himself up and approached the crowd.

"May I be of some assistance?"

The crowd turned and stared at Meredith.

"I saw the whole incident," he continued in his best superior voice.

Inspector Watts turned. *What's a man like you doing in Wellsbury?* he thought.

"Let me through!" shouted a small voice.

Harry, still dressed in his school uniform, was pushing his way through the crowd. He stopped in his tracks and stared at his mother holding the damp towel to her cheek and Jasper with a supportive arm around her.

"Who did this?" Harry demanded, his watery eyes scanning the crowd.

At that moment, Nigel and Harry's eyes met. Harry's expression morphed into one of Carmichael hatred.

Lawson, who was watching Harry, gasped. The face he saw was a young Jasper's, the day Lawson accused him of killing the newsagent.

Kate took Harry's hand. He looked into his

mother's eyes, tears running down his cheek.

"I'll kill him," he uttered.

Kate knelt by her son. "You shouldn't say things like that."

"I don't mean now, but when I'm bigger."

Kate, still holding Harry's hand, walked towards the inspector, who was talking to Nigel.

"I would be grateful," Kate interrupted, "Inspector, if one of your men would call tomorrow. I'll give a statement; you can have a copy of the video and hospital report."

She turned away. Nigel leapt towards her, gripping her shoulder. The atmosphere suddenly became charged with anticipation; Jasper's sudden bursts of violent temper were well known.

Jasper forcibly snatched Nigel's hand off Kate's shoulder. In one swift move, Jasper's hands tightened around Nigel's neck.

Lawson's gasp echoed. He had witnessed Jasper's temper accompanied by that angry, hateful expression with dead eyes and mouth tightly closed before. Lawson knew only too well what was about to follow. Inspector Watts raced towards the two men.

But it wasn't the inspector or Lawson's gasp that caught Jasper's attention, but a gentle hand on his shoulder and a soft murmuring in his ear.

"Not now, my love."

She had never referred to him as her love. A sideways glance, and he met his wife's loving green eyes. His grip on Nigel's neck slackened.

The inspector moved closer and Lawson held his breath. The crowd was so quiet that you could have heard a pin drop.

Kate gently caressed her husband's face. He turned his head into her hand, his eyes momently closing as his hands dropped from Nigel's neck.

Nigel fell to the ground, coughing and spluttering, gasping undistinguishable venomous words at Jasper.

"I'd shut up if I was you, Mr James," said the inspector.

"Run him in," Nigel choked.

"You both should thank Mrs Carmichael."

Eyes turned to Jasper and Kate. Harry had joined them, and Jasper held him in his arms. Kate kissed Harry's forehead while her hand ran through Jasper's hair.

Meredith Spencer couldn't believe his eyes. He had never witnessed the like; his granddaughter had so much power over a man like Carmichael. The power of love, which they both shared with so much depth and intensity.

Chapter Fifty

Harry sat on Jasper's lap, head nestled in his father's shoulder. His tears had subsided. The soft touch of Jasper's hand stroking Harry's hair was having the desired effect: sleep.

The waiting room doors swung open. Kate's eyes settled on father and son. Jasper went to stand but Kate shook her head. She kissed Harry's forehead, and his sleepy eyes slowly opened. A smile crept across his face.

"Home," she whispered.

The doctor appeared, carrying a folder. "A copy of my report."

It was Harry's hand that clutched the folder.

***

Jasper didn't argue when Kate tried to make light of her bruised cheek and black eye. She wasn't going to admit how much pain she was in, or that she couldn't wait to get home to take her painkillers.

Clare and Malcolm were waiting. They refrained from asking questions when they saw Jasper's scowl and tight lips. He brushed past them on his way to Harry's bedroom while Kate took Oliver from Clare's arms. He had obviously been crying from the colour of his cheeks, but he smiled at Kate while his chubby hands tried to grab her hair.

She didn't hear Jasper join them in the kitchen.

Kate was too occupied with swirling effervescent painkillers around half a glass of water.

"We should talk," he said in a tone that made Clare grab Oliver and hurry from the kitchen. "I want to kill him. He deserves nothing less. I knew you were in pain." They stared at one another, each trying to read the other's eyes. "You can't hide things from me, Kate."

"Back at you," she calmly murmured.

"But you were right to stop me. Not the time or place."

"I could have just been plain selfish. I couldn't cope with you being in prison, the strain of a trial." Her green eyes flickered, and her lips formed a half smile.

"There's not a selfish bone in your body," he calmly said, taking a step towards her.

"I think we should grab a couple of blankets and gaze at the stars." Her eyes watered as she cringed at the sharp pain when she tried to smile.

***

Meanwhile, a stubborn Harry was searching the house. "Where are they? I'm not going to school until you tell me," his small voice shouted in defiance.

Malcolm nodded towards the terrace. Harry pulled open the bi-fold doors. Jasper was just making sure Kate was warmly wrapped. Harry silently tiptoed over to his mother. He glanced up at Jasper, who had his finger over his lips.

"She'll be okay?" asked Harry, as Clare checked his school bag.

"Do you want to know what will make her very happy?"

Harry nodded.

"You coming home with gold stars and an empty lunch box." She grinned.

Harry jumped off his stool and raced to Clare, stretching his arms around her thick waist.

***

It was mid-morning by the time Kate walked into the kitchen carrying the blankets.

"Have they gone?" she sleepily asked, reaching for a glass.

"Food first," said Clare, taking the glass from Kate's hand. "There's some soft toast, and I'll make a fresh pot of tea."

An hour later, Kate lay on her chaise longue gazing out of the studio's bi-fold doors. Oliver was busy playing, throwing his toys at the bars of his playpen.

"You have a visitor," Clare tentatively said. "Should I send him away?"

"No," said Kate, thinking it would be the inspector.

To her surprise a tall, distinguished-looking elderly man stood behind Clare.

"Meredith Spencer."

Kate went to stand.

"No, no," Meredith said, pulling up a chair.

Oliver glared at Meredith, shaking the bars of his playpen.

"I have a rather urgent matter that I must talk to you about," Meredith began, finding himself unusually nervous. "I have a story I must tell you. I will start at the very beginning, when I'd just qualified as a lawyer. I was in a hurry to own my own practice. The quickest route was to marry into a law family, if you follow my thinking. She was a lovely woman. She gave me two boys.

But I didn't love her. And to be perfectly honest, I longed to be swept away by love. Then one lunchtime, I was having lunch with a group of colleagues, and there she was, writing down our order."

He paused while Clare placed a tray of tea and cake onto a small antique wooden table next to Kate.

"She captivated me. Her sparkling green eyes, a smile that lit the room, and the manner in which she flicked her long hair back." He stopped to sip his tea. "Does this sound familiar?"

Kate nodded as she carefully chewed on a mouthful of cake.

"My affair with Helen went on until she died. We had a girl. Oh, how I loved her! She was everything my boys weren't. Clever, kind, caring. She went off to Oxford. I don't know how or when she met Reynolds, but that bastard made her pregnant. In a mad fit of temper, I said things I shouldn't have. She left and never returned. Her mother persuaded me to at least put a roof over her head."

"The house we lived in," Kate thoughtfully murmured.

"You're just like her. The same sparkling green eyes, the irresistible smile and the flick of the head. I fell in love with her when she smiled and flicked her long blonde hair. I'm sure Jasper did too."

Kate had been so enthralled by Meredith's story that she hadn't noticed Jasper enter the room. He confidently strode towards her, planting a soft kiss in her hair. Kate wasn't surprised to see him. Clare had brought three cups with the tea.

"I did fall in love with her when she smiled and

flicked her long blonde hair. I didn't know it at the time; I was so wrapped up in my own selfish needs. What's that saying? 'You don't know what you have until you don't have it.' I've been there. I know what it's like to have a life without a purpose. To gaze into the abyss, wallowing in your own self-pity because you let the one you love fall through your fingers. What do you want, Meredith?"

An uncomfortable silence filled the studio.

"I don't suppose you'll believe me if I said to meet my granddaughter?"

Jasper scoffed in disbelief.

"I worked for your grandfather, Jasper—a self-made man rich beyond dreams. He wielded power like waving a wand. He had four sons. Colin, your father was the bonus, if you like. His mother ruined him. Spoilt beyond recognition. When she died, Colin went off the rails. It didn't help that Jasper was having an affair with a younger woman, Alice. The story has it that Colin fucked her the day she married your grandfather. I was there the day you were born. Colin had agreed to get rid of you. It was obvious that he didn't care for you or Alice. But he had me fooled. He took you to that filthy gangland-ridden area to be brought up by that whore." Meredith couldn't hide the disdain from his voice. "And now! You claim to love my blood."

"If you were so concerned about your blood, why didn't you rescue her from Eric and that evil bastard Reynolds? You didn't care. You didn't know you had a granddaughter." Jasper's angry voice made Kate grab his sleeve.

"I know what you're really like," Meredith said. "I know what you've done. Colin got you off the hook. No doubt he called in many favours.

Lawson knows." Meredith momently paused while he gathered his thoughts. "Do you know why he sent you to Wellsbury? He knew the place. The airfield you own was the one used to bring in the Dutch diamonds. Colin knew the streets of Wellsbury. No doubt he visited every dive in this godforsaken place. He visited this house; the Isaacs worked for him. Their job being to keep an eye on you and his precious diamonds."

The air was filled with a venomous tension.

Meredith broke it with a slightly calmer tone. "You have Colin's diamonds. That's why Colin had the Isaacs keep an eye on you. But before he could claim them back, he found himself the head of the Carmichael clan. His brothers were all dead. Jasper was a broken man, but he insisted that his blood was head of the Carmichaels. Colin and his family moved into the ancestral castle, took his place in the Freemason Lodge and various political groups, his son and diamonds taking second place to his new responsibilities. And you!" Meredith pointed his finger at Jasper. "A murderer, fraudster, money launderer. What crime haven't you committed? You are not fit to call yourself a Carmichael. And you!" Meredith looked at Kate. "You're not fit to have my Laura's blood flowing through your veins. You married this scum. Had his children. Every time I think of him touching you, I want to be sick."

"I think you'd better leave," said Kate sternly, glancing over at Oliver, who sat mesmerised by what was going on.

"I haven't finished."

"I think you have," retorted an angry Jasper.

"You have the diamonds. You're in cahoots with that scum Zak Cohen. I don't care how you're fencing Colin's diamonds, but I want five million."

"For?"

"Keeping my mouth shut."

"Or you'll do what?" Jasper stepped closer to Meredith.

"With what I know, I'll put you behind bars. You'll never see your precious Kate again."

Meredith turned and walked out of the studio.

***

It was past midnight when there was a gentle tap on the studio doors. Jasper sat without a light, sipping a very large malt and staring into darkness, his mind focused on Meredith Spencer. Kate had long gone to bed.

"Mr Carmichael?" said a nervous voice. "It's Higgins."

Jasper slid the bi-fold doors open, and Higgins took a step inside.

He was struggling with a large, heavy box. "I had no idea how much stuff there was."

Jasper took the box from him and placed it on Kate's workbench.

"I can't stay long. He'll know I'm missing."

"I'm sorry, Higgins—I don't know what you're talking about."

"I'm Meredith Spencer's butler. He has to be stopped. I think he's going mad."

Jasper looked at the box. "And that is?"

"All the information he has on the Carmichaels and your charming wife."

Jasper guided Higgins to a chair and poured him a large malt.

"He was always jealous of your grandfather. He thought he was better than him, but he wasn't. Nowhere near. He fancied his chances with Jasper's second wife, but Colin beat him to it.

Colin was wild. No respect for anything or anyone.

"Meredith tried to blackmail Colin into giving him a cut of the diamonds. It didn't happen. I reckon Colin had something on him. Probably his affair and Laura. If anyone found out, it would have ruined him." Higgins paused to regain his breath. "I can't stand by and let him ruin your lives. I must go—I have a long drive."

"Where's your car?" asked Jasper, somewhat puzzled.

"Through the hedge at the bottom of the garden."

"I'll walk you," offered Jasper.

Chapter Fifty-One

Inspector Watts strolled into Kate's gallery. He stopped in the doorway, briefly mesmerised by the light streaming through the new glass roof. Paintings were being hung on the off-white walls. The inspector couldn't decide if the floor was marble. Bruce, the bear, was barking instructions to his team. Kate had just picked up Oliver and placed him on the kidney-shaped counter.

"Inspector. To what do I owe this visit?" she said, in her calm, soft voice.

"What a change, Mrs Carmichael," he commented approvingly.

"Inspector, you didn't come here to praise my gallery."

The inspector smiled. "No. Business, I'm afraid." He paused, gathering his thoughts. "A Meredith Spencer visited?"

Kate nodded.

"What did he want?"

"You'll have to ask him, Inspector." The inspector raised his eyebrows. "It was private and personal."

"Meredith Spencer is dead, Mrs Carmichael."

"Dead? When? How?!" Kate stuttered.

"Higgins found him lying on his balcony with a golf club in his hand." It was Kate's turn to raise her eyebrows. "He practised his golf swing on the balcony."

An ashen Kate pulled a high stool towards

her and sat on it to steady herself. "What do you want from me, Inspector?"

"Why did he come to see you?"

"In a nutshell: he claimed I'm his granddaughter. He had a long-time affair; my mother was the result. She was the apple of his eye, until she went to uni and met Reynolds. Then she had me. Meredith disowned his daughter, but made sure she had somewhere to live."

"Did you believe him?"

"That's immaterial." The inspector raised his eyebrows. "I want to remember my mother with my memories, not a bitter old man's. If he was so concerned, he would have come to see me sooner."

"You're in his will. Laura's daughter, Kate Carmichael. But I'll put that to one side. Meredith controlled the Carmichaels' finances. Most of the ancestral home is run by the Carmichael Trust. The Carmichael cousins have a good life off the trust fund. Of course, there's the farm, but that's run as a separate business.

"The thing is, Mrs Carmichael, Meredith denied Jasper his birthright. The trustees of the fund will be contacting him."

"You're well informed, Inspector."

"I have friends in high places. The trustees are divided. Some want a Carmichael back in control, arguing that Jasper has the bloodline. Others want nothing to do with Jasper—he's Colin's son, with a reputation to match. Such a man can't be in control of the Carmichaels' fortune. Don't you agree, Mrs Carmichael? A murderer, fraudster and money launderer can't be in control of such a fortune." The inspector became animated when he talked about Jasper. "He has a network—people owe him, he calls in favours. I look around this gallery that's been finished in record time... What rules have been broken? Money passed, favours called in to buy the materials?" The inspector's eyes settled on the floor.

"I'll tell you what type of bloke Jasper Carmichael is." Bruce's loud voice filled the gallery. Unbeknown to the inspector, he had been listening to his mini tirade. "He looks after his men. Pays on time. A boss that brings bacon butties and tea when it's cold. Sits by a brazier warming his hands. Listens to complaints. He's the best. And you say a man like that wouldn't be good for the Carmichael fortune?"

Kate slipped off the stool and lifted Oliver off the counter. Oliver had been so good Kate had almost forgotten he was there.

"I think you should leave, Inspector," she firmly said.

"I could get you and Jasper down the station," he retorted, equally firmly.

Kate eased her phone from her jeans pocket. Two missed calls and four text messages.

"Who're you calling, Mrs Carmichael?" the inspector sneered. "Your husband?"

"Her husband's here, Inspector." Jasper's voice was controlled and measured. "And we'll attend any station with our solicitors present."

Oliver reached out to Jasper, who lifted him from his mother's arms.

Chapter Fifty-Two

Nigel James sat outside the George, smoking a joint, his eyes glued on the Carmichael Centre. He knew she was at the gallery and Watts was questioning her. Every customer carried some news about her and Carmichael.

"I wish you'd stop smoking those," said Lawson, slipping into the seat next to Nigel. "Come inside."

"Meredith no doubt told her."

"Does it matter?" commented Lawson.

"He was my last meal ticket. I should have fucked her before Reynolds kicked the bucket."

"It's all too late." Lawson kept his voice sympathetic as he didn't want to upset Nigel.

"Those were the days. Michelle couldn't get enough. When I told her of my plan for Kate, she went ape-shit. I had money from Anton, Reynolds and Meredith. Anton and Meredith paid for information. Reynolds was blackmail."

Lawson slowly turned his head and stared at Nigel. "Blackmail?"

"He knocked her about, Kate's mother. I threatened to tell Meredith. Reynolds paid me to keep quiet."

"You bastard," said a shocked Lawson.

"Carmichael would agree with you. But if Michelle hadn't stopped me, I would be married to Kate, have my fingers in the shop money—and the money Meredith undoubtedly has left her." Nigel took a long drag on his joint. "Instead, my business is going under. Michelle won't fuck and Beth is having my baby."

Lawson stood, pushing the chair away with some force. "I hate Carmichael, but he would get off his ass and do something. I suggest you do the same."

"Fuck off, old man. Kate Carmichael will pay. I'll have my pound of flesh," Nigel sneered.

"What're you going to do?"

"Fuck her, of course."

Lawson left Nigel wallowing in self-pity and re-joined the crowd in the George. The conversation was all about Kate and the gallery. How Jasper spoilt her. Most agreed that she deserved it; they remembered how Reynolds treated her, how she'd saved his business. And now Lawson knew why Reynolds had treated her so badly: Nigel had been blackmailing him, and if Kate had found out, Reynolds would have been toast. Lawson couldn't stand blackmailers. As far as he was concerned, they were the lowest of the low.

Lawson left the George by the side door. He walked into the Carmichael Centre and purchased a burner phone from one of the cheap shops that were taking advantage of Jasper's low rents.

He put a handkerchief over the phone and dialled Jasper's home number. His message was short.

"Protect Kate. She's in danger," Lawson managed between coughs.

He dropped the phone in a waste bin and continued window-shopping.

***

Jasper was still with Kate at the gallery. She

had flounced off to supervise the hanging of her paintings after refusing to talk about Inspector Watts.

"Malcolm," Jasper said as he watched Kate.

Malcolm took a step closer to Jasper. "Clare has just had the strangest of calls."

"Well?" Jasper was a little irritated.

"Protect Kate. She's in danger."

"What the fuck?"

"The thing is, Clare said he couldn't stop coughing. Now, who do we know who has a bad cough?"

"Lawson! He'd never warn me; he hates my guts." Jasper paused, his mind whirling. "He doesn't hate Kate though."

At that moment, Nigel James strolled into the gallery, moving towards Kate and Bruce.

"Sorry, sir," said Bruce. "We're not open yet."

Nigel pushed past, his evil stare on Kate.

Bruce, sensing trouble, grabbed Nigel's collar and dragged him away from Kate, throwing him onto the cold marble tiles. Nigel peered up at Bruce's hulking form looming above him, and realised he'd messed with the wrong guy.

"Now what?" Kate's impatient tone surprised Bruce, but she was looking at Nigel, not at him.

"He doesn't know what he's doing," shouted a husky voice that immediately started a bout of coughing. "He's high," gasped Lawson.

By this time, Jasper had joined them. Lawson and Nigel noticeably quivered.

"Do you wish my wife harm?" Jasper's voice was as cold as ice.

"He's still in love with her. That's his problem," explained Lawson, trying to cover for Nigel.

A thick tension filled the gallery. Jasper Carmichael was in charge—not the new Jasper, but Jasper of old. His body stiffened, lips tightened, and his eyes were as cold as his voice.

Lawson had seen this look before. He bent down and held his arm out to Nigel. Jasper clenched his fists, fighting the urge to thump Nigel.

"You think you're so high and mighty," snarled Nigel. "But we'll see how high and mighty you are when you no longer have her."

"Take him out." Jasper's temper was rising.

"Jasper, if anything untoward happens to Nigel, the police will put you in jail. I'll see to that," said a breathless Lawson.

Jasper turned his cold eyes to Lawson. "I wouldn't waste the energy. Drugs will do the job for me. Richard, your son and my half-brother, is rolling in some gutter somewhere, and Nigel is on the same slippery slope."

"You could help him."

"Help?! Have you any idea how many times I've dried Richard out?" Jasper's bitter tones echoed through the gallery. "Go and do your Good Samaritan bit with Nigel."

Jasper turned his head, searching for Kate.

In the still room, no one dared utter a word; they were waiting for Kate or Jasper to break the heavy silence.

Kate handed Oliver to Malcolm. "Take him home and collect Harry for me."

***

They sat on Kate's favourite bench, looking towards the confluence of the Wells and Bury, holding hands. Kate waited for Jasper to speak. She felt the anger still bubbling inside him.

"He wants you." Jasper's cold words broke the silence, making Kate shiver.

"I don't want him." She lay her head on his shoulder. "Only you."

"Why?"

"Can you explain love? I can't." Her words were soft and low and full of meaning.

In one swift move, Jasper lifted Kate onto his lap. She smiled and planted a soft kiss on his lips.

"You know what's going to happen tonight?"

She grinned. "Three-orgasm sex, I hope."

***

Jasper slid out of bed, not wanting to wake Kate. She'd worry that he couldn't sleep.

He stopped by his study and poured a more than generous malt into his favourite crystal glass before opening the studio's bi-fold doors, which led onto the terrace. He'd taken to using the studio doors. This was the place where she was with him, whether she was painting or not. Everything was his Kate: paintings scattered in no particular order; paints, jars, brushes left in easy reach of her easel; her camera and tripod stored at the back of the room, out of Oliver's reach; her apron draped over a stool. The studio didn't smell of paint, but his Kate. Even on the terrace, he felt her presence. She'd recently bought a very large wicker chair, big enough for cuddling both Harry and Oliver. He smiled; Oliver wasn't into cuddles—he was into mischief.

He'd always enjoyed sex with Kate, but since Meredith's visit and the men in grey suits, it had become more intense. It was as if she wanted to be inside him. With every kiss, touch, move, he felt as if she was ripping the anger out of him. But the anger was very deep, and he knew the only way it would be satisfied was the death of Nigel James.

Kate had made it perfectly clear to the grey suits that she wanted nothing to do with Meredith's will and his sons could contest all they liked. The suits didn't understand Kate, but she already had what she desired the most here with him, Harry and Oliver. Money was secondary; she had more than enough, and that's all that mattered to Kate.

However, she had agreed to go with him to the Carmichael ancestral home. He could tell she didn't want to go, but she had agreed for him.

He guessed Kate saw problems with him becoming head of the Carmichaels, but he saw potential, opportunities. He would have access to powerful men: politicians, heads of industry. Deals to be made—some legal, some not. He would enlarge his network, offer assistance, with the intention of making the rich beholden to him.

He smiled when two arms wrapped around his waist and she nestled into his naked back, planting soft kisses on his shoulders. The effect was immediate; all the tightness in his muscles disappeared. He couldn't live without this woman. She read his needs, his mood, his mind; she truly was the power behind him.

She trailed her fingers down his spine and rested her cheek on his shoulder.

"Tell me." Her words were soft and caring.

"You should be asleep."

"No secrets, remember?"

"I'll make a deal," he said, somewhat playfully. He turned and whipped her into his arms. She giggled. He loved that he made her giggle. "When I have everything sorted, I'll tell."

He felt her body stiffen. "That means I won't like it."

"Not necessarily."

Chapter Fifty-Three

"Wow!" exclaimed Harry as Jasper turned into the long, straight, single-track road that led to Carmichael Castle, Jasper's ancestral home.

Jasper silently mimicked his son's word. He was impressed that this was his. Jasper Carmichael, bastard son of Colin Carmichael, who was disowned by the powerful Carmichael family for being a criminal. He wondered if the Carmichaels were so lily white.

He glanced over to Kate. She oozed disapproval.

They parked in the visitor's car park, paid the fee and followed the long line of visitors to the castle. Oliver was safely attached to his father's back, keeping those little hands away from mischief.

They dutifully followed the procession of people in and out of the four ground-floor rooms that were open to the public.

"Look at this place," whispered Jasper in Kate's ear. "It's a gold mine."

Kate was admiring the silver cutlery and place settings, and Jasper was trying to recall the price of silver.

They carried on, dawdling through the dining room. Their shoes clicked on the polished floorboards; the carpet had long gone.

Harry stopped to look at family photographs that filled a small oval table.

"Are these Dad's relatives?" Harry asked.

"We don't know," Kate quietly replied, trying

not to attract unwanted attention.

"Why are there so many paintings?" Harry said, shaking his head. He caught Kate's hand. "I don't like it here. It smells funny."

Harry was right. It smelt cold, damp and possibly of mould—or was it cat pee?

"We'd better go. Oliver has a strong desire to wreck the place," commented Jasper, who was trying to move his head out of Oliver's reach.

Kate and Harry tried to stifle their laughs as Oliver pulled on Jasper's ears.

"It's not funny," Jasper said, trying to sound disagreeable.

"Mr Carmichael!" called a reedy voice.

Jasper stopped and tried to think where he'd heard that voice before. "It's Higgins."

"Who's Higgins?" asked Kate.

"I thought it was you." A breathless Higgins caught them up. "I come every first Sunday of the month. Meredith liked me to check the books."

"But you no longer work for Meredith." Jasper couldn't help himself.

"I like your style—coming unannounced with the visitors. The family will be shocked. Carmichaels don't normally behave that way. What do you think of the place?"

"Higgins, I think the place is a disgrace. The Carmichael Trust want a kick up the arse. The car park is expensive for a waterlogged field. The entrance fee is likewise too expensive for the few downstairs rooms that are open to the public."

"Oh! It's not the Trust's fault. It was Meredith and the family. They refuse to plough money into the castle. I attend all the meetings—I think the Trust won't renew the current agreement when it expires."

"You mean Meredith dangled a carrot that was full of promises then backtracked," Jasper said bitterly.

"Of course, you have no authority, Mr Carmichael, until you agree to the terms set out by the trustees."

"Higgins, I have no intention of agreeing to those terms. How many hangers-on live here?"

"Jasper fucking Carmichael," bellowed a husky female voice. "'bout time you turned up. I knew your dad—what a charmer! He charmed the knickers off Alice. I suppose not much charm was needed." The old lady chuckled. "Ran rings round this lot. He made the Carmichaels a lot of money. But that thief Meredith helped himself."

"Now, Connie, I'm sure Mr Carmichael doesn't want to hear about that," said Higgins, taking the old lady's arm.

Jasper stood statue-like, trying to remember a Connie. "You came with grandfather."

"That's right. He wanted to see you, where you lived. He was disappointed. I remember his words as we drove away: 'There's a Carmichael, Connie. Might be the last one.'" She shook her arm free from Higgins. "These are yours?" Her crooked finger pointed first at a frightened Harry and then Oliver. "The older one's a Carmichael, not sure about the littlun. Takes after his mother, I suspect." The old lady's eyes wandered up and down Kate. "Come again. Just ask for Connie." She turned and tottered along a passageway that had a *Private* notice tangling from a chain.

"You shouldn't pay much heed to what Connie says. She has dementia," commented a red-faced Higgins. He knew Connie had already said too much. "Nice to see you all. I have a feeling we'll meet again, Mr Carmichael."

Higgins turned and went down the same passage as Connie.

The Carmichaels continued to the grounds—a well-mowed field and a duck pond. Harry and Oliver enjoyed a run about while Kate walked over to a wooden shed for ice cream and feed for the ducks.

Oliver made a scene when Kate took the ice cream from him. Most of it covered his face and hands, very little went into his mouth. He shook his head and screamed when she tried to feed it to him.

All was soon forgotten when Jasper handed Harry the duck food. Oliver eagerly followed his older brother to the water's edge where the ducks had gathered to be fed.

Kate nestled between her husband's legs, watching the boys feed the ducks.

"I'm a lucky bugger," Jasper murmured into Kate's neck. "I'm happy, Kate. You make me happy, and so do the boys. I want to kiss you."

"I wouldn't if I were you. Unless you want to make the tabloids."

Visitors had their phones out, taking photos.

***

"We had ice cream, fed the ducks, and Oliver pulled Dad's ears," chuckled Harry to Clare and Malcolm as he skipped towards his bedroom.

"He's happy," commented Malcolm, watching Harry. "Had a bit of an incident here. Nigel appeared at the studio doors, thumping and shouting."

"You didn't let him in?"

"Nah! Phoned the police; they took him away. High as a kite. The thing is, Watts turned up wanting to know how he got on the premises. Nigel had broken away some of the bottom wall. Watts helped me make an emergency repair."

Chapter Fifty-Four

It was early—but not too early for Kate, who was comforting a grizzly Oliver—when Inspector Watts knocked on the Carmichaels' door.

His stern, business-like voice boomed through the silent house. "Mr Carmichael!"

The inspector followed Malcolm into the kitchen, where Kate was struggling with Oliver.

"Here. Give 'im to me," offered Clare, lifting Oliver from Kate's arms. Oliver was having none of it, his little chubby legs kicking frantically. "You've 'ad no sleep."

"Up all night, Mrs Carmichael?" commented the inspector, trying to show sympathy as memories of his youngest boy flashed into his mind.

"How can we help?" said Kate, filling the kettle while dropping two slices of wholemeal bread into the toaster.

A pyjama-clad Harry joined them, rubbing his eyes. "I don't want Coco Pops."

Kate exchanged a quick glance with Clare.

"My stomach hurts."

Jasper appeared, dressed for the office in a crisp white shirt and grey Armani suit. "Welcome to early morning madness."

"You're going to the office early," commented Kate as she rested her hand on Harry's forehead.

"I can't work here in this mayhem."

His curt words made Kate's head whip round. "Well, I'm sorry if your son kept you awake."

"Don't start, Kate." Jasper angrily turned his

foul mood towards the inspector. "Well?!"

"Nigel James was found dead at the bottom of your garden."

Jasper stopped walking towards the door. Kate's hand fell from Harry's forehead. Even Oliver went quiet.

"Drug overdose. My men went looking for him after they raided his home. Beth and Lawson were sleeping there."

"I'm not seeing the connection," said a bemused Kate.

"You mean Jasper hasn't enlightened you? Shame on you, Jasper."

The inspector intensely watched Kate and Jasper. It was obvious from Jasper's sheepish expression that Kate didn't know. *What's he hiding?* thought the inspector.

"We've been keeping an eye on Beth, Lawson and Joanne. Beth and Lawson were arrested for drug dealing." The inspector paused for a long moment while his statement sank in. "Beth wants to ring your solicitor, Mr Carmichael, but she needs your permission. Joanne suggested that you would fund their legal costs."

"What am I missing?" said a very miffed Kate.

***

They were the last words Jasper heard from Kate. They repeated in his mind over and over. He'd taken his Carmichael birthright—Lord Carmichael, living in the ancestral home. He had power, high-society friends, brushed shoulders with politicians and powerful men. He had taken the Carmichael seat in the House of Lords and as a Freemason.

He should have told Kate that he was

financing Joanne's boutique expansion. He should have told her that Beth and Lawson had seen a business opportunity after Anton's demise. Zak had warned him to keep away, but he hadn't listened.

He opened a velvet box. Inside was a diamond pendant that Zak had cut from one of Colin's diamonds. Kate had returned the matching ring and earrings.

He moved to the window. The boys were waiting for her. Harry stood statue-like holding his holdall. He didn't like his new school. Oliver didn't like his nursery. Joanne had insisted they'd had their hair cut, a buzz cut. He knew Kate would hate it. She resented him having custody of the boys and Joanne's interference. There were lots of tears that day when the judge gave Jasper custody. She hadn't looked at him; she hadn't contested the case, for she knew Jasper's strength and determination.

Zak had told him that she'd shut herself in the studio for a week: "She's aged, more grey than blonde. Her eyes are dead. I've seen you do many hurtful things, but I never dreamt that you'd do them to the woman you loved."

Zak had become his eyes and ears on Kate. Their diamond arrangement was working well. Jasper dripped Colin's diamonds through Zak's many outlets. He skilfully made them unrecognisable.

"She's here." Higgins' curt words broke his thoughts. He had never liked Kate.

Joanne pushed past him. "Jeans. And to think she's Lady Carmichael. You really must divorce her, Jasper." Joanne's bitchy tone reminded Jasper why she wasn't in his bed.

"That car, sir," said Higgins.

"The car's hers, and so's the house."

"She could take you to the cleaners," said Joanne.

"You don't know Kate." A lump rose in Jasper's throat as her name slipped from his mouth.

Kate stopped alongside Harry and Oliver; she read from their stiff, stern body language that all was not well. No smiles, kisses or hugs.

Harry silently picked up their bags and opened the tailgate. Oliver climbed into the rear seat. Harry dropped the bags.

"Mum," he choked.

And with a speed any professional runner would be proud of, he flung his arms around her neck. Kate lost her footing and fell backwards onto the gravel drive. Harry was on top of her, kissing and laughing. Oliver jumped out of the car and joined Harry.

Jasper hadn't seen his sons smile, let alone laugh, since the court hearing.

"Does that woman know nothing else but chaos?" Higgins' disdainful words brought happy memories into Jasper's mind. Chaos brought happy boys, like he was watching.

Oliver took off, running around the car with Kate after him. He was giggling; his beaming smile filled his face. Harry was skipping on the spot, hands waving, and shouting.

"Lady Carmichael!" a security guard shouted. Kate didn't look or answer. "Excuse me, Lady Carmichael."

Kate turned. An out-of-breath security guard held out an envelope. Kate dropped it on the front passenger seat.

"I must see you open it, and you must sign here."

Jasper looked at Higgins and Joanne, both

had cocky smirks on their face. Jasper pushed past them and ran along the corridor and down the stairs, taking them two at a time.

"Stop!" he bellowed as Kate was about to open the envelope. Jasper skidded to a halt, sending stones flying on the gravel drive, and snatched the envelope from Kate's loose grip.

"Sir, I have to have a signature," said the guard, somewhat nervously.

"Who pays your wages?" Silence. "I pay your wages, not Higgins or Joanne."

The security guard reddened.

"So, you're Joanne's dirty little secret," Jasper said.

"It's my wife—if she finds out..." stuttered the embarrassed guard.

"I suggest you tell your wife. Now go."

"I don't like school," Oliver commented.

"School?!" Kate hadn't expected her voice to be so shrill.

"It's nursery not school." Jasper hadn't expected his voice to nervously quiver.

His hand rested on the pocket where he had hidden the velvet box. He eased the box from his pocket and handed it to Kate.

"Open it."

With shaking hands, Kate slowly opened the box. She gasped.

"Zak finished it. The pendant's from one diamond." Silence. "I had it made for you and no one else."

"That means he loves you," whispered Harry. "We're doing relationships at school. Men always give the woman they love gifts."

"Out of the mouth of babes," whispered Jasper.

Kate closed the box and lifted her head, unsure what to say. Jasper was close, very close. Their heads brushed against one another. In an instant, his eyes focused on her slightly open mouth, and with desperation and need, he claimed it.

Chapter Fifty-Five

Jasper made an excuse to go to the Wellsbury office. Higgins, who somehow had manoeuvred himself into the position of butler, had shown his disapproval, particularly when Jasper had insisted he stay behind to run the castle.

Jasper parked the Range Rover outside the Isaacs House. Clare had cried out when he walked past the kitchen window. Harry and Oliver clambered onto the Belfast sink drainer.

"He's come for his make-up sex," said Harry.

"Harry! I don't know what that school is teaching you," Clare said.

Kate was leaning in a chair with her legs draped over another. Without moving her gaze, she softly said, "I expected you sooner."

Jasper lifted her legs and sat with his hand resting on her shin.

"I'm going to fight you, Jasper." Her voice was low and calm. "Harry is so withdrawn. He sobs in his sleep. Oliver is bouncing back, but he's not as sensitive as Harry."

"They want for nothing."

"Except love." She turned her head to meet his gaze.

"I survived."

"Did you?" She raised her voice.

His hand was slowly caressing her shin, up and down, up and down. She tried to move, but he gripped her leg.

"I haven't fucked since you." He paused

and stared at her leg as if it was the most interesting thing in the world. "I've been doing a lot of thinking… I don't think Colin fitted in with the Carmichael set. If he did, he was up to no good. The Carmichaels got very rich; that's why Meredith didn't want to let it go…

"The boys are unhappy, but you've worked that out… You're no match for me, Kate. I'm utterly ruthless. You don't know what the word means. That's what attracted me to you. Your innocence, thoughtfulness, loyalty."

"Ok, Jasper, you've made your point. What do you want?"

"Do you have any idea how rich I am?"

"No!"

"Higgins said you only know chaos. I watched you and the boys. You chasing Oliver, and Harry skipping. Chaos, as he put it, equalled happiness. That morning I left—it was chaos. I was angry you had left our bed for Oliver. You were more concerned about Harry not wanting Coco Pops than me. And I had kept secrets from you. Joanne, Beth, Nigel, drugs."

"All this because I left our bed." Disbelief and bitterness echoed as Kate tried to release her leg from Jasper's grip.

"Taking my place in the Carmichael hall of fame appeared to be the answer. A completely different life."

"Money isn't everything, Jasper."

"I realised that when I saw happiness spread over the boys' faces. You were giving them something money can't buy."

"So! What is it you want?"

Jasper continued as if Kate hadn't spoken. "The thing is, could I settle for the old life? Could I go back?"

"You honestly think your new Carmichael existence is a step forward? Mixing with moneyed people? Clever talk that achieves zilch, except possibly more money?"

"Joanne and Higgins want me to divorce you. Have a trophy wife. Grandfather had one of those, and Colin fucked her."

"Harry's a bit young for that but, give him a year or two—I think he'll manage." She tried to make light of the conversation, but it was lost. Jasper was in a dark place.

"I'm desperate to fuck you. Bury myself inside you until I've made a decision." He pushed her leg off him and stood staring at the garden. "These feelings of despair have been with me for some time. A bottle of malt helped, but no longer. Joanne offered cocaine, but Richard came to mind."

"So you came here. I haven't the answer, Jasper. I could offer advice, but only you can decide."

"You think I should go to a shrink."

"No. I think you need a rest."

"It's not that easy, Kate. If I rest or appear to be weak, the vultures will start to circle."

She stood behind him, itching to put her arms around him.

"They know I'm in a dark place. They know I'm here. They'll be preparing."

"Preparing for what?" She moved beside him.

"To take over. Make me penniless. Make me grovel like Richard in some gutter."

"You'll never grovel, Jasper. You'll have Wellsbury, come what may. And if the worst comes to the worst, I could step in. Zak would help. And Bruce would look after the centre."

His arm slowly reached out and pulled her into his chest.

"I've been a bastard to them. They won't want to help," he whispered into her ear.

"They'll do it for me."

Jasper sat on the wooden bench and held his head in his hands. The dark emotions he had kept bottled up since leaving at that fateful breakfast were stirring. He no longer had the strength to keep them locked inside.

"Let's walk," she calmly said, holding out her hand.

"Walk?"

"I'll show you the orchard me and the kids planted. Malcolm and Bruce prepared the land, and we went to the garden centre and the kids chose the fruit trees."

"Why?" His eyes filled.

"I love you, Jasper. You need that love. Remember, no questions."

He remembered using those words when she first worked for him.

"I'll go and change while you decide."

"You better not hurt her." Harry's determined voice surprised Jasper.

He was confronted by two miniature Carmichaels. They both had the angry Carmichael glare and stern features.

"I may not be big enough now, but I'll remember, and when your back's turned..."

Harry's hateful words brought the newsagent into Jasper's mind. Jasper *had* waited until he was big enough.

"I'm not going to hurt her." Jasper stood and made for the stairs.

Harry looked at Oliver. "Make-up sex," he quietly said in his mature manner.

"What's make-up sex?" asked a bemused Oliver, mimicking his brother's quiet tone.

"It's a secret. Can you keep a secret?"

Oliver nodded, moving closer to his brother, eager to learn the secret.

"When mummies and daddies disagree, instead of fighting they have make-up sex." Oliver's eyes grew wide and his mouth opened. "It's true—the boys in my class told me. They all spy on their parents."

Chapter Fifty-Six

Jasper sat cross-legged, hands behind his head, leaning against the headboard, waiting for Kate to finish showering.

"I was hoping we could have some alone time. Quality time. Just the two of us."

His words faded as Kate walked into the bedroom, wrapped in a bath towel. The towel dropped as she opened her underwear drawer. She had lost weight. The C-section scars were visible, but her breasts were still full. He tried to muffle a sigh when she turned to face him, dressed only in a lace white bra and matching panties. He felt his Armani trousers tighten as he became hard. Joanne had called him impotent; he showed no interest in her or any other woman. His sole interest had been in proving he was worthy of being a member of high society, even though some of their practices and attitudes towards the people who he thought of as friends enraged him. The anger of his youth boiled inside him, but he'd locked it away deep inside.

"What have you got in mind?" she said innocently, slipping on her jeans and white blouse. She draped a towel over her shoulders and began to dry her hair.

"I could ravish you on the bed," he said, somewhat playfully. "But talk must come first."

"No lies, Jasper. If you've fucked around, tell me."

"Why do you have to be so perfect? Why

hasn't one of your art dealers wined, dined and fucked you?"

"We never wined and dined. It was always business. Never frequented the theatre, cinema." Her words drifted, as thoughts of what they had missed surfaced in her mind.

Jasper stared into her green eyes and was surprised to see tears. *I've lost her,* he thought. The realisation fell like a stone.

She was walking towards the bedroom door. He had seen that determined look before.

He had to stop her. If she walked away, it would be over and divorce would follow.

"Kate, don't go." His voice echoed desperation.

"I'm not going to join you in the Carmichael hall of fame." She paused, turned and stared at him. "That doesn't mean I'll stop loving you."

Jasper's legs wouldn't move. She was ending their marriage. A little voice inside urged him to do something—move, slam the door, kiss her. And that's what he found himself doing. The door closed with a loud thud, and before she could fight, she was pinned to the door, arms firmly held above her head while his mouth devoured hers. All resistance ebbed away; this was the Jasper of old who took what he wanted. And he wanted her.

At that moment, she didn't care if he was Lord Carmichael or Jasper the criminal; he wanted her, and her body wanted him. And that was how she'd felt the first time sex-on-legs had taken her body to places she hadn't known existed.

Her legs grew weak. She had no idea how long the kiss lasted; time had stood still. They were both breathless, full of desire and longing.

"We'll go away. Alone. Off the grid. This will be sorted. Once and for all."

***

Harry and Oliver had cried when they left, but older than his years, Harry had slung his arms around Kate's neck.

His small voice had been full of emotion. "I'll miss you. Come back happy."

"Stop worrying," said Jasper as he drove far too fast. "Malcolm has an emergency number."

"You said we were going off the grid," Kate answered, somewhat indignantly.

"I have a satellite phone. I am Lord of the Manor." He grinned. "So to speak. It's Higgins—I don't trust him or Joanne. They visit Beth."

Kate sat silently, mulling over what Jasper had just said. Beth hated her. She would go to any lengths to destroy her relationship with Jasper.

"Higgins?" Kate mumbled. "He appeared to hate everything Meredith stood for."

"Money corrupts."

***

It was dark when Jasper parked the Range Rover at the rear of a log cabin.

"It was grandfather's. He probably brought his women here," he explained. "One room—kitchen, living and bed. Decent bathroom."

Kate carried their bags while Jasper started a fire. They shared the bed, Kate one side and Jasper the other.

Kate tossed and turned while Jasper slept like a lamb. At first light, she walked along the lakeside. She came across a large stone, which served as a seat for her to watch the dawn. Her mind was awash with Jasper thoughts. She had to decide what compromises she would make.

***

"What time is it?" Jasper's husky voice was full of sleep.

"Lunchtime."

"You let me sleep."

"You needed it. Bacon sarnie?" she said, turning the rashers.

Jasper strolled from the bathroom with one towel around his waist and rubbing his wet hair with another. Kate flushed; no hot-blooded female could resist a half-naked Jasper. He smiled that Carmichael smile. His blue eyes sparkled, his broad chest slowly moving with every breath.

"Uncomfortable?" He grinned. She could feel his warmth. She wasn't expecting his lips to trail her neck. "Missed this, Kate?" His voice took on a sexy tone.

His arms surrounded her waist. Kate's head slipped back onto his shoulder. A slight groan escaped her mouth.

"I bet you're wet. You're mine." He felt her shiver slightly.

"I'll make you a deal," she stuttered. "A day in bed after we've decided a way forward."

"No matter the outcome?"

"Yes." A lump formed in her throat. *This is it,* she thought. *No going back. Divorce or marriage.*

Their deep kiss brought tears to Kate's eyes. Could she let this man go to the likes of Beth and Joanne?

"I see it this way," Jasper began. "Option one: I live in London and come home every weekend. Option two: I live in Wellsbury and commute to London by helicopter."

"There's a third option," she nervously suggested. Jasper raised his eyebrows in surprise. "You could live in Wellsbury. Run the centre, develop the Carmichael brand."

"You want it all, Kate. That's not going to happen. I've given you my two options." Jasper was slightly annoyed. "Compromise. That's what you always told me. Now it's your turn."

"I don't understand why you want to live in that mausoleum. It wants millions spending on it. And what for? So a private trust can open it to the public. Far better to give it to the National Trust or English Heritage," Kate calmly said. She didn't want to provoke Jasper.

"People live there. Have you forgotten?" Jasper snapped.

An awkward tension developed.

"Let them live in a Carmichael property."

"What about the Carmichael investments?" Jasper retorted.

Kate was on a roll. "You have a team of people already looking after them. A visit two, three times a year should suffice." She paused. "So what would you miss? Freemasons. House of Lords. Social events. Dinner parties. Have I missed anything?"

Yes, Jasper thought. *You.* "How do you propose I spend my time?"

"Running the Wellsbury centre. Developing the Carmichael brand. Expanding the Carmichael Centre concept. Don't forget the airfield."

They had moved from the cabin to the lakeside.

"Do you know, I have no idea where we are?" Her words were lost on the gentle breeze.

"Does it matter?"

"Not really."

"What will you do?" said a thoughtful Jasper.

"The book shop needs a lot of attention. It's just taking off. The old library staff are invaluable."

She paused. "I'll have to watch costs though. I can use some of the art gallery profits. There's still a problem with teenagers though—nowhere to go. Some are congregating in the book shop. Others need something more physical. A gym. Boxing. Football."

Silence settled as they walked.

"I was thinking, instead of demolishing the old Victorian school building—"

"Kate, they're poorly built."

"—you could employ those out-of-work builders. Create apprenticeships for the school leavers. Involve them in a worthwhile project."

"Kate, it'll take years. Planning permission. No return."

"I see it this way. If we—*you*—don't create something, Beth's drugs will find a way in. At the moment, Watts has it under control, but that won't last forever."

He gripped her arm so she faced him. "Have you any idea what you're suggesting?"

"Yes. I'm talking about saving a community. You have the money, resources. I admit you won't get a return, but surely the satisfaction is in putting the money to good use. Giving the youngsters a worthwhile start. Giving the adults jobs. Wellsbury can buck the trend of decline."

Silence.

"You can be your own version of a Carmichael. Be your own man. Not a mirror image of Colin or your grandfather."

"Did you pack the malt?"

Chapter Fifty-Seven

"They're back!" shouted Harry, running through the kitchen door and towards the Range Rover.

"You owe me a day in bed," commented Jasper as he switched off the engine.

"We haven't got a deal."

"We'll see about that."

Jasper had hardly spoken since Kate had ranted on about the future of Wellsbury. She'd thought he'd reject the idea, as he could get a better return on his money. But to her surprise, he was giving her ideas some thought.

Kate smiled at Harry, hugging and kissing him.

"I'm too big for kisses," he murmured quietly in her ear.

Kate ruffled his hair and, still smiling, thought, *Don't change, my gorgeous boy.*

Oliver had no such reservations. He raced into Jasper's arms for a twirl, giggling and shouting, "More! More!"

"It's Zak!" shouted Clare, trying to make herself heard.

Kate watched Jasper and Zak walk down the garden towards the recently planted orchard.

"Here," said Clare, handing her a cup of tea. "Why so pensive?"

"I don't know, Clare. I just have that uneasy feeling. I've never taken to Zak. He's done nothing to me, but there's just something."

"You'll be thinking he's going to set Jasper astray."

"Jasper seems to attract people who run close to the law."

"He loves you and the kids. Be thankful."

"Yes. You're right. I'm probably looking for something that's not there." But Kate's gut told her Jasper and Zak were up to no good.

***

Jasper and Zak walked into the orchard, well out of sight of the house.

"How good are your diamond contacts?" asked Jasper in a low voice.

"They can't sell me enough. Always pushing to buy more."

"Buy as many as you can. Good stuff."

"I only deal with good stuff. Money?" said Zak in a low voice.

"Cash only. No paper trail. No text or email. Only use burner phones once and when necessary."

"Cash, Jasper!"

"I have cash. Have you got diamonds?"

Zak grinned. "You son of a bitch. You've still got cash stashed."

Jasper didn't answer. He just walked, his mind whirling with how he was going to put this business together.

"Give me a price on the diamonds you already have. Got to be cut—I can't get rid of uncut. That involves too many people."

"Jasper, this could be a huge operation. Are you sure?"

"Let me worry about selling the diamonds. Deal?"

Zak spat on his hand and held it out. Jasper did likewise. The deal was sealed.

They walked back to house in silence, Zak

thinking about the diamonds locked away and Jasper thinking about how he was going to rekindle old contacts that would be receptive to buying diamonds with dirty money. This time, he wouldn't involve banks.

Any excess money would disappear into Kate's project. He already had contractors that would work for cash, no questions asked. His biggest problem would be Kate and that enquiring mind of hers.

***

"You and Zak were a long time walking," she said in a matter of fact way. She stood in the doorway to his office.

"You owe me a day in bed." Jasper looked over his laptop and grinned.

She raised her eyebrows. "We haven't got a deal."

"What if I suggest that Wellsbury becomes my main office? What if I donate the Carmichael ancestral home? What if I convert the ancestral home into luxury apartments? What if I develop those falling down Victorian slums into a gym and workshops?"

Kate slipped onto his lap, looping her arms around his neck.

"Go on." Her lips grazed his neck.

"You can have all that, providing..." He paused for effect. "...You're on my arm for Lord Carmichael's social occasions."

"You're kidding, right? I don't fit in. I don't do small talk."

"I want you in the finest designer dresses, hair down instead of pulled back." He pulled the tie that secured her ponytail. Her hair fell onto her shoulders. "I prefer you in heels so I can admire your legs. You'll wear the best diamonds."

She tried to move off his lap.

"Kate, you're a successful artist. These people are dying to meet a new and up-and-coming artist. They'll try and sponsor you, try and impress you with their money. But I'm the only sponsor you'll ever have." He kissed her neck.

"Can I think about it?"

He shook his head. "This is a one-off offer. What's to think about? You get what you want, and me in the bargain." After a long moment, Jasper whispered, "I want you in my bed, Kate."

"I'm in your bed."

"I want to be inside you. I have an idea about that. We can meet at the penthouse apartment. Spend the afternoon there. Alone. We can visit the cinema, theatre."

"You'll do all that?"

"Yes."

She turned her head and their lips met.

"I need words, Kate."

"I'll do it," she murmured between kisses.

Chapter Fifty-Eight

Jasper stood gazing at the greying sky, waiting for the sun to rise. He was in his favourite room, Kate's studio. This was the room he was most comfortable in. This room was Kate; paintings, paints, a paint-stained apron draped over a stool, her nineteen-thirties easel that she'd seen in a second-hand shop. He closed his eyes, and she was painting, smiling—she was happy. But guilt spread through him.

Before his first coffee, he'd woken his property manager, instructing him to find homes for his relatives that lived at Carmichael Castle. His next call would be the architect. He wanted the castle split into luxury apartments. Amanda would set up a meeting with Wellsbury Council. And the grey suits responsible for the Carmichael Trust were about to get a kick up the arse.

He felt two arms stretch around his waist. A sigh escaped his mouth as Kate lifted the coffee from his hands.

"You don't like coffee," he said in a soft voice.

"I like your coffee." He could hear the happiness in her voice.

"Come."

They walked out onto the terrace. Kate nestled between his legs, holding the coffee.

Jasper draped a couple of blankets over them. "Any left?"

She handed him the coffee without taking her eyes away from the sky.

"Are you going to tell me?" she asked.

"I've instructed my people to—"

Kate didn't let him finish. "I'm not interested in that. What's bothering you?"

For a long moment, she thought she wouldn't get an answer, but then he spoke. "I'd like to tell you a story about an unloved baby that grew up to be very rich. His father paid a whore to bring him up. They lived in a terrace house in a run-down part of London. He was streetwise and wild. His dad would visit to check on things, but the real reason was to fuck the whore and organise a diamond heist.

"There was a newsagent that owed him money. The newsagent took the piss out him. He came to a sticky end.

"This unloved lad was angry; dark moods controlled him. He would fight until the darkness went away.

"His dad could see his son was on the slope to destruction, and with the help of his best friend, the lad was introduced to sex.

"The local neighbours hated this lad and his dad. Then one day, his dad told him to move to Wellsbury and start a business. He gave him a box and a little black book.

"The lad's company was successful until outsiders tried to take over his business. The lad knew he had to get out, but he wasn't ready. He needed someone to watch his back. And she changed his life with a smile and a flick of her blonde hair.

"The lad was in deep with an unsavoury character from South America. Knives were thrown in his back, but she saved him with her kindness and loyalty."

"Jasper. Stop. Just tell me what you've done," she interrupted.

"Don't you want to know how the lad survived?"

"I'm not a fool. I know about Max, the Wilsons, Anton."

"I told Zak it was just between me and him. No paper trail, no text or calls, use burner phone once. I knew if you caught sight of any files, you would put two and two together and make four."

"Zak!"

"Colin's box was full of diamonds. His stash from his many heists. Some cut diamonds and many uncut. Over the years, I have sold many of the cut diamonds, but I needed someone to—"

She interrupted. "You needed a Zak."

"He's very talented, but the Cohens didn't want to know him. I gave Zak one or two diamonds, and he'd cut and polish them to sell them on. Then it struck me: some of my new and powerful friends might be interested in high-end diamonds. I have my own network of people that buy diamonds, and I have Colin's black book. Names, addresses."

"You have three outlets for your diamonds," she commented.

"Word will travel that I'm in the diamond business."

"So, the respectable Lord Carmichael is an illegal diamond dealer. I don't understand why you're telling me."

"I thought I could do it without you. But you have my back, Kate. Your loyalty means more than you would ever know. We don't have just sex. It's a deep love. You give yourself to me. Time stands still as we share our love. I can't betray or deceive you, Kate. You've turned my darkness into light.

"You see, that unloved lad has found love. He wants to give and share." His soft words caressed her ear while his large hands cupped her breasts.

"You want me to keep records?"

"Do you care where the money comes from for the gym? Do you care how the materials are paid for? Do you care how the men are paid?"

She flipped over so she was lying on his front. Her index finger covered his lips. "Enough."

She stretched so her mouth covered his. His hands lifted her night dress.

"Oh, Kate! No panties," he mumbled, taking control of the kiss.

It was his turn to flick her onto her back. Her nightdress bunched up around her waist. He slipped inside her.

"Deal?"

"Deal."

***

Harry tightly held Oliver's hand as they tiptoed back to their bedroom.

"Can I sleep in your bed?" whispered a very sleepy Oliver.

"Only if you can keep a secret."

Oliver snuggled into Harry's chest.

"Love you, Harry."

Harry smiled and kissed his brother's hair.

Author Profile

After spending many years in the industrial and academic worlds, Frances Parker-Smith now has the time to pursue her dream of writing.

Her imagination is sparked by visiting new towns and countries, beach walking, and of course, the people she shares conversations with. You'll always find a notebook tucked away in her pocket, ready to record new ideas. When at home, you'll find her relaxing in the garden.

Carmichaels' Diamonds is her third novel and has simmered in the back of her mind for many years. The main character has kept her awake many a night, and they've shared many glasses of malt.

Life has so many strands.
Never look back.
Follow your dreams.

For updates from Frances Parker-Smith follow her
on Twitter @fparkersmith
or via her website francesparkersmith.wordpress.com

To contact Frances Parker-Smith please email
francesparkersmith@icloud.com

Publisher Information

Rowanvale Books provides publishing services to independent authors, writers and poets all over the globe. We deliver a personal, honest and efficient service that allows authors to see their work published, while remaining in control of the process and retaining their creativity. By making publishing services available to authors in a cost-effective and ethical way, we at Rowanvale Books hope to ensure that the local, national and international community benefits from a steady stream of good quality literature.

For more information about us, our authors or our publications, please get in touch.

www.rowanvalebooks.com
info@rowanvalebooks.com

www.ingramcontent.com/pod-product-compliance
Lightning Source LLC
Chambersburg PA
CBHW032137190626
46814CB00005BA/1736